Caribbean *...*

MAYAN
WATERS

A Rick Waters Novel

ERIC CHANCE STONE

Published by Lost and Found Publishing

Printed in the United States of America

ISBN: 978-1-959020-03-5

First Edition

10   9   8   7   6   5   4   3   2   1

MAYAN
WATERS

FIND THE OFFICIAL SYNOPSIS MUSIC AT:

ERICSTONE.GUMROAD.COM/L/MAYANWATERS

CHAPTER ONE

Rick showed his ID to the woman behind the glass at the Okaloosa County Evidence & Property Recovery Office in Shalimar.

"Rick Waters?" she read aloud.

"That's me. I'm here for 'The Black Strat'," he said with a wink.

The woman eyed him for a moment, then nodded. "I'll be right back with it," she said.

Rick flashed a smile at Jules as they waited for the woman to return with the Stratocaster. *The* Black Strat was originally owned by David Gilmour of Pink Floyd but had sold at an auction at Christie's for almost five million dollars to raise money for Earth Client, a charity that helped homelessness and hunger. Jack Raynes, owner of the Red Ruby Casino in Biloxi, had bought the guitar for six million from the winner of the auction. Jack had already faxed over a request to turn The Black Strat over to Rick so he could return it to him in Biloxi. The guitar had been taken by Jack's musician son Tyler and played at every one of his shows, hidden in plain sight beneath a plaid lumberjack-looking cloth wrap. Tyler was currently awaiting trial for larceny and second-degree murder.

"Here you are, sir," said the woman. "If you can just sign on the dotted line."

Rick signed the document releasing 'The Black Strat', and took the guitar gingerly in hand. "Come along, Jules. Let's get this home to Jack."

He and Jules headed for Biloxi. The guitar's value had doubled since the theft. It was now valued at over twelve million, and Rick's reward for returning it would be a cool million dollars. It was going to be a huge payday for him and his private detective agency. He planned on depositing the check, spending the night at Jack's casino, then he and Jules would continue on to New Orleans for a well-deserved week-long vacation in Tulum, Mexico. They'd booked a nonstop flight to Cancun on Spirit Airlines. As much as Rick hated flying commercial, he didn't have much of a choice, as his partner Gary Haas had taken his private jet down to Costa Rica to research a possible business venture.

Gary had been a hard-working blue-collar man until he won Powerball a few years back. Now everything he touched turned to gold and made even more money. Gary's newest venture was to get his hands on the best coffee bean strain in Costa Rica and import it into Mississippi, where he would go into business with a man named Tungsten and grow the beans in a specially controlled environment. His idea was to produce the world's richest, most aromatic coffee science could create. He could've done it in Florida, but the tax incentives to open the business in Mississippi were too good to pass up. Plus, he felt indebted to Tungsten, who had helped him and Rick's team not long ago in a major time of need. He wanted to pay it forward.

Once they arrived at the casino in Biloxi, Rick opened the back door of the Bronco and carefully pulled out 'The Black Strat'. They'd each brought a small carry-on suitcase for the trip to Mexico. Jules pulled them both as Rick carefully carried the valuable guitar.

"Come on in, Rick. Good afternoon, Jules," said Jack as he walked them into his office on the top floor of the casino.

Rick followed Jack into his opulent office with The Black Strat wrapped in a linen cloth. He placed it on Jack's desk.

"Hard to believe that thing is worth twelve million dollars. I'm just glad to have it back. You did a great job, Rick."

"Any word on Tyler's case?" asked Rick.

"I've spoken to my lawyers, and he says the DA is dropping the charges in regards to the theft of the guitar and the ransom money, since most of that was returned. He's still pressing for second-degree murder though. Because Tyler killed his kidnapper, then placed him in the trunk of a Cadillac and buried it, they feel he has some culpability in his death. My lawyers are framing it as a case of self-defense. It was stupid of him to bury the car and not contact authorities, but he was not in his right mind after all of the psychological torture the kidnapper made him endure. I feel good about his chances for an acquittal."

"I see. I'm just glad he's home safe and getting some therapy," replied Rick.

"We all are, and I can't even begin to thank you enough for all you and your crew did."

"It's our job, Jack. We are glad it all worked out."

"Well, here you go," said Jack as he slid an envelope across the desk to Rick.

Rick picked it up and was about to place it in his pocket. "Open it. I insist."

He slowly opened the envelope and slightly pulled out the right corner of the check, revealing the amount. His eyes widened.

One Million and Five Hundred Thousand Dollars.

Rick shook his head. "That's not the reward amount, Jack. It's too much."

"You're right, Rick." Jack grinned. "The reward for the guitar is one million, but because you didn't really listen to me and used your gut instinct to tie the return of the guitar to the kidnapper, that's a bonus for you and your crew."

"I don't know what to say."

"No need to say anything. Consider us even and it's for a job well done. Oh, and there's a little something in your room as well. Y'all have fun in Mexico."

Rick stood up and they shook hands.

Jack hugged Jules and handed her a little envelope and keys to the presidential suite in the casino. "Now you make sure Rick buys you a steak tonight downstairs."

Jules giggled. "I will."

"Oh, and Rick, since you like that Caymus Cabernet, I had it stocked in the steakhouse. It's become one of my favorites as well."

"You're too kind, Jack."

"Don't mention it."

They waved goodbye and Rick and Jules took the elevator to their floor, and stepped into the massive suite. It was adorned with flowers and a huge gift basket in the center of the twelve-seat dining table. Jules picked up the card and read it aloud.

Rick and Jules,

Since you told me you planned to go to Tulum and hadn't decided which resort to choose yet, I went ahead and booked the best one down there. My treat. It's called Dreams Tulum. It's an all-inclusive on the Caribbean Sea. Y'all have a blast.

Jack

"¡Ay, Dios mío!" exclaimed Jules.

"Wow, that guy is something else." Rick shook his head again, chuckling. "I've heard good things about that place, Jules, and it was one of the ones I was gonna look at this afternoon and probably book. I guess that frees up the afternoon. Resort research is over. Let's just chill the rest of the day. How about some pool time? This room automatically comes with a free cabana at the pool. We can take that wine from the gift basket and head down. Deal?"

"You don't have to ask me twice."

Jules threw open her suitcase and grabbed a little red bikini and cover-up and stepped into the bathroom to change. Rick kicked off his shorts and put on a pair of swim trunks, flip flops, and a tank top.

Ahhhh, officially on vacation.

Rick dipped his toe into the water. The pool was heated and it was bathwater warm. Jules set up the wine and two glasses on the cabana table with a bowl of grapes and other assorted fruit. When Rick saw the grapes, he thought of

Chief, his beloved cockatoo back home. He missed him, but he knew Johnie, his first mate back on his charter boat *Nine-Tenths*, would be taking great care of him. Bringing Chief into Mexico on a commercial flight would be a major hassle.

Jules did a cannonball into the pool, splashing Rick a little. He tried to do a swan dive to follow her in but ended up doing a most embarrassing belly flop. Jules laughed so hard she almost choked on the water. She swam over to Rick.

"Nice one, Greg Louganis," she said.

"Ha-ha-ha," replied Rick.

Jules wrapped her arms and legs around Rick and comforted him.

"It's okay, Rick, I don't think anyone saw. That little boy over there was looking the other way," said Jules with a grin.

Rick kissed Jules, knowing she loved to mess with him and give him a hard time. It just meant that she loved him.

"We're gonna have such a great time in Mexico, Jules. I've been to Cozumel, Isla Mujeres, and Playa Del Carmen, but I've always wanted to go farther south on the Yucatán Peninsula. We can take a bus down once we land in Cancun. Maybe we should consider renting a car, so we can do some exploring. What do you think?"

"I think a car would be great. How about something fun, like a convertible?" asked Jules.

"Better yet, how about a dune buggy?!"

"I love it!"

"There's a 10:20 a.m. flight from New Orleans to Cancun. I think we should chill here today, then take the scenic route along the beach to New Orleans through Bay St. Louis. One of my high school friends owns a little barbeque and blues joints in Gulfport called Murky Waters. His last name is Waters too, but we aren't related as far as I know. Then after lunch, we can head to Bay St. Louis. It's only an hour from the airport in New Orleans. We can spend the night there, eat at this killer place I like called Cuz's, then drive to the airport the next morning. Sound like a plan?" asked Rick.

"Sounds like perfection, Rick. I'm so happy we are taking this time off. We both need it."

They played around in the pool for a couple of hours, then chilled in the cabana. Jules opened the wine and they sipped it while munching on some mango slices and grapes. Instead of drying off and eating in the restaurant, they ordered sandwiches from the pool waitress. It was a glorious day of relaxation and recharging.

Afterward, they decided to head up to the room for a little afternoon delight. They were so in tune with each other that even that came naturally and words were never spoken.

Rick opened his MacBook to look at some photos of Dreams Tulum. It was a beautiful all-inclusive resort, just south of Akumal in Quintana Roo, Mexico. It was also close to Reserva de la Biósfera Sian Ka'an, a tropical jungle reserve to the south. It was full of rivers and cenotes. Rick pinned that as a place to explore. The resort offered two pools, and one had a splash park he was sure Jules would enjoy. There was free use of kayaks and complementary greens fees at the Riviera Maya Golf Club and El Camaleon Mayakoba Golf Course. They had six à la carte restaurants, one buffet style, and seven bars.

"Come check this out, Jules! A swim-up bar."

Jules leaned over his shoulder to get a closer look. "Wow, it looks so beautiful, Rick. I'm so excited, mi amor."

Now that Jules was out of the shower, he took his turn. They planned to go to the steak house and have dinner around seven. That would give them a couple of hours to gamble. Jules put on a black dress with sequined shoulder straps. She looked stunning as usual. Rick put on a pair of slacks and a sport coat that Jules had picked up for him. When he looked in the mirror, he thought he looked rather dapper.

"Shall we?" asked Rick as he stuck out his arm for her.

They went down to the casino. Rick handed her three hundred-dollar bills and told her to win big. Her eyes lit up.

"Let's walk around first and see what's hot," said Rick.

The craps table was slow with only one player and didn't entice Rick at all. He stopped at the three-card poker table and watched a few hands. The dealer seemed to be the only one winning.

"Have you ever played pai gow poker, Jules?"

"I learned the game when I trained as a dealer, but I've never actually played. You wanna try it?"

"Sure, we can play side by side for a while and get some free drinks."

They grabbed the first and second seats at the table. In order to win a hand in pai gow poker, the player needed to have two hands that beat the dealer. One hand was a five-card hand and the other was a two-card hand. So, if a player had a royal flush on the five-card hand and a pair on the top hand and the dealer had a larger pair, it would still be a push. It was basically a game of pushes. Rick knew it was the slowest way to win or lose in the casino, which made it the best game in the casino for free drinks. When the cock-tail waitress came by, Rick ordered a Crown and soda and Jules got a martini. Rick tipped her ten dollars for the first round to ensure she'd be back often.

They both started with a hundred-dollar bill each. After about an hour, Rick still had ninety-seven dollars left and Jules, who had won a few hands and one with a bonus, was sitting on a hundred and sixty. Even after tipping the wait-ress and dealers, they walked away from the table in the black with a free buzz to boot.

"Let's go try a five-dollar Wheel of Fortune!" exclaimed Rick.

They found one with a bonus deluxe spin if you bet seven or ten dollars a pull. Jules put in a hundred and so did Rick. They sat together on the large bench chair and took turns pulling the handle of the one-armed bandit. Jules got the first spin. The wheel stopped at a hundred and twenty, the smallest number on the wheel.

"Figures," said Rick.

They kept pulling the handle. Rick hit a couple of triple bars, which kept the game alive. He finally got a spin, but this time it was a deluxe spin, which was a bonus wheel on the bottom that gave them anything from one to six times whatever hit on the big wheel up top. He hit three times. Then asked Jules to push the button again. The big wheel went round and round then landed on six hundred.

"Yay! Six hundred, Rick!"

"No, Jules, that's eighteen hundred," he replied as he pointed at the three times bonus wheel.

"Oh shit, I forgot. Woohoo!"

They waited for the slot attendant to hand pay their winnings, then headed to the hostess stand of the steakhouse. They followed her to a private room Jack had arranged for them.

"Mr. Waters, I am Kevin and I'll be your server tonight. Jack has arranged for a six-course meal personally prepared by our chef. He said you are free to order off of the main menu but feels you will enjoy the special menu more. Will that be all right?"

"Sounds great, Kevin. Let's go with that."

"Wine?"

"Wine not?" Jules grinned.

Kevin poured a glass of Caymus Cabernet, and Rick gave him the thumbs-up. He poured them both glasses and placed the bottle on the table. Soon he returned with a steaming hot order of escargot. Along with some brie and pâté. The food just kept coming, and the tomahawk steaks were the size of a small truck. Jules did her best to eat as much as she could, but they were massive. She finally gave up. Rick knocked a nice hole in his before dessert arrived. It was a double chocolate hot lava cake. They both only had a few bites as they were beyond stuffed.

"Can you just bring us the check, Kevin? We are ready to bust open."

"There is no check, Mr. Waters. It's on Jack."

Rick just shook his head and smiled. He pulled out the $1,800 they had just won from the casino and placed it on the table. He wrote a thank-you note to Kevin for his wonderful service, and they slipped out before he returned. Rick felt good about paying it forward. He didn't know Kevin or his circumstances in life but felt like he was a good person and deserved a huge tip. They hobbled back up to their room and sat on the bed, almost too full to sleep.

"Rick, can we change and take a walk? I need to walk off this meal. That was insane."

"I couldn't agree more, Jules."

They both put on shorts and jogging shoes and decided to take a stroll down the sidewalk on the water. It was a beautiful night, and the stars were twinkling like little lanterns in the heavens. They walked hand in hand over a couple of miles each way. Rick was glad to finally be on a little break from work. For the past few months, once case had seemed to run into another, and they really needed this time off. After their walk, they were feeling better and decided to call it a night.

Once back in the room, they got comfortable and sat up in bed to watch *Forensic Files*. The narrator's voice always made them sleepy. Before he knew it, Rick was snoring upright in the bed. Jules gently awakened him and turned off the TV. They both slept like babies that night and were out before ten p.m.

CHAPTER TWO

The sound of a maid's cart bumping into the wall awakened Rick from the wild dream he was having. He bolted up with chills but couldn't remember a thing about it. The clock on the nightstand read 8:17 a.m. Jules shifted in bed but didn't wake up. Rick made a pot of coffee and tiptoed around the room, trying not to disturb her. Their flight was supposed to leave tomorrow at 10:20 a.m. from the Big Easy, but he pulled out his laptop and moved it to the 3:10 p.m. He figured that way they could sleep in a little in Bay St. Louis and then make a quick side trip to the French Quarter before the flight.

Jules murmured something Rick couldn't make out. He sat down on the bed beside her. He kissed her forehead, and her eyes slowly opened to a smile. She was so beautiful, he thought; even with no makeup and bed hair, she was still stunning.

"Good morning, Mr. Waters," said Jules.

"Good morning, Miss Castro. Did you sleep well?"

"I did, but I kept dreaming about cows. So weird!"

"Well, we damn near ate an entire one last night. No wonder."

"What's the plan, Rick?"

"If we can get out of here in the next half hour, we can stop by my friend's place in Gulfport I mentioned and have lunch before we hit the resort in Bay St. Louis. Tomorrow morning, we can swing by the French Market. They have some cool souvenirs there, t-shirts and whatnot. It's pretty cool. I think you'll like it."

"Sounds good, let me jump in the shower," said Jules with a yawn.

Rick emptied the chest of drawers and packed his suitcase. Jules dried off and hollered at Rick that it was his turn. He quickly showered as Jules brought up a luggage cart from downstairs. Once dressed, he texted Jack to see if they could say goodbye, but he responded that he was in Memphis on business and told them to have a great trip.

Rick put the carry-ons in the back of the Bronco, and they were off to New Orleans. He turned onto US 90, westbound for Murky Waters. It was only about a half hour drive up the coast. The place didn't open until eleven a.m., and they arrived at 9:15 a.m. Rick stuck his face up against the glass front door of the blues-styled eatery and spotted his old friend Leonard from high school, sweeping the floor.

When Rick knocked on the door, at first, Leonard just waved him away, indicating they weren't open yet. Rick knocked again, and Leonard looked over and squinted, finally recognizing him. He jogged over to the door and opened the deadbolt.

"Rick Waters in the flesh! What the hell are you doing here?" asked Leonard.

"Hey, Leonard, we are on our way to New Orleans and thought we'd stop by. Oh, forgive me, this is my girlfriend, Jules. Jules, Leonard. Boy, do we have some stories!"

Jules reached out her hand to shake Leonard's, and he pulled her in and gave her a big bear hug. He hugged her so tight he almost crushed her.

"Any friend of Rick is a friend of mine. Holy shit, you're gorgeous!"

Jules blushed and thanked him.

"Well, sit down. We don't open for a couple of hours, but the beer is cold and we can catch up," said Leonard.

Leonard went behind the bar and pulled out three frozen pint glasses and poured them each a frosty Andy Gator IPA without bothering to ask them if they wanted a beer at 9:45 a.m.

"Just like the old days, huh Leonard? A beer buzz in the morning," replied Rick with a grin.

"I'm sorry, what was I thinking? Jules, would you like a beer this early?"

"Yes, please, and a Bloody Mary chaser."

"I like this girl!"

Leonard also made three Bloody Marys and brought out a bowl of homemade cracklings. They sipped on both drinks and chatted.

"Jules, did Rick ever tell you about the time I got my income tax check back from the IRS and he talked me into going to Panama City for spring break?"

"I don't believe he did. I'm all ears."

"So, we had graduated a year before, I think, and I had a little trailer over near where Rick lived. He came over almost every day after we got off work. One Friday, he came over and I checked the mail and there was my income tax check. I had recently split with my wife and wanted to do something fun. He kept going on and on about Panama City and how it was the mecca for spring break. After several beers, we worked ourselves into a frenzy. The plan was to leave the next morning, but we were so excited, we made a pot of coffee and left for Florida 'round midnight. We took turns driving and barely slept. Once we got past Destin into Miramar, we were both so tired we couldn't see and I pulled the car off into the woods. We ended up sleeping in the car until two p.m. When we arrived in Panama City, the place was a ghost town. We checked in and the man behind the desk said, 'Y'all should have been here last week; the place was crawling with college girls.' We both just looked at other in disgust. We had missed spring break by a week."

"Oh no!" Jules laughed. "That's awful."

Leonard shrugged and grinned. "We managed to have a great time anyway. We befriended some touring rock band and hung out with them a lot. We fished some and did the tourist thing. It was our first time in Florida for both of us. I guess it struck a nerve with Rick, as he moved there a few years later after he got that job with the airline. You still working for them?"

"Naw, I got bumped so many times, I finally started doing something else."

"What are you doing now?"

Rick pulled out his business card and slid it across the desk to Leonard. On one side, it read: *Rick Waters—Boat*

Captain—*Nine Tenths*. On the other side: *Rick Waters— Private Investigator*.

"Damn, son. You're a P.I. and a boat captain now?"

"Well, sort of a boat captain. I barely get to drive the boat with all the cases we've had lately."

"Cool, I'll hang onto your card. I might need a P.I. one day."

The continued to catch up until about 10:15 a.m. Several employees started showing up, and Rick motioned to Jules that it was time for them to leave. Leonard tried to get them to stay for lunch, but they had already decided to go to Cuz's in Bay St. Louis.

"We'll catch you on the way back from New Orleans after our trip to Cozumel, okay?"

"If I'm still in business, haha."

"What do you mean? Your reviews are great and the place is fabulous."

"Oh, business is great, that's not the problem. It's the damn interest on the loan for the building. My credit was in the doghouse when I started this; the only way I could open was to get a loan from some unscrupulous peeps."

With his thumb and forefinger, Rick bent his nose and gave Leonard a serious look. Leonard just nodded.

"When we get back, let's get together and see if we can refinance that loan of yours. I have done well and have a nice line of credit at Synovus Bank."

"Rick, I can't do that, that's not why I mentioned it. You don't need to get involved. I'll figure it out."

Rick waved his protest away with a hand. "Nonsense. We are lifelong friends, and if I can help you out, consider it done. We can discuss if you wanna be partners or just have me hold the loan. Don't worry, it'll all work out."

Leonard came from behind the bar and hugged Rick as tears welled up in his eyes. "You were always a good guy, Rick." When he pulled away, he said, "You take care of him, Jules. He tends to overdo things and get hurt. When we were youngsters, I never saw him skip a chance to jump on a bronco or young bull in a field just to see if he could stay on for a few seconds. He's a little cray-cray."

"I'll keep an eye on him. It's my favorite pastime."

"You are one lucky SOB, Rick Waters! Hang on to her."

"I'm holding on to her like the time I jumped on that calf in the shoot and it took off like a rocket slamming my legs against the rails. You remember that?" Rick chuckled.

"How could I forget? You could barely walk for a week and your legs were covered in bruises and cuts. What an idiot you were. Are?"

"Were, no more indiscriminate bull riding. Those days are long gone."

Rick patted Leonard on the back as they left. Leonard grabbed Jules one more time for a hug.

"He's a nice guy," said Jules once they were outside.

"Salt of the earth, Jules, salt of the earth."

"Why do you bend your nose?"

"Oh, that's a sign for the mafia, aka crooked nose as they are known. I guess Leonard took out a loan from one of those scumbags. The vig alone is enough to shut down any business."

"Vig?"

"It's just another name for interest. If you take a loan from a shark, they often have you pay back the loan for more than you took plus the vig, so just to make it easy to understand, let's say he borrowed $50k and the payback was $75k. He would have to pay back $75k plus the interest on the $50k, which could be 40–50 points, which is insane. If he was paying back like five hundred a month, only about $250 of that would go to the loan and the rest would be the vig. It's a never-ending cycle and if you don't pay, well, let's just say you better pay."

"Why, what would happen?" asked Jules.

"You'd end up wearing cement shoes and get dumped in the middle of Taylor Bayou. My guess is he got the loan from the Guidry boys. They are basically known as the Cajun mafia from the area we grew up in. They aren't true connected mafia but they are just as violent. All they care about is money and respect. I've had a run-in with them a few times. When we get back, we'll sick Gary on their ass and get that loan paid off ASAP. I'm sure Gary will wanna be a part of it. He hates the Guidrys. He has more history with them than I do."

Jules shuddered. "I'm getting chills, Rick. They sound scary."

"They are. But money comes first with them. I'm sure we can set Leonard free from their greedy grip."

They hopped in the Bronco and continued on to Bay St. Louis. As they approached the bridge, Rick grabbed Jules's hand and squeezed it.

"You recognize this bridge, Jules?"

"Yes, it's where I kicked that carjacker in the nards!"

Rick burst out laughing. He assumed Jules might feel a little anxious or traumatized about driving over the bridge again, as it could bring back bad memories of when she was carjacked, but she took it in stride as if it meant nothing to her. Therapy had done wonders for her.

Once in Bay St. Louis, Rick found a parking spot by the beach road, and they strolled down to Cuz's Old Town Oyster Bar & Grill for lunch. They sat at the bar and each had a bowl of seafood gumbo for an appetizer. Jules decided on the ahi steak, while Rick went with the blackened redfish. Everything was spicy and cooked to perfection. They decided to take a walk down to the end of the fishing pier.

"Any luck?" Rick asked an old guy with three rods leaning against the rail.

"I caught a jack and two sheepshead but that's about it. Been kinda slow."

He lifted a towel off the bucket, revealing the fish.

"You eat those?"

"I do eat the sheepshead, but I use jacks for fertilizer. If you stick a jack in a hole then plant a tomato plant on top of it, it will produce more 'maters than any other plant. Works every time."

"Well, that's a nice tip. Good luck and have a great day," replied Rick.

As they continued on, he put his arm around Jules. "Jules, I was planning to put us up in the Hollywood Casino and Resort, but I'm kinda casino'd out. How would you feel about going into New Orleans today since it's still early? We can stay at this haunted hotel on Poydras Street called Le Pavillon Hotel. I read that one paranormal investigating team cited catching nearly one hundred undead entities roaming the property throughout the night."

Jules pulled away from him to give him a wide-eyed look. "Are you crazy? A haunted hotel?"

"You're not skeered, are you?"

"Scared?! Hell no. Let's go."

Rick grinned, knowing full well she was scared shitless but refused to admit it. He thought it might be fun. Maybe he could spook Jules a little and she would be forced to hold him tight all night. A win-win.

As they parked the Bronco outside the hotel, Jules scanned the top of the building, taking in the ornate facade of the structure that was built in 1907. It was truly a beautiful structure. The decorative railing and massive pillars were awe-inspiring. When they walked in, Jules instinctively grabbed Rick's arm as they made their way to the front desk. She was squeezing harder than normal. She was trying not to show fear but she was nervous. Struggling to be strong and overcome the fear she had about haunted hotels. Now, ghosts scared her, but criminals didn't anymore. What Rick didn't know was that deep inside, the carjacking had lit a fire in her to become as self-reliant and tough as she possibly could. It had brought out the Lara Croft in her.

"Good afternoon, we'd like a king room tonight if you have one," said Rick.

"May I have an ID and credit card, sir?"

Rick slid them over as the man behind the desk typed briskly on his keyboard.

"I have a traditional king in room 1017 on the tenth floor. Will that be to your liking?"

"Sure, is it a super haunted room?"

"It's considered our most haunted floor, sir."

"Perfect!"

Jules's eyes were huge as she looked over at Rick.

"It's not really haunted here, is it?" asked Jules.

"You tell me, ma'am,' said the man as he slid over a scrapbook.

Jules opened up the leather-bound book and scanned through article after article written about the historic hotel dating back to the early 1900s. Toward the end pages of the book, she even read that the TV shows *Ghost Hunters* and *Ghost Adventures* had both filmed episodes here. A cold chill ran down her back.

"Okay, sir, here are your keys. Please check out our signature restaurant and bar, Cachette 1907. We also have a fitness center and there is a pool on the roof."

"Sounds amazing."

The lobby was exquisite. As they approached the elevators, Rick pinched Jules, no doubt trying to scare her. She jumped and smacked his arm.

"Stop it!" she yelped.

"I thought you weren't scared?"

"I'm not. You just caught me off guard."

"What's that?" exclaimed Rick as he pointed behind her with big, scary eyes.

She jumped toward him and grabbed his arm. Rick laughed so hard he had to hold his belly. She gave him a dirty look as she stepped into the elevator.

"This isn't gonna go on all night, is it?"

"Okay, Jules, I'll lay off. How about we check out our room then head over to Bourbon Street. Want a big-ass beer?"

"Uh, no, but I do want a big-ass martini!"

"Okay, let's see if we can sort that out."

Their room was lovely and decorated with modern furniture as well as antique replicas of days gone by. It was extremely clean and comfortable, which made Jules relax somewhat. She unpacked the suitcases and put them in the dressers. Then she changed into her walking shoes and grabbed a light windbreaker in case they went into someplace cold. Right before they left for the lobby, she put her pistol in her purse. Rick always carried a handgun, but for Jules this was new. Her abduction in Mississippi had been the catalyst for her to start carrying a concealed weapon.

The walk from Le Pavillon to Bourbon Street was only about a ten-minute walk via Baronne Street. They walked hand in hand. Rick had tucked his .38 into the rear of his waistband just in case. New Orleans had become one of the most dangerous cities in America.

They stopped at a place called Prohibition. It had a sign under it that said Huge Ass Beers, which made Rick laugh.

"They have a full bar, Jules, and I can get a Huge Ass Beer instead of a big-ass beer. You can get a martini, that work?"

"Sure, I'm game."

They made their way upstairs, and Rick ordered for them both. It was a dive bar at best, and they only stayed for one drink each.

"Let me see if I can find someplace a little nicer." Rick pulled out his phone and did a quick search and decided to try the Foundation Room above the House of Blues.

It was quaint, small, and only had a few patrons inside when they arrived. Jules ordered a Belvedere Vodka martini with three olives, and Rick went for a classic Pimm's Cup, a drink created at the Napoleon House in the 1040s. After a few drinks and a recommendation from the bartender, they decided to go to the restaurant he suggested. It was a place called Galatoire's just up the street on Bourbon. It featured French creole cuisine and was considered by many to be the best restaurant in New Orleans.

They had a glorious dinner of shrimp etouffee and crab au gratin. Afterward, they decided to slowly walk back to the hotel via Royal Street to get away from the tourists that had started to stagger all over Bourbon Street. As they walked, Rick started to notice that several of the street-lights were out. He pulled Jules to the opposite side of the street where some guys were smoking. Rick glanced over his shoulder as they continued to walk. Two of the guys began to follow them. Once they got about a block from Canal, it was obvious they were about to be mugged or worse.

As Rick reached back for his pistol in his waistband, Jules spun around and pulled her gun from her purse.

"Step back, motherfuckers, or I'll blow your Goddamn heads off!"

They froze, and Rick released his fingers from around his .38. She raised the gun and fired a shot just over their heads. They ran as if they were in the Olympics. Jules tucked her pistol back into her purse and waved with her head for Rick to follow her. Rick was stunned and amazed at the same time.

They hurried one street over to Carondelet Street and crossed Canal toward the hotel without speaking. Sirens rang out as they quickly stepped into the hotel and went up to their room. Jules let out a big sigh when they got to the room. She pulled out her pistol, unloaded it, and took her cleaning kit out as if it was just a normal day. She began to clean her gun before Rick had even spoken to her.

"Are you okay? That got sideways kinda fast."

"I'm fine. Why?"

"Jules, you just fired a .9-millimeter bullet inches over two men's heads.

"So?"

"So?" asked Rick.

"I'm fine, Rick. I promise. I just need to clean my gun before we head up to the pool, okay?"

"Uh, okay, Jules," replied Rick, still sort of shocked at her calm demeanor.

Once at the pool, they sat in the shallow end, still not discussing what had just happened as they took in the New Orleans skyline. Rick was concerned that she had almost zero reaction to the incident but decided to table it for another day.

CHAPTER THREE

The clock read 5:17 a.m. when Rick was awakened by a sound. He lay in bed staring at the ceiling, listening. The room was deadly silent with the only sound being the whirr of the ceiling fan.

Knock, knock, knock

There it was again. It seemed to be coming from the floor above. Rick rolled over, figuring it was someone stomping on the floor in the room above them. As quickly as he shut his eyes, they flew back open as he remembered they were on the top floor and there were no rooms above them. Jules was softly purring beside him. He figured it was best not to wake her.

Knock, knock, knock

The sound returned, this time louder. The hairs on the back of his neck stood up. Rick had booked the hotel as a joke mostly to spook Jules, but he was acutely aware of the significance of three knocks. After his experience with the voodoo queen in Haiti, his inquisitive interest had arisen and he'd studied as many books as he could find on the occult, demons, ghosts, poltergeists, really anything on the subject he could get his hands on. Three knocks were otherworldly. They always came in threes. Every book on the afterlife mentioned three knocks. He waited again and listened.

Knock, knock, boom!

The ceiling fan slammed to the ground just inches from Jules's head, who woke up with a startled cry. She instinctively reached for her gun on the nightstand. Rick grabbed her arm and pulled her back.

"No, Jules, it's okay. No one's here."

"What happened?" she said, still half asleep and confused.

"The ceiling fan fell. Look!"

Rick pointed to her side of the bed on the floor. The fan sat there, bare wires showing, still rocking from its fall.

Knock, knock, boom!

Two knocks and a loud bang came from the hole where the ceiling fan was.

"What is that?!" shrieked Jules.

"Pack the bags, Jules. I'll tell you in the Bronco."

They both packed their suitcases as fast as they could and threw on their clothes for the flight. Jules was shaking. They hopped in the elevator without speaking, and Rick dumped the keys in the drop box.

Once in the Bronco, Rick rubbed Jules's legs.

"Jules, when I booked that hotel, I was merely trying to spook you a little, but it turns out the place is really haunted.

You slept through several of the sets of three knocks before the fan fell. Three knocks signify a poltergeist. I'm not trying to scare you now, just letting you know."

Jules looked at Rick's hands. They were trembling.

"Oh baby, you're scared too?" asked Jules.

"Just a little unnerved. That fan missed you by just a few inches. Whoever or whatever that was didn't want us around, and I was obliged to agree. Let's get some coffee and beignets and try to catch our breath."

Jules held out her hands, and they too were shaking. She was fully awake now and finally comprehending what Rick was saying. It was hard to process.

Ghosts? thought Jules. *Real ghosts?*

Rick found a great parking spot near Café Du Monde, and they grabbed a small table by the sidewalk. Rick held Jules's hands in his as they waited for the puffy, powdered sugar treats to arrive. He got a large coffee with chicory and Jules got the French roast.

"Let me see if I can find us a sooner flight," said Rick, pulling out his iPhone. "Looks like Southwest has a nonstop at 7:40 a.m."

"Book it," said Jules.

They arrived at the airport an hour early and got through security quickly, since it was so early in the morning. They got A Group as the flight was nearly empty. Both Rick and Jules had put their pistols in the locked compartment of the Bronco before they proceeded into the airport. Rick chose two seats in the emergency exit row, and they stowed their bags overhead. Within minutes, the plane was up in the air and on its way to the Mexican Riviera. Jules looked at

Rick with a *did that really just happen* look. He nodded and squeezed her hand.

"No more haunted hotels, mister!" said Jules, motherly like.

"You don't have to say that twice! Phew!" said Rick.

"What about the room? Do you think they will think we trashed that fan?" asked Jules.

"Good point. I'll call them as soon as we land."

They both rested their heads back and drifted off to sleep.

The next thing they knew, the wheels chirped as the plane hit the tarmac. Jules glanced out of the window at the Cancun airport building. It was much larger and more modern than she expected. At the gate, they went through customs and immigration. Jules hated leaving her pistol behind, but she knew it was too risky to try and bring it into Mexico. Besides, it was time to relax and kick back. It was their first real vacation together. No work, all play. Still, she felt an uneasiness waft over her without her beloved .9 millimeter in her purse.

"Ready for some fun, Jules?"

"Si, señor!"

"Oh, I forget sometimes that you speak Spanish as a first language. That's gonna make our trip that much better!"

Once they got to the car rental area, they were ambushed by vendors trying to push every conceivable excursion on them, from a jungle trip to Xcaret to deep sea fishing off of Isla Mujeres. Rick scanned the room for the most honest-looking guy and waved him over.

"Hola, señor, do you want to go shopping at Playa Del Carmen?" he asked.

"Nope, listen up and I'm only gonna say this once. I'm not doing any excursions or shopping, but if you can get me a clean, dependable dune buggy for a week, I'll give you this as a tip."

Rick held up a fifty-dollar bill and spun it in circles. The man's eyes widened.

"Hold on, mister, I got chew."

He pulled out his cell phone and starting speaking Spanish so fast even Jules could barely understand him. She nodded at Rick and whispered in his ear.

"He's getting the car from his cousin. He said it was just painted and has a new motor."

The man hung up. "Follow me, the car is coming."

They both followed the man out the side doors of the airport to the curb and waited. He ran behind the corner and returned with a bottle of tequila and two shot glasses, a huge grin on his face. Rick and Jules clinked their glasses together and both downed the shots. The tequila was smooth.

"What is it? I mean, what brand?" asked Rick.

"It's Los Tres Tonos. I get it from a friend of mine, Luis, who works at the Chile Tequila Factory Outlet in Cozumel. If you go, please tell him I sent you. Oh, here's my card."

His card read, *Pancho Vasquez—Riviera Maya*, and that's it. No phone number, no email, nothing. Rick stuck it in his pocket and promised to let Luis know if they ended up in Cozumel somehow.

"You wanna sell that bottle?" asked Rick.

He thought for a minute then said, "Yes. One hundred dollars, plus the fifty for the Jeep."

Jules rolled her eyes. He was trying to rip them off—no way was she going to let him. She walked up to the man, speaking Spanish faster than Rick had ever heard her. The man began to cower a bit. He then said, "Eighty dollars altogether, okay?"

Rick agreed and handed him the money as the dune buggy pulled up.

"You've got to be kidding me!" exclaimed Rick.

Jules was bent over laughing. The dune buggy was hot pink and had a large sunflower painted on the hood. Rick shook his head, signed the papers, paid the man, and immediately handed the keys to Jules.

"You are D.D. this week. I ain't driving this damn thing."

Jules threw her bag in the space behind the seat and jumped in. She was super excited to drive. Rick did almost all the driving back in Florida, and she was happy for the change. Rick reluctantly climbed in the passenger seat and turned his cap around for the long drive down to Tulum. He held up one finger for Jules to hold on a second while he was on the phone. Jules waited while he called the hotel back in New Orleans.

"Hello, this is Rick Waters. We were staying in room 1017 last night, and the ceiling fan fell and almost hit my fiancé. That room is freaking haunted. I ain't paying for that fan!" he said over the phone.

There was a long silence as he waited, then he hung up.

"All good, Jules. They said it ain't the first time and it won't be the last."

Jules squealed the tires as she took off out of the airport, knocking Rick back in his seat. She was still not used to the brand-new clutch that had recently been installed on the upgraded ride, but after a few false starts, she was feeling like Mario Andretti. Jules was having so much fun driving the dune buggy, she figured Rick was now happy the damn thing came in pink. She couldn't stop grinning. She had all but forgotten about the paranormal experience they had just had a few hours prior in New Orleans. That seemed like ages ago now, as if it was just a bad dream before their trip.

They stopped in Playa Del Carmen, and Jules spotted a couple of gorgeous his and hers Blue Opal and Tungsten Carbide rings.

"Can I try it on?" asked Jules with a childlike look on her face toward Rick.

"Of course."

She was gleaming with the ring and slipped the other one onto Rick's ring finger.

"Rick Waters, will you…"

Rick held his breath, and Jules could see in his eyes he was sort of freaking out before she finished the sentence.

"Will you be my boyfriend forever? These can be our promise rings."

"Awe, how sweet, Jules. But I can't be your boyfriend forever."

She frowned as he continued, "One day, I hope to be much more."

A huge smile sprouted from her face, and she wrapped her arms around him. Rick paid the man for the rings, and they continued on toward Tulum. Rick had a huge Tecate in between his legs, while Jules sipped on a Diet Pepsi. She was taking this D.D. thing seriously.

As Jules drove, Rick pointed at the signs for Xcaret and other tourist stops. If they had time and the gumption, he planned to take Jules to a few of the places. He just didn't wanna use a third party to book them. After all, he had Jules. She would get them the best price for anything they did with her charm and finesse.

They arrived at Dreams Resort in Tulum midafternoon, and Jules zipped right in and stopped on a dime by the massive registration doors at the entrance. The grounds of the resort were stunning and meticulously manicured. They both snatched their carry-ons from the buggy, and Jules tossed the keys to the valet.

"Park it, Paco," she said with determination.

They arrived at the front desk, and Jules began speaking Spanish to the man behind the desk. Rick tried to follow but she was too fast. Soon a manager walked back from behind the desk. Jules got Rick to look down at her hand, and she flashed five twice, indicating ten.

"Congratulations, Mr. Waters, on your anniversary," said the manager.

Thinking on his feet, Rick said, "Yes, ten wonderful years already. How time flies when you're in love."

He spun his ring around with his fingers.

"We don't normally do this, but your wife has convinced me to upgrade you to one of the swim-out rooms. The rooms have a veranda on the first floor that has steps down into a lazy river that encompasses the entire garden area, as well as many other upgrades."

"Why thank you so much. That is so kind of you."

Jules winked at Rick and spun her ring around as if to say, *See, I told you these rings were a good idea.*

A man brought Rick and Jules some champagne, and they toasted to a great start to their vacation. They strolled through the grounds of the stunning resort, taking in all the flora and fauna. Rick pointed out birds, which made him think of Chief back home.

"Look, Jules," said Rick as he pointed at a black bird walking in the grass. "You know what kind of bird that is?"

"A crow?"

"Nope, it's a long-tailed grackle. That other yellow one over there is a great kiskadee."

"Wow, Rick, you really know your birds."

Rick just grinned as he glanced down at his bird identifier app on his phone when she wasn't looking.

"Do you know what kind of plant that is, Rick?"

He studied it for while, trying to make an educated guess. "Honeysuckle?"

"Close, it's a *ceiba pentandra*, aka kapok tree, the most sacred tree to the Mayan people."

"I give up, you win," Rick laughed. "Let's get wet!"

They opened the door to their room. It was quite opulent with lots of marble and decorative dark wood accents. It did seem a tad dated, but it was Mexico and they were just happy to be anywhere but work. They quickly changed into their bathing suits and stepped hand in hand into the lazy river. Rick carried the bottle of tequila he had gotten from Pancho. He took a swig and passed it to Jules. She took a small sip then asked if they could order some cold drinks from room service.

"It's all-inclusive, baby. We can order whatever we want!"

Rick tiptoed into the living room, as if that would cause less water to get on the floor, and called room service.

"Hi, can I get two frozen piña coladas? Yeah, just knock loud as we are in the back by the pool. Oh, okay."

He hopped back into the water.

"They will deliver right to the veranda, Jules. Now that's service."

They settled into the water, basking in the sun as the neighbors next door to them stepped out and into the water.

"Hello," said Rick.

"Hi, how are you two today?"

"Right as rain. I'm Rick Waters and this is Jules."

Rick swam over and shook the man's hand as his much younger hot wife stepped into the pool. She was easily twenty years younger than him, but Rick didn't judge. Love is love.

"I'm Paul Giovanni, and this is my wife Kirsten."

"It's a pleasure to meet you both," said Rick as Jules waved at them and came closer.

"Where are y'all from?" asked Rick, noticing an accent.

"We are from Kimberley, South Africa. And you, let me guess. Georgia?"

"Nope, I'm from southeast Texas and Jules is from Columbia. What brings y'all here?"

"A little mix of business and pleasure."

"Oh cool, I won't pry."

"No worries, mate. I'm in the wholesale diamond business. We are here to deliver an order to Diamonds International. Just another day in the jewel business. What do you do for a living?"

"Well, that's a loaded question. I'm a boat captain, treasure hunter, and private investigator. We have a small firm in Destin, Florida. But I am here strictly on pleasure. We have been slammed for months and all we want is sun, fun, and rum...ahem...make that tequila."

They all hung out in the water and chitchatted until they were pruned. A young woman and a man who looked like he was in his mid-thirties stepped onto the veranda.

"This is my daughter Ava and her boyfriend Maxx."

Rick stood up to shake her hand, but she just spun around as if he wasn't there and disappeared into the living room.

Maxx shook Rick's hand and whispered, "She's a little high maintenance."

Rick winked his acknowledgement.

"Can we go check out the beach, Rick?" asked Jules.

"Sure thing, baby."

They said their goodbyes and promised to share dinner one night. Jules dried off and threw on a cover-up. Rick just donned a t-shirt and flip flops and air dried.

The sun was setting as they approached the beach. There was a massive pool on the right with a swim-up bar and bridge over one part of the pool and an even larger pool to the left. Just past a small, short cement wall was the soft sand and the Gulf of Mexico. A small flock of monk parrots in a palm tree were yipping and yapping, which caught Rick's attention. High above flew the great frigates with their massive wingspan that kept them floating on the thermals. Frigates were Rick's favorite bird, next to his beloved Chief.

"You getting hungry, Rick?"

"I'm famished, but I don't wanna ruin dinner. Oh look, they have a hot dog grill over by the adult pool. Want a dog?"

"Yeah, a hot dog sounds great right now."

They both scarfed down a hot dog and got another piña colada. They decided to head back and get dressed for dinner. Jules showered first and slipped into a lovely black dress with a long split down the side. When Rick saw her, he knew his shorts and flip flops wouldn't work, so he showered and grabbed a pair of slacks and a Henley. They decided to go to the fanciest of the seven restaurants on the property: Bordeaux, a French-inspired fine-dining restaurant. The food was excellent, and they both felt super sleepy after dinner and decided to call it an early night. They were passed out by ten p.m.

The next few days were much like the first. Lots of pool lounging, eating too much, and soaking up the sun. Soon Rick was getting restless and wanted to do some exploring. Always the treasure hunter, he had been researching some wrecks off of the coast of Xcalak at the bottom of the Yucatán peninsula near Belize.

"Wanna do a road trip?" asked Rick as he poured Jules a coffee.

"Yes, please!"

"I was reading about this little town called Xcalak. Several British and Dutch wrecks have been discovered there. It's not Spanish gold, but we might be able to hire a boat and some scuba gear and find some porcelain or something. It could be fun."

"I haven't ever done a dive in a wreck, Rick. Are you sure I'm ready?"

"You'll be fine. It's fairly shallow there. There's a long reef that claimed most of the ships. Don't worry, I'll be right beside you the entire time."

Jules smiled at him, reassured. "How far of a drive is it? Should we bring a change of clothes?"

"Yeah, let's just load up one suitcase with a few overnight things and a change of clothes and bathing suits just in case."

Rick pulled out his iPhone and mapped the trip to Xcalak.

"Wow, it's a three-hour drive. Are you sure you're up to it?"

"To be honest, as nice as this resort is, I'm kinda getting bored. Maybe we can get into some trouble down there, ha-ha."

"Well, hopefully not too much."

Jules drove the entire way down and made the trip in under three hours. It was around ten a.m. when they pulled into Xcalak. Rick found the only dive shop and they met the owner. The town was very primitive. It was more of a village than a town. No cell service and no ATMs. He was glad he'd brought lots of cash.

"Hello, do you speak English?" asked Rick.

"Si, I mean yes. I am Jose Batun. Would you like to go diving today?"

"We would, Jose. Actually, we were wondering if we can do some exploring of any of the dive sites that may have shipwreck remnants."

"I have been diving and dive mastering here for over twenty-five years. I know all the spots. It's very slow right now and I have no one booked for the day. If you want, you can charter the entire boat for yourselves and I can provide a lunch, drinks, and four tanks each and do a six-hour trip. They are normally four hours. Would that interest you?"

"That sounds great. Jules?"

She nodded in agreement.

"Do you have any metal detectors?"

"As a matter of fact, I just got in two brand-new Pulse 8Xs. We can break them in on this trip."

"Excellent. I have one at home and I'm very familiar with it. When can we leave?"

"Give me a half an hour to get the boat ready and meet me at the dock. If you want anything special to snack on, there's a little market just up the road."

"Okay, we'll see you shortly."

They stopped at the market, and Jules got some sun-block, which she had forgotten to bring from Destin. Rick grabbed some snacks for later. Once back at the dock, they climbed aboard Jose's boat, and he slammed the boat into gear and they were up on plane in seconds. The trip to the reef didn't take long, and they were all geared up when he dropped the anchor.

Jules fell off of the boat first, and Rick did a giant stride to join her. Once they checked each other's gauges, they descended down to the edge of the reef, a mere thirty-two feet down. The reef was alive with fish and invertebrates. Jules was snapping photos with her Go Pro, and Rick was scanning the floor for any signs of ship wreckage. On the first dive, he didn't find anything. But on the second dive, he found some broken porcelain plates. Rick was disappointed; he'd been hoping to find more interesting pieces.

After their last dive, they all cracked open beers and Jose began to tell them stories about growing up in in Xcalak. He was a likeable guy and had one yarn after another. His English was exceptional, and he rarely slipped into Spanish unless Jules did first.

"How many wrecks do you think there are around here?" asked Rick.

"I'm no expert, but I've heard they have found over seventy. I'm sure there's many more that haven't been discovered. If you wanna try and find more wrecks, I suggest you talk to Manuel Polanco in town. He's an old fisherman and the local expert of old shipwrecks. He's from Port Sisal but down here to fish for the season. He personally discovered two wrecks in Sisal and is somewhat famous in the area."

"How will I find him?"

"Oh, that's easy. He will be the loudest one playing dominos by the pier. He's not the easiest to approach. Do you play dominos?"

"I've played before. Why?"

"They love to gamble and dominos rules the night here."

Jules piped up, "I'm very good at dominos. I've been playing since I was a little girl."

They rinsed off, thanked Jose, and changed into street clothes in search of Manuel Polanco.

Rick folded up twenty-thousand pesos and gave it to Jules to hold for the dominos game. It was roughly a thousand US dollars. He doubted they'd get that crazy gambling. Jules parked the car a few blocks from the pier, and they began to walk down as the sun set. From nearly a football field a way, they could hear a man hollering and cheering.

They both looked at each other and simultaneously said, "Manuel!"

They slowly approached the table to stares from the men sitting around it. Rick felt like a fish out of water. Jules took the lead.

"¿Puede una niña jugar?" she asked.

The just shook their heads and focused on the dominos. She had asked them if a girl could play. They obviously didn't know who they were dealing with.

"¿Estás jodido?" she said aggressively and flapped her arms like wings.

The men stopped and looked up at her acting like a chicken. One man laughed and pulled up a chair and waved her over.

"Ven aquí niña," he said with a smile.

Money was sitting on the center of the table, and once the game finished, Jules pulled out a thousand pesos and slammed them on the table. Silence fell over the men as she had just tripled the normal ante for a game. One man pushed his chair away and shook his head. It was too rich for his blood apparently. Jules had learned the art of the shark from Rick's pool hall days. She would throw the first few games and increase her bets. She mostly wanted to get on Manuel's good side. He was a great dominos player, and every game she threw, he ended up winning the entire pot. He hugged her for good luck after the third win.

They began to talk in Spanish. Rick tried to keep up, but her Spanish was way too fast. He did make out the word *naufragio*, which meant "shipwreck" in Spanish.

On the final game, Jules plopped down the rest of her money, roughly eight hundred US dollars. It was obvious they had never played for that much before. Everyone but Manuel and Jules got up from the table. Manuel was sweating profusely and looked worried. He dug in his pockets for all of his money but couldn't match Jules's eight hundred. He opened a small backpack and pulled out a gold watch and leather tube with a lid on it. He uncorked the lid and pulled out an old, ratty piece of paper with burned edges. He laid it on the table and stared into Jules's eyes. He said one thing and one thing only:

"El tesoro de maya."

Rick typed in the words, but then pulled out his translation book since his phone was useless.

The Treasure of Maya

Jules rolled her eyes at the man as if the map was worthless, but his stare into her eyes was genuine. He did not want to lose the map. Rick had to wonder if that meant it was real. At last, they'd stumbled upon something intriguing.

Manuel scattered the dominos around and the game began. On the final play, Jules laid down her domino and the men gasped as she slammed the table. It was customary to slam the table after a big win. Dominos flew up into the air and she reached over and slipped the money, watch, and map over to her side of the table.

The old man looked defeated, devastated, as if his dog had just died. Jules eyes welled up. She hugged him and whispered in his ear and he perked up. They shook hands, and she took the map and Rick's hand and they headed back to the dune buggy.

"What did you whisper to him?"

"Let's be partners. Fifty-fifty!"

CHAPTER FOUR

It was too late to drive back to Dreams Resort. They could make it, but driving on a Mexican highway at night was more dangerous than walking in New Orleans after dark. They had to find a place to crash for the night. Without the use of phones, they just had to drive around and find something. Jules drove south down the coast past the dive shop, and they ran into a place called the Xcalak Caribe Lodge. It was only seventy-seven dollars a night and had Wi-Fi. The rooms were clean and the restaurant was surprisingly good with lots of fresh seafood.

The next morning, they met with Manuel over breakfast and set up a meeting with him and some of his crew in a few days over in Sisal. Jules realized now they would probably be in Mexico more than just a week.

Back at the resort, they settled into their routine of swimming and eating. Jules and Rick studied the map together several times and kept it in the safe in their room. The map was more words than map, and all in Spanish, of course.

"It says…the bells of three low in the street," said Jules, translating it. "Look toward Christ, the way to gold is in reverse. The church of lime is where the route is found. The second map is inside the book of Paul… Some kind of riddle, huh?"

"Seems like it."

If there was treasure to be found, it was going to take them a long time to find it, but that wouldn't stop them from trying.

After dinner, they decided to stay in the room and watch a movie. There was a ruckus in their neighbor's room next door and they could hear yelling and stuff breaking. Someone was having an over-the-top argument. Jules turned up the TV, trying to drown it out, as it was making them both feel uncomfortable. After about a half hour of yelling, they heard a door slam and then silence.

"I guess someone's pissed off," said Rick.

The next morning, there was a knock on Rick's door. He threw on a robe and stumbled across the cold tile floor and opened the door. It was Paul and he was visibly upset.

"Come in, come in, what's wrong?"

"It's my daughter Ava. Well, and her boyfriend Maxx. They were gone when we came back from dinner last night and they haven't returned. Something is wrong. Did you hear anything last night?"

Rick frowned. "Yes, we did. They seemed to be having a loud fight, then around 9:45 p.m. the door slammed and it was over. That's all we heard. We didn't want to make a big deal about it. I mean, people do have fights. Tequila can do crazy things to people."

"Can we sit down, Rick? I need to tell you something."

"Sure. Jules, can you make some coffee, baby?"

She nodded as the two men sat at the table.

"This is kind of embarrassing, but I've been dealing with it for so long now I'm just gonna say it. First off, I apologize about the noise. It wasn't tequila driven, I assure you. My daughter has BPD."

"BPD? Is that Bipolar Disorder?" asked Rick.

"No, but that's a common misconception. It's actually Borderline Personality Disorder. It's caused from early trauma as a child. Actually, Ava's was caused by my ex-wife. She had postpartum depression after Ava's birth and refused to hold her or give her any attention. She would just let her cry and cry for hours and leave her alone. She felt abandoned as an infant and it messed her up as an adult. I was working in the diamond mines then and away from home often. She started showing traits as an early teenager. She tried to cut herself a lot and attempted suicide several times. After the second attempt, we committed her to an institute for a while, and she was official diagnosed with BPD. I've already contacted the front desk and they called the local police to help search for them."

"What does the BPD have to do with her disappearance?"

"Everything. BPD has nine traits. A person only needs five to be diagnosed, and Ava has eight of them. They are fear of abandonment; unstable relationships; unclear or shifting self-image; impulsive, self-destructive behaviors; self-harm; extreme emotional swings; chronic feelings of emptiness; and explosive anger. She is literally a ticking time bomb.

My new wife and her don't get along at all. I met my new wife at a convention in Cape Town. She's twenty-five years younger than me and only a few years older than Ava. They are jealous of each other, and it makes things extremely difficult at times."

"You certainly have your hands full. Her boyfriend seems older, no?"

"Yes, he's thirty-eight. I don't approve, but what can I say? I'd be a hypocrite if I kept them apart after marrying a girl twenty-five years younger than me. I just had to keep my feelings to myself. He seems to make her happy. Well, as happy as she can be when she's not throwing dishes. The reason I'm telling you about her BOD is because time is ticking. She didn't take her Effexor with her and she is already unstable."

"Effexor?"

"It's a drug for depression. She also takes Xanax but not all the time. We need to find her. Quitting Effexor cold turkey is dangerous for the nervous system. Can you help? I came here because you said you were a private investigator. We don't know anyone here, and I don't have a ton of faith in the local police. Hell, we called them an hour ago and they still aren't here."

"Sure, Paul. We'll help. Anything else you can tell me about her that may help us track her down?"

"She loves animals and she's been obsessed with iguanas ever since she got here. Maybe they got lost in the rainforest looking for iguanas. Who knows?"

"Okay, we'll start looking now. Can I have your cell number? Mine is on the card I gave you."

"I'll go back to my room and text you so you have mine."

"Perfect. I'll keep you posted."

Rick got dressed as he sipped on his coffee, and Jules pulled out a map of Tulum. They got in the dune buggy, and Rick texted Paul back and asked for a recent photo. He sent him one they had taken by the pool just the day before. Rick cropped the others out and zoomed in on Ava's face. He tried to memorize every detail. The last thing Rick wanted to was be working. Sure, he was getting a little bored, but instead of working he could be on a treasure hunt. But he could feel the man's fear and knew he had to help.

They drove around for hours, stopping at several places and showing Ava's photo to store owners and bartenders. On their last stop at a place called Caribe Swing, they both grabbed a swing chair and sat at the bar. Rick waved the bartender over and ordered two Dos Equis and showed him the picture on his phone.

"¡Si esa puta estuvo aqui!"

Rick recognized the word *puta*, which meant whore. Jules commandeered the conversation.

"¿Estaba aquí sola?"

"No, ella estaba con un tipo mayor."

"¿Cuándo se fueron y dijeron adónde iban?"

"Eché a la perra repugnante a medianoche después de que me arrojara una botella. No dejaba de decir que se iba a follar a su novio encima de las ruinas."

"Gracias!"

Jules slid a twenty-dollar bill toward the man.

"Let's go, Rick."

"Where?"

"The ruins!"

When they arrived at the entrance to the Mayan ruins, they were closed. They closed at dark. Rick pulled out two small flashlights and handed one to Jules. The moon was full so they might not need them, but at least they had them.

They snuck through the woods around the gate where a security guard was sitting on a chair playing with his phone. They searched the entire area, including the tops of the ruins they could climb to. The kept yelling her name and got no response.

At the far edge of the ruins was a small trail through a wooded area that led to a cliff's edge. The sign made it obvious it was dangerous to crawl past the guide rope. Rick stepped over the rope and shined his flashlight down. About ten feet down, before the final drop of over a hundred feet, lay a crumpled body of a woman who looked like Ava. She was motionless and covered in blood. Her right shoe was missing, but other than that, she was fully clothed.

"Oh my god, Jules. It's her! Help me down and call the police."

Jules wrapped her arms around the rope, and Rick lay on his belly and gently lowered himself to the lower cliff.

"I have a pulse, Jules. She's unconscious but she's breathing."

Jules immediately called the police and began spewing Spanish.

Suddenly, headlights were coming her way fast. It was the security guard on a large ATV who must've heard them yelling Ava's name. He stepped off of the ATV as if he was coming to arrest Jules. She put him right in his place and pointed to the cliff. He looked over the cliff then ran back to the ATV, secured it to a tree and lowered a winch down the side of the cliff.

Rick picked up Ava and draped her over his shoulders, then wrapped the leather strap through and around his belt and they slowly ascended to the top. Once at the top, they placed her on the back of the ATV and directed the man to drive back to the resort.

"The damn EMT didn't believe me that there was an accident at the ruins because they're closed. I can't get over that!" exclaimed Jules.

They arrived at the resort before any authorities. They quickly rushed Ava to Paul's room. There was a gash on her head, and her face was covered in dirt and grass. Paul grabbed a washcloth and cleaned up her face. He was beside himself. They placed her on the bed. He instructed his wife to stay with her, while he and Rick ran to the front lobby to wait for the EMT. Just as they were going out the door, she started coughing. She was coming to.

Paul moved back to her bedside. "Ava, can you hear me? It's Dad. What happened?"

She was in a fog and looked dizzy as she tried to sit up. He helped her back down onto a pillow. She held her head.

"My head hurts, Daddy."

"Kirsten, mix her up a BC powder quickly."

"What happened, Ava? Where's Maxx?

As if she had just been given a shot of Naloxone, through tears and pain, she said, "He raped me, Daddy, and threw me off the cliff."

"What?! I'll kill him!" shouted Paul.

Ava fell back on the pillow holding her head.

"Are you okay, Paul?" asked Rick.

"Yeah, I'm fine. Please come with me to the lobby. She needs medical treatment ASAP."

Jules went back to her room to get her notepad and wait for instructions from Rick.

Thirty minutes went by before the ambulance arrived. While they waited, Paul made a quick trip to the bathroom in the hotel lobby. When he came back, the ambulance was finally pulling up.

"It's about fucking time!" yelled Paul.

Rick waved the EMTs to follow them with a gurney. When they arrived at Paul's room, Kirsten was screaming.

"Help, help!"

They rushed past the living room and into the bedroom. There was vomit on the floor leading to the bathroom. Rick ran into the bathroom first and saw Ava face down in the toilet. He grabbed her hair and pulled her out. Vomit was everywhere. She wasn't breathing.

"What the fuck happened?" asked Rick. "She was fine thirty minutes ago."

Kirsten pointed to the bed. Beside the bed and on the nightstand on the floor was half a bottle of pills scattered about. Rick walked over and picked one up. Effexor.

"How many did she take?"

"I don't know. It was a brand-new prescription."

From the look of the bottle, it appeared she had ingested a lethal dose. At least half of the bottle.

"Son of a bitch!" yelled Rick.

Jules rushed in to see Kirsten and Paul crying and Ava's body on the floor of the bathroom. The EMTs were giving her CPR, but she was blue and looked cold. Jules put a hand over her mouth in shock.

They covered her body after twenty minutes of futile CPR. She was gone. Rick put his head in his hands and slumped down. There was nothing he could do. They wheeled her body off to the ambulance.

"I'm so sorry, Paul."

Rick walked over and wrapped his arms around his new friend, trying to console him. The sadness in the air was almost too much to bear. Rick and Jules comforted them for a while then returned to their room to try and wrap their heads around what had just happened.

"How could this happen, Jules? She was hurt but she was fine. Why would she kill herself?"

Jules began to cry uncontrollably. Rick hugged her, but she wouldn't stop. Through tears, she tried to speak.

"I, I, huh, huh, I know why, Rick. I've never told you this, but after I was carjacked, the trauma was so bad I thought about suicide. The feeling of not being in control and that freak holding what I thought was a gun to my back really affected me. Ava was raped, so her pain must've been ten times what mine was, plus she has BPD. She was already so unstable."

"Yes, you're right, Jules. It must've been unbearable for her. It was the final straw that put her over the edge."

"It's a tragic accident, Rick. I feel so sorry for Paul and his wife. I guess maybe Ava is in a better place now, though. She was such a lost soul according to Paul."

"I guess that's one way to look at it. I'm sure Paul wants to get on with his life and bury his little girl, but one thing about the whole incident really bothers me."

"What's that?"

"How the fuck did she overdose on Effexor in less than thirty minutes?"

"It's a strong drug," replied Jules.

"I know that. I immediately pulled up on my phone *can you overdose on Effexor.* You definitely can, and she took more than enough to do the trick. What's bothering me though is one thing—time. The Effexor she was taking was in capsule form. It takes a solid thirty minutes for capsules to dissolve in the stomach."

"Maybe she died from the head trauma and had a brain bleed? Could she have drowned in the toilet? Wasn't her face under the water?"

"You're right, Jules. There could be other reasons than an overdose," he said, thinking fast. "The vomiting could've been a side effect of a concussion instead of drugs. She needs a thorough autopsy. I'm calling in the cavalry."

Rick picked up his phone and dialed an old friend. He put his phone on speaker.

"Carson, it's Rick. Jules is here with me. Can I call in a favor?"

"Hi, Jules. Sure, Rick. Whatcha need?"

"I need a forensic M.E. stat."

"I don't know any medical examiners in Destin, but I can call around."

"I'm not in Destin. We're in Tulum."

"As in Mexico?"

"The very one."

"Let me call some of my friends in DC and see if I can talk one into helping. They'll need airfare and a large fee, I'm sure."

"No worries. I'll send Gary and his new jet to rendezvous."

"Okay, Rick. Give me an hour and I'll get back to you."

"Thanks, Carson."

A short while later, a knock came on Rick's door, and he was surprised to see it was Paul.

"Hey, Paul, how are you doing?"

"Not great," said Paul. His eyes were still red from crying. "Just trying to keep it together."

"I'm here if you need anything."

"Thanks, I appreciate that. I just came by because I thought you might want to know...something else has happened. My safe has been breached, and over half a million dollars worth of uncut diamonds are missing."

"No shit." Rick's eyes widened. "Are you sure?"

"Positive. As if I needed another problem to deal with right now." He glanced over his shoulder, back in the direction of his villa. "I better get back to Kirsten. But I'll let you know if anything else comes up."

Gary's jet arrived before sunup with Carson on board, as well as Jason Almose, lead M.E. out of Quantico. It had been two days since Ava was found dead in the bathroom of the five-star resort. Rick had taken as many photos as he could, with the approval of her grieving father, and also tracked down blurry video surveillance footage showing someone had indeed walked back into Paul's villa while he and Rick were in the lobby waiting for the EMTs, and then walked back out carrying a baggy that had to hold the missing diamonds. But the footage wasn't helpful at all in identifying who the person might've been.

Now the crime scene was a mess since the local police had little experience in such types of investigations. Luckily, Rick's photos and the evidence he collected happened before the main Federales came in and basically destroyed the crime scene, assuming it was a drug deal or something.

Since possibly multiple crimes had occurred, Rick asked Jules if she wanted to take the lead on the missing diamonds and he would focus on Ava's untimely death. The two may or may not have been connected, but they both considered it a strong possibility. Jules had come into her own since she was carjacked. The event changed her and she had become a great investigator and assistant to Rick. Everyone was a suspect in the diamond heist. Jules focused on Maxx and Paul. Maxx was still missing, which raised him to the most suspect of the two. Paul was grieving terribly, as was his young wife.

There was a knock on Rick's door just as he was about to spread the evidence across the bed so he and Jules could go over it.

"Hola, amigo!" said Possum.

"What are you doing here?" asked Rick.

Possum had his right arm behind his back and moved it around, revealing Chief sitting on his wrist.

"Chief!" exclaimed Rick, taking his pet bird from Possum.

Possum had been Rick's best friend and sidekick since high school. He now split his time between his home in Houston and his new condo in Destin.

"I had no idea you were coming. Where's Gary and Carson?"

"They are at the front desk arranging a room for us."

"How'd you get Chief through customs and immigration?"

"One word: money! Gary tipped the ramp guy who brought the plane in, and he personally brought Chief around to the front of the airport after we rented a car. We landed at the FBO Cancun International Airport. It's the private area where executive flights arrive."

"I'm so glad you're here. Let's give Gary and Carson a few minutes. I wanna go over what we have so far. I haven't been hired by Paul yet. He doesn't even know that Ava's death to me seems suspicious. As I mentioned in the email to Carson, which I assume he showed you?"

"Yes, he did."

"Good. Jules will be heading the investigation of the missing diamonds, and I will be handling Ava's death."

"Hi, Possum!" piped up Jules from the veranda.

"Hey, Jules. Where is Ava's body now?"

"She is being held at the Casa Funeraria Sanchez Villfaña Tulum. She will be transferred to the medical examiner's office in Cancun tomorrow, so y'all got here just in time."

Just as Possum was stepping into Rick's room, Gary, Jason and Carson walked up.

"Rick, Jules, this is Jason, our M.E., here with his forensics kit. I worked with him on many cases when I was in the FBI. He's here unofficially as he took vacation time to help us out."

Jason was tall, thin, and had a tightly cropped salt-and-pepper beard. His grayish-brown hair was short and wavy. He shook Rick's hand.

"Now that you're all here, let me get you up to speed."

Rick put on some latex gloves and laid out all the photos, screenshots from the surveillance video, and other evidence methodically on the bed. It was the only place large enough for all of it to fit.

They all gathered around and glossed over the photos. The bathroom was a mess from all the vomit. Water or possibly urine coated the floor as well.

"Did she micturate?" asked Jason.

"Did she what?" asked Rick.

"Did she piss herself??"

"Oh no, there was water on her blouse and pants, but if you look at this photo, you'll see she was dry in that area. I think the water came from the toilet."

The photo from the bedroom showed a pill bottle with the cap removed lying on the nightstand with pills strewn all over the floor.

"That's a lot of pills. Do you know how many she took?"

"According to Kirsten, her stepmother, it was a new prescription and it appears that about half of the pills are missing," replied Rick.

"What's that?" Jason pointed at a wad of toilet paper on the floor.

Rick unraveled the paper to reveal half of a pill capsule.

"I found it behind the toilet. I assumed she threw it up and the other half got dislodged in her stomach."

"Was it dry?" asked Jason.

Rick thought for a minute.

"Come to think of it, it was dry. I didn't think much of it though. I figured it just dried on the floor."

"Have they done an autopsy yet?"

"It was ruled a suicide. The local authorities did the autopsy. I'm not sure how thorough it was. I do know the father, Paul, wants to have her body flown back home as soon as possible. At the moment, he still isn't aware of my suspicions. What is your gut feeling telling you so far, Jason?"

"I can't really tell much now. I have to see her body as soon as possible."

"Should we bring the father in on this yet?" asked Rick.

"Yes, I think so. But only him and in the strictest confidence," replied Jason.

Rick had purchased a box of latex gloves at the pharmacy, in case anyone wanted a better look. Possum put a pair on and his strongest readers and picked up one of the photos. He stared at it intently. It was taken from behind Ava as she lay on the floor. Her hair was draped forward and the back of her neck was clearly visible.

"What's that?" asked Possum.

"A birthmark?"

"Do you have a magnifying glass?"

"I think Jules does," replied Rick.

"She got one yesterday so we could study the map."

"Map?"

"Oh, that's a whole different thing and we can't get into it right now, but trust me. We will!"

Possum grinned at Rick knowingly. He had to know Rick was talking about a treasure map.

Jules jogged over with the magnifying glass and passed it to Possum. They all gathered around.

"That doesn't look like a birthmark to me. It's too rectangular, and see the little circle in the middle?" asked Possum.

"Yeah, when I took the photo, I wasn't even noticing that. What do you think it is?"

"It looks like an impression," said Jason.

"An impression of what?"

"No idea, but I will look at it closely when I do the autopsy. Do you think they'll allow me to examine her?"

"Let me take care of that. I may not know a lot about Mexico, but I do know one thing: the cops here are as corrupt as they come. A few hundred pesos will get us inside with no problem."

"Rick, before we move forward, I think it's time we speak to the father," said Jason.

"Jules, baby, can you get Paul on the house phone and ask him to come over alone?"

"Consider it done."

A few minutes passed and Paul knocked on the door. He stepped in and looked confused at all the people in Rick's room.

"Hi, Paul. Please sit down, we need to talk to you," said Rick.

Paul sat down on a chair beside the bed, taking notice of the photos and other items lain across it. His eyes welled up when he realized the photos were of Ava.

"Paul, let me introduce you to everyone first," said Rick. "This is Possum, Gary, Carson, and Jason. Possum and

Gary are on my crew back in Destin, Florida, and Jason and Carson are with the FBI unofficially."

"Is this about the diamonds?"

"Yes and no. This is gonna be difficult to say, but we believe Ava's death was not a suicide. We don't know for sure yet, but Jason is one of the US's leaving medical examiners and with your permission, we'd like to do a thorough autopsy just to make sure."

"What? Not a suicide? An accident then?"

"No, I'm afraid not. We believe it may be a homicide."

"That's impossible." Paul shook his head. "The only people near her were myself and Kirsten. There's no way Kirsten would have done anything like this. I know her too well."

"That's probably true, but remember when we ran to the front desk to wait for the EMTs? We left the front door wide open. Anyone could've come in—and someone definitely did, since we know someone also went into your room to steal the diamonds. It could be a coincidence. It could be a suicide or an accident, but we want to make sure. I'm sure you want closure, right?" asked Rick as he put his hand on Paul's shoulder.

Paul ran a hand through his hair and sighed. "Yes. Do it!"

CHAPTER FIVE

Carson, Gary, and Possum left right away for the funeral home. It was the only building with refrigeration for the demised. Jules approached Paul as he was about to leave and asked him to step onto the veranda.

"Paul, Rick has asked me to assist you in finding the culprit and possibly recovering the diamonds that were stolen from your room. At this point, we don't have proof that Ava and the missing diamonds are connected, but it's highly probable. Would you be interested in my help?"

Paul thought a minute. He was clearly still reeling from the possibility that his daughter may have been murdered.

"I contacted the insurance company and I will get reimbursed. But if you think it may be connected to Ava's death, then I definitely want to know. What do you normally charge?"

Jules wasn't ready for that question, as she had never been the lead on an investigation yet. She had no idea what to say.

"Whatever you think is fair," she replied.

"How about this—I had the diamonds insured for $2.5 million. They were uncut and would bring much more than that once they were designed and fastened into rings and earrings. If you recover them and find out who was responsible, I'll return the money to the insurance company and give you 20 percent of the final sale. I was planning on selling them to Diamonds International for $1.9 million. Let's call it a finder's fee. That's roughly $380,000. I'll round it up to $400k. Are you good with that?"

"That's more than fair, Paul. I'll do my very best to get the truth. Thank you for the opportunity."

Jules smiled and shook Paul's hand, and he left to check on his wife.

Rick was on his laptop looking up BPD. He was so unfamiliar with it and he wanted to know more. He came across a guy named Vebjørn Bråthen from Lillehammer, Norway, who was one of the leading experts on personality disorders. He clicked on his Facebook page and found he had a website called Coach Bråthen. The page was for survivors of what he called cluster B relationships. Rick had to look that up and it turned out that cluster Bs were people with personality disorders. The main ones were Borderline (BPD), Narcissistic (NPD), Histrionic (HPD), and Antisocial (ASPD). He sent him a private message on Facebook, and Vebjørn responded within minutes.

Rick: Hi Mr. Bråthen, my name is Rick Waters and I am investigating a possible homicide of a girl who was diagnosed with BPD. Could you answer some questions for me?

Vebjørn: Please call me Vebjørn. Before we start, are you familiar with my services? Have you looked at my webpage?

Rick: Okay, Vebjørn. Yes, I read about your service and about the nine traits of BPD. What is the likelihood of a young woman with BPD committing suicide?

Vebjørn: Well, it is known to happen, but statistically it doesn't happen often. So generally, the likelihood is not high. Do you know if she had any comorbidities?

Rick: Comorbidities?

Vebjørn: Yes, like anxiety,
bipolar, etc. Comorbidities
and meds CAN make the
condition more volatile.
And they may impair their
assessment of risk and
danger.

Rick: I do know she was
taking Effexor and Xanax for
anxiety and depression.

Vebjørn: Can you tell me
more about why you're
asking, and what's your take
on the situation that led to
this poor woman's death?

Rick: She was found dead
from an apparent overdose
of Effexor in a bathroom
in Tulum, Mexico, but it
seems staged. We'll know
more after an autopsy.
I'm bringing in a medical
examiner from the FBI as
the local authorities here
aren't very sophisticated.
She was in a very loud
argument the night before
she died with her boyfriend,
we think. We heard lots
of yelling and breaking of

things. She seemed to be completely out of control. I don't really know much about BPD and only found out from her father. I really wanna get as much knowledge about it as I can in case it's related to her death. Could she have had a breakdown? I've honestly never heard someone scream such vile language at someone she supposedly loved. At this point it's been ruled a suicide, but I have reason to believe that's wrong.

Vebjørn: Okay. What is known about her boyfriend? And about her relationship with him? Was it constant turmoil?

Rick: I do know he's quite a bit older than her. Maybe a daddy complex? He's still missing at the moment. He's wanted by the police for possible rape and assault on Ava. He's probably out of the country at the moment.

Vebjørn: Yes, people with BPD seek out partners

that can be caretakers, with nurturing qualities. This might be somewhat good for them, but due to their condition, they see their partners as either all good or all bad. When they split, they can be wildly confusing for partners that are reasonably healthy, but they sometimes end up with partners that are bad for them too. What is common for both types of relationship is the more or less constant turmoil. Does her partner have a criminal record? Or something that might indicate that he is somewhat unstable?

Rick: We don't know much about the boyfriend since this is a brand-new investigation, but we will be looking into him closer.

Vebjørn: I hope you get to the bottom of this. People diagnosed with BPD tend to bring out the worst in others, due to their way of gauging what other people can take and handle before they leave them. They are hypersensitive and pick up on clues that pass other people by. This might often be confused with empathy, but it isn't. Not really. Simply put, their brain works differently from yours and mine. It's hard to explain in just a short dialogue. Anyway, I hope you figure it out. Nobody deserves to die like this.

Rick: Thanks for all the insight, Vebjørn. If I have any questions, can I call you? I'm happy to pay for your expertise.

Vebjørn: Nonsense. Feel free to call me anytime. I'm happy to help free of charge. Please let me know how the case progresses.

Rick: I'll keep you posted.

Rick closed his laptop and thought a lot about what Vebjørn had written. BPD sure seemed like a horrible thing to deal with on a daily basis. If people suffering from the disorder could turn on their partners—or caretakers, as he called them—so fast, he could see how her boyfriend Maxx may have just gotten his fill and maybe overreacted and attacked her in a fit of reactive abuse. A person could only take so much. He hoped he was wrong.

Chief was still snuggled on Rick's lap when he got up from looking at his MacBook. Rick placed him on the top of the travel cage and broke off a piece of banana he had gotten for breakfast the other day. Chief was content and seemed to purr like a cat, although he hated cats. Having Chief with him in Mexico brought a sense of calm to Rick even with the chaos they were dealing with. Rick's phone rang.

"Rick, it's Carson. I'm gonna put Jason on speaker."

"Okay, Jules is outside talking to Paul, but I'll relay what you say."

"I did get some DNA from the rape kit. She definitely had intercourse before her death. There is also some bruising around her arms and shoulders and petechial hemorrhaging around her face and eyes."

"That can be caused from violent vomiting, can't it?" asked Rick.

"Yes, that's true, but you know what can't be caused by vomiting?"

"What?"

"She has a broken hyoid bone in her neck. She was definitely strangled. There are also marks around the front of her neck that could be from the toilet bowl. And that mark on the back of her neck is definitely not a birthmark. It appears to be some sort of impression, most likely from someone pressing down on her neck with something like a shoe. I would check all the shoes in the victim's room and see if there is a match. I'll text you the image I just took with my phone."

"Anything else?"

"Yes, she has major irritation and redness in her throat. I opened her stomach and did not find any capsules even partially digested. I'm gonna send the rape kit and a few other items to Quantico and try and get a DNA profile. It'll take a couple of days. We can run it on CODIS and see if we get a hit."

"You did a tremendous job, Jason. Thank you. Now I have to break the news to Paul."

Rick stepped out onto the veranda where Paul and Jules were finishing up. Jules told Rick about the agreement they had made for her to attempt to recover the diamonds.

"I need to leave for Playa Del Carmen soon," said Jules.

"I'd feel much better if I could go with you. Playa Del Carmen can be dangerous. Several bodies have been dis-covered dead on the beach in abandoned taxis in recent years," said Rick.

"I'll be just fine. Besides, you have your hands full now, helping Paul. I know I can do this."

Jules was determined, and Rick couldn't talk her out of it. He had to let her do her own thing. She stepped into the room to pack her carry-on for the trip, in case it took longer than a day.

Rick grabbed the half-empty bottle of tequila and two glasses. He filled them and handed one to Paul.

"Paul, I need to tell you something."

Paul took a long swig of the tequila and listened intently.

"Ava didn't commit suicide. She was murdered."

"Are you certain?"

"One hundred percent. She was strangled. Jason, the medical examiner confirmed that the hyoid bone in her neck was broken. That can only be caused by strangulation or asphyxiation with pressure to the neck."

Paul put his face in his hands and began to sob.

"How, why, who would do this?"

"I don't know, but if you will allow me, I will find out. I want to bring justice and closure for your little girl. I know she had some serious mental struggles, but no one deserves to die like that. I have to tell you also that she was raped. We believe raped, anyway. She definitely had intercourse the night she died. It all seems heinous."

"What's next?"

"You're not gonna like this and you will probably not agree, but I need you to take Kirsten to the beach or something and give me an extra key. I need to examine all the shoes in the room."

Paul looked at him sharply. "You don't think Kirsten is responsible, do you? There's just no way."

"Honestly, at this point everyone is a potential suspect. Let me ask you. How was Kirsten and Ava's relationship?"

Paul rubbed his forehead and sighed. "Truthfully, like most of Ava's relationships, it was volatile. They both vied for my attention. I believe they were both a little jealous of each other. But not enough to commit murder. I know Kirsten is way too young for me. I have a dad bod. I'm not stupid. I'm sure my money was a huge allure to her in the beginning, but she loves me and she loved Ava too. Besides Ava's BPD, we all seemed to get along quite well considering. There has to be another person responsible for this."

"Based on the timeline and the fact that Ava was alone with Kirsten after she was returned from the ruins, and that you and I went to the lobby, I have to put her as a prime suspect now. I need you to act normal and not let her know I'm looking into this. Can you do that?"

"Yes, I'll do my best to keep it on the down-low. How much do you want for your services?"

"Paul, I'm down here on vacation. If I get paid, then I'm working." Rick chuckled. "So, let's call this a pro bono for now. I feel I have to do this. Don't worry about the money."

Paul nodded in agreement. They shook hands, exchanged cell numbers, and he handed Rick an extra key to his room before heading back next door. Jules was finished packing and ready to leave. She kissed Rick goodbye and strolled out the door with fierce determination. Rick was worried about her being all alone but also knew she was extremely capable of taking care of herself in almost any situation. He had to focus on his side of the investigation. Still, letting her leave was tough.

Jules arrived in Playa Del Carmen around lunchtime. The town was bustling with tourists. She used the map on her phone to find Diamonds International. The first thing she planned to do was corroborate Paul's story that he indeed planned to sell them the large bag of wholesale diamonds he'd brought from South Africa. She was wearing a short red dress and high heels. She knew she would attract attention, and it wasn't long before the cat calls came as she walked down the street. She ignored the lusty men. As she opened the front door of Diamonds International, she was greeted by a middle-aged salesman named Javier.

"Hola," said Jules.

"Hola, señorita. ¿En que le puedo ayudar?"

"¿Habla Ingles?"

"Yes, I speak English. What can I assist you with today?"

"I'd like to speak with your buyer, please."

"You're talking to him."

"Oh good. My name is Juliana Castro, and I have some uncut diamonds I'd like to sell you if you are interested."

"We normally deal exclusively with a company out of South Africa, but I'd be happy to take a look."

"Oh, I don't have them with me. It's far too dangerous to carry those around here without security, as I'm sure you know."

"I misunderstood. I thought you meant a couple of diamonds. How many are you trying to sell?"

"I have a large bag, forty-five to be exact."

Javier frowned. "Oh, I'm sorry, we can't do that large of a transaction this month. We already have a seller coming in the next couple of days. You could try one of our stores in Cancun."

"You must be referring to Paul Giovanni."

"Yes, you know Paul?"

"Yeah, we are acquaintances in the industry. I guess you didn't hear what happened?"

"What happened?"

"I can't really discuss it. I'm sure Paul will be calling you in a couple of days. But please take down my number. If you decide you want to make a purchase, I can arrange a time to return with the diamonds."

"Thank you, Miss Castro. I'll be in touch."

"Call me Jules. I'm Jules with the Jewels."

Javier graciously laughed and put her number in his top pocket. Jules left, never intending to return, but took notes on her entire conversation with Javier so she'd remember all he said. She needed to find a fence in the area. She knew that the people in the know would be the bartenders. She stopped at a tourist shop and bought a large cubic zirconia diamond surrounded by sapphires. It would serve its purpose for what she had in mind.

She did a search for the most dangerous bars in Playa Del Carmen and came across one called Bar Loco. She would start there. It looked like a typical Mexican bar with a mix of locals and tourists. Sitting down at the bar, she ordered a margarita. The bartender was checking her out in the mirror.

Time to turn up the heat.

She licked the salt off the glass's rim in a seductive way. The bartender never took his eyes off her.

"¿Eres local?" he asked.

"No, I'm from Columbia."

"Aye, Columbian. What brings you to Playa Del Carmen?"

"I came down here on vacation and spent way more money than I should have already. I was wondering if you knew anyone who would be interested in buying my ring? I need money fast."

"Have you tried the Jewelry store on 10th Street?"

"I can't really sell it in a normal store, if you catch my drift." She winked at him.

"Ahh caliente."

"Can you keep a secret?" she asked. "Some rich bitch left it on the little table by the pool. She was a rude American, so I swiped it. I need someone who makes purchases that others won't. You understand?"

"Yes, I can't help you. Go see Miguel over at the Tequila Barrel. He usually hangs out at a back table. He's easy to recognize as he has a spider tattoo just beside his left eye. He can help you. Tell him Santos from Bar Loco sent you. Make sure you tell him that."

"Gracias," said Jules as she dropped a twenty-dollar bill on the counter.

Jules strolled up to 5th Avenue and found the Tequila Barrel. The outside was an unassuming cement building with a small neon sign, but inside was a full-blown nightclub. It hadn't quite transformed yet because it was midday, but all the tell-tale signs of debauchery were there. A sign by the restrooms read: *No Bullshit, No Drugs, and No Sex in the bathroom.*

Classy.

She leisurely made her way to the rear of the bar and saw a group of men sitting at a round table. She immediately spotted Miguel. She walked up to the table in a sexy manner and held her finger to her bottom lip seductively.

"Are you Miguel?"

"Who's asking, chica?"

"I'm Julia. I got your name from Santos over at the Bar Loco. He said you might be interested in something I have to sell."

Miguel waved the other two men away from his table and patted the seat beside his, encouraging Jules to sit down. She obliged.

"So, what does a pretty girl like you have to sell?"

She covered her mouth with her left hand and pointed at the ring on her finger. Miguel began to laugh.

"Is that all? I deal in much larger quantities. Go away, I can't help you."

"Please, I'm desperate. I'm almost out of money and I need to dump this ASAP."

He considered her for a moment. "Okay, step into my office and let's see if we can come to an agreement."

Jules didn't like the idea of going somewhere hidden but didn't have a choice. He waved her to follow him. Behind a curtain on the back wall was a door. He opened it and escorted her inside. It was a small office with one bare light bulb hanging from the ceiling. He locked the door behind them and held out his hand. She removed the ring and walked over to his desk, hoping he couldn't hear her heart pounding with nervousness. He pulled out a diamond tester pen. Jules got flushed knowing it was fake.

He held the tester to the diamond and yelled, "¡Chinga! ¡La maldita batería está muerta!"

The battery was dead on the tester. Jules breathed a sigh of relief. She sat on the edge of his desk, revealing her tanned thigh to distract him as he fumbled though his desk trying to find a battery. He set the ring down and moved toward her.

"Maybe you have something else you wanna sell? Or trade?"

"I'm not that kind of girl, Miguel."

He reached up and rubbed her thigh with his hand. She pulled away.

"¡Puta!" he exclaimed.

He reached back to slap her with the back of his hand, and she caught it in midair and spun him around, revealing the bulge of a small caliber handgun behind his back. She quickly removed it and put it the back of his head. The self-defense classes she'd taken after her carjacking really paid off.

"Look, you piece of shit. I came in here to do business, not to be felt up by a perv like you. Now, if you wanna keep your head on, listen to me and answer honestly, or I'll splatter that spider all across the wall. Did someone contact you about selling some uncut diamonds?"

"Fuck you, bitch. What are you, policia?"

"Fuck me? Fuck you!" she said as she bent his arm upward until it cracked. He writhed in pain and grunted."

"Okay, okay! A man came by asking if I wanted to buy a bag of diamonds. He didn't have them with him and planned to meet me here tomorrow."

"What time?!"

"He said he'd be here around 9:30 p.m. once the club was hopping."

"What did he look like?"

"I don't know. Like a white dude! Maybe mid-thirties. I didn't pay much attention."

"Okay, here's what's gonna happen. I'm gonna a leave now, and you are gonna count out loud to a hundred. You can keep the ring. It's fake. I'll be keeping your peashooter though. This will come in handy. I'll be back tomorrow for the drop."

"You're making a big mistake. Do you know who I am?"

"Yeah, you're a perv named Miguel. Now shut the fuck up and start counting."

She smacked him upside the head with her free hand and pointed the gun at him as she backed toward the door.

"Uno, dos, tres…"

She closed the door and tucked the pistol in her purse and slowly walked out of the bar as if nothing had happened.

Time to go undercover.

CHAPTER SIX

The blackout curtains were closed when Rick used his key to get into Paul's room. He used his iPhone light to find his way to the bedroom. Once inside, he turned on the light on the ceiling fan. In the closet, he found six pairs of shoes. Two men's and four women's pairs. He flipped them upside down and took photos of each pair. Most of the shoe brands he had never heard of, but he jotted down each name. They had to be South African brands. None of the bottoms of the shoes had anything that resembled the rectangle mark on the back of Ava's neck. The only pairs left to check were the ones Paul and Kirsten were wearing at the moment. He turned off the light and proceeded to the bathroom. He searched the entire bathroom for any object that could've made that mark on Ava. Nothing.

He decided to try and find Paul and Kirsten and hopefully get a look at the bottom of their shoes. He texted Paul.

> Hi Paul. Where are y'all?

> We are at the spa. Kirsten thought it might do us some good to come here and do some meditation and get a couple's massage to help us deal with the grief.

> Gotcha. Let's talk after.

Rick needed to see those shoes. He jogged down to the spa and stepped into the dressing room. He threw on a robe over his shirt and shorts and began to look for Paul and Kirsten's room. He wasn't having any luck and stopped at the front desk. The girl behind the counter was on a cordless phone and gave Rick a sign to hold on. As she turned around, he opened the appointment book.

Bingo! Room 3.

Once at room 3, he stuck his ear to the door. He could hear soft music playing and smelled incense. He slowly opened the door. Both masseuses were facing away from the door and didn't hear him open it. Just to the right of the door, he saw their shoes. He leaned in for a closer look. Kirsten's shoes were flats with smooth bottoms, and Paul's were Birkenstocks. Rick knew those shoes well and knew they couldn't leave the mark either.

Dammit!

He gently closed the door, hoping they wouldn't hear him, and returned the robe to the dressing room. He had struck out. Whatever or whoever left that mark on Ava's neck didn't come from any of their shoes.

He returned to his room to research more on Kirsten. At first, he'd thought she might be involved but was now getting a different vibe. She seemed to be honestly grieving at the loss of Ava. Rick logged onto his Nexus account. Nexus was one of the best info sites online, and Rick used it often to find out about people he was investigating. After a search on Kirsten didn't reveal anything, he focused on Maxx. He called Carson and asked him if he could check the FBI and Interpol database to see if Maxx had any priors.

On Nexus, he found out that Maxx was from Oregon and had moved to Cape Town in his twenties to pursue a career in animal husbandry. His main focus was cattle, but after a few years, he'd opened a surf shop and all but quit his intended career. The surf shop was still thriving and he was partners with a local man named Joey. He decided to give them a call. It was 7:40 p.m. in Cape Town, but he'd leave a message and hopefully get a call back. On the third ring, someone picked up.

"C Town surf shop, how can I help you, mate?"

"Oh hello, I didn't think you would be open."

"Not really open, mate. I live in the flat above and popped down to grab my cell phone. The house phone rang so I picked up. You need a surf lesson? I have openings tomorrow."

"No, actually, I'm trying to get some information on your partner, Maxx."

"Oh, Maxxi-Pad. What's that wanker up to now?"

"I was hoping you could tell me."

"Mate, I haven't seen him in three years. He's still a partner in the shop, but after his wife died, he took a hiatus. I literally haven't heard one peep from him since."

"He was married?"

"He was. Cyndi died of mysterious circumstances. She went missing and was found raped and dead with a massive head injury at the bottom of a canyon."

"Oh my God."

Hearing what Joey said sent Rick's mind racing. Maxx's wife dying of a similar fall was just far too much of a coincidence to overlook.

"How is he?" asked Joey.

"To be honest, we don't know. He's missing. His girlfriend Ava was found raped and beaten. She later died."

"That doesn't sound good. Maxxi-Pad has a bit of temper, but I don't see him doing anything like that. Is he a suspect?"

"Everyone is at this time. If you hear from him, will you please call me back? As far as we know, he could've been beaten to death and thrown in the ocean himself. The only reason Ava was found was because she landed on a small ledge before the big drop on a cliffside. Who knows if Maxx went all the way down."

"Wow, okay, I see your number on my caller ID. Oh, what's your name?

"I'm sorry. It's Rick, Rick Waters."

"Okay, Mr. Waters. If I hear from Maxx, I'll let you know right way, mate."

"Call me Rick. Mr. Waters is my father."

"Ha-ha, okay mate, Rick it is. My name is J-man. Joey but everyone calls me that."

"All right, J-man. I'll be in touch."

Maxx had just moved up in position as the number one suspect. As soon as Rick hung up with Joey, his phone rang. It was Carson.

"Anything new, Carson?"

"I'll say. I just got an email from Interpol. Did you know Maxx was married twice and both of his wives died of mysterious circumstances? Almost identically."

"Twice?"

"Yeah, he was married to a girl in Oregon named Vanessa, and she died two months after the wedding. Her daddy had money, and shortly after her death, Maxx cashed in a $500,000 life insurance policy and moved to South Africa, where he met wife number two."

"Cyndi!" interjected Rick.

"That's right. Cyndi. And she was found deceased in a canyon near Johannesburg. He was questioned and released. No charges were ever filed, but he did have a charge for domestic violence twice in Oregon before his wife Vanessa met him. Neither of the girls agreed to press charges, so they were dismissed. He never got them expunged though."

"Damn, that's quite the coincidence. Two wives, two deaths, and now Ava. We need to find this guy and fast. Let me call you back. Jules is calling."

Rick ended the first call and answered the second. "Hi, Jules, how's my little crime fighter doing?"

"Good, Rick. Listen, I need to stay tonight. I have a lead on the diamonds and I need to be at a certain club tomorrow at 9:30 p.m."

"Do you want me to come meet you?"

"No, you work on the case and I'll handle this end. I'm going undercover soon. I just need to pick up a few items. It should be fun."

"Please be careful."

"Oh, I will. I have a nice little .9-millimeter now. I sort of borrowed it." She giggled.

"Don't get caught with that damn thing. They'll throw you under the jail."

"I'll be careful. I promise. Anything new on the Ava case?"

"Lots! Too much to discuss now. I'll create a Google Doc, so we can keep each other updated on both cases. I've got a feeling they must be connected somehow."

"Okay, Rick. I love you. See you soon."

"Love you too, baby. Bye."

Jules opened her Safari browser and looked for a costume store. She found a place called La Isla del Disfraz—The Island of Disguise. Once there, she found everything she needed for her transformation: a rubber nose, a salt-and-pepper man's wig, latex, and a complete Hollywood makeup kit. She also made a quick stop at a nail salon and had her acrylic nails removed so her hands wouldn't give her away.

At a men's department store, she bought a suit, then checked into the AMAITE Playa Hotel Boutique, just kitty-corner and across the street from the Tequila Barrel. She booked two nights and chose a room that overlooked 5th Avenue. She stayed off of the street and ordered room service. She did not wanna risk being spotted by Miguel or one of his goons before the drop.

She had brought a spotting scope for Rick to look for birds and had it in her bag. She placed that and the tripod by the window. And then she waited.

The next morning, Jules was awakened by a loud sound in the street. She jumped out of bed and ran to the window. Lying in the street were two men with large pools of blood near their heads. The alarm clock read 4:05 a.m. The night club had just closed. She peered into her spotting scope at the men lying in the street.

¡Ay, Dios mío!

She could see clearly that both men had taken gunshots to the back of the head. It looked as though they were ambushed. Based on their attire, it appeared they had just come from the club. Both men were dressed to the nines. She looked at their hands and saw a stamp. Squinting hard to see it, she recognized the design. It was the top of an agave plant: the Tequila Barrel's logo.

Sirens rang through the streets, and within minutes, both men were covered with sheets. Not long after, several ambulances and Federales' trucks with men holding machine guns arrived. The men were loaded into the ambulances and another man pressure-washed the street. By sunup, it was as if it had never happened, and tourists began to trickle into the popular entertainment district. Anxiety crept up in Jules. She knew this place was dangerous, and this morning's murders solidified that.

She had to brush it off and get into character. The meeting wasn't until 9:30 p.m., but she wanted to be certain she would not be recognized. She needed a trial run. After an hour in front of her bathroom mirror, the transformation was complete. She took a selfie and sent it to Rick.

Rick, do you know this guy?

After a minute, Rick texted back.

No. Who is he? Do you need me to find out?

No honey, I'll explain when I return.

Okay, baby, be safe.

She smiled, feeling better. If Rick didn't even recognize her, no one would. She put it to the test. There was a rear exit out of the small hotel that led to the Hotel Maya Azul and then to 1 Avenida Nte. She made her way through both hotels and stepped into an OXXO convenience store. She picked up a box of Polvorones, the orange-flavored cookies she was so fond of, and made her way to the counter.

The woman behind the counter looked up at her and said, "Hola, señor. ¿Eso es todo?"

Jules nodded and took out a fifty-peso bill and handed it to the woman. She did her best job to lower the register of her voice and replied, "Gracias. ¿Puede decirme dónde está el banco más cercano?"

The woman thought for a second then told Jules where the bank was. Jules stepped out and ripped open the cookie wrapper, feeling confident she passed for a man. She returned to her room and had her cookies with some coffee at her desk, as she reviewed her plans for tonight's encounter.

With the help of several cups of strong java, Rick exhausted his online search for Kirsten and Maxx. It would be a couple of days before the DNA results would be back from Quantico. He texted Possum to see if he wanted to join him to meet Manuel over in Sisal and go over the treasure map, as the meeting was still on for today. He was knocking on the door within minutes of Rick's text.

"Hola, amigo!" said Possum in his best Spanish accent. "¿Cuál es el plan?"

Rick quickly translated what Possum had said and replied, "We're going to meet a man who claims to know where some treasure is buried. I don't know how real he is and my Spanish is rusty. Since Jules is in Playa Del Carmen, you'll have to do most of the talking. I assume you've been honing up on your Spanish?"

"Si, señor!"

"That'll work."

Possum checked with Gary and Carson to see if he could use the rental for their little trip to Sisal and to check if they wanted to join them. Gary declined, saying something about he and Carson meeting up with some senoritas later. They had shifted into tourist mode.

Possum brought the rental up to the front desk as Rick came up the side stairs with Chief in tow in his travel cage. Possum drove, since Rick wasn't on the rental agreement. He drove a little ways into Tulum then turned onto México 180, which would route them through Valladolid then Mérida and finally into the coastal town of Sisal. The trip would take roughly four and a half hours. They would have to spend the night in Sisal or Campeche.

When they arrived in Valladolid, they stopped and got some street tacos from a vendor near a beautiful colonial building in the center of town. The town had many old buildings and churches and was extremely clean. After the tacos, they continued their journey and arrived a couple hours later in Mérida, the capital city of the Yucatán. It was a vibrant city rich in Mayan and colonial heritage. As beautiful as it was, they didn't have time to play tourist, but Possum urged Rick into going to the Mayan World Museum of Mérida later if possible. He agreed. Once in Sisal, he followed directions to the house that Manuel lived in.

It was late in the afternoon when they arrived. Manuel was in his front yard repairing a fishing net that was strewn from one side of his lawn to another. Possum honked and Rick waved. Manuel squinted, trying to figure out who they were. Once Rick stepped out of the rental car, Manuel waved him over.

"Hola, señor Rick. ¿Dónde está Julio?"

Possum stepped up.

"Hola, soy Possum. Jules está haciendo negocios en Playa Del Carmen. Somos ella para discutir el mapa del tesoro."

Possum's Spanish was right on the money, and Manuel understood perfectly that Jules was on business in Playa Del Carmen.

"Hablas bien español, pero. ¿Por qué no hablamos en inglés?" asked Manuel.

"You speak English?"

"Yes, don't you?" replied Manuel with a laugh.

Rick was relieved he wouldn't have to have too much translated back to him. His Spanish was adequate, but the more excited Manuel got, he figured his Spanish would be so fast he'd get lost. At least he'd have Possum as a translator if he needed him somewhere else.

Manuel had them follow him into his house. Rick was carrying Chief, and Manuel was fixated on him. Once inside, Rick pulled Chief out of the cage and set him on Manuel's shoulder. He took a couple of photos with Manuel's phone, and Chief stayed there as they sat at the kitchen table. Manuel fed him a piece of tamarind, and Chief shook his head at the sourness of it.

Rick spread the map out on the table. It was barely a map, with more words than a drawing.

"Where did you get the map, Manuel?"

"I got it from a dying man who was a former treasure hunter. He and I crossed paths many times. He had no family to leave anything to, and this was the only thing he had of value."

It was in Spanish, and Manuel grabbed a piece of paper and pencil and pushed it toward Possum. Possum quickly translated the words, just as Jules had done before.

"The bells of three low in the street. Look toward Christ, the way to gold is in reverse. The church of lime is where the route is found. The second map is inside the book of Paul."

"What the hell does that mean?" asked Rick.

"Well, let's think about this. Bells of three? Church of lime? Does that mean anything to you, Manuel?" asked Possum.

He thought for a long while, then shook his head.

"Maybe it's under a lime tree by a church," said Rick.

Possum scratched his head and kept saying, "Church of lime, bells of three," over and over.

"Limestone!" he exclaimed. "Church of lime. Maybe it's a church made of limestone. But that has to be half of the churches in the Yucatán."

Just then, as if a light bulb had gone off, Manuel jumped up from the table and ran to the bookcase at the far end of his living room. He pulled out a large coffee table book titled, *Casa Mexico: At Home in Merida and the Yucatán.* He placed it on the table and frantically started flipping pages. He suddenly stopped and spun the book around so Possum and Rick could look. On two pages was a stunning photo of the Cathedral de Mérida. Manuel pointed to the bottom of the photo, and in the small courtyard were three large bells sitting at street level. Rick and Possum looked at each other as Possum read aloud.

The Cathedral de Mérida began construction in 1562 on the site of Mayan ruins T'ho. It was one of the oldest cathedrals build in the Americas.

"Oh my God, I think I got it!" yelled Possum, startling both Rick and Manuel.

Possum pointed at a statue tucked into a niche in the side of the cathedral. It was the statue of St. Paul. In his right hand was a sword and, in his left, a large book.

"That's it!"

"The treasure's inside an old cement book?" asked Rick.

"No, not the treasure, the real map to the treasure. This is a map to the treasure map!"

Both Rick and Manuel's eyes grew wide.

"How are we gonna get up to that book without being arrested?"

"I know," said Manuel. "We're gonna use Manuel labor, get it? *Manuel* labor?" He grinned.

He went to the backyard and into a shed and returned with three orange vests and hard hats.

"Here you go. The standard Mexican drag-your-feet uniform. The slower we work, the more we'll be accepted."

Rick laughed and passed one of the vests and hard hats to Possum, and tucked one under his arm. Merida was an hour back the way they came, and they wanted to be at the cathedral before sunup. Rick did a quick search for the closest hotel to the church and found one of the same name, in walking distance to the great cathedral: Hotel Cathedral Merida. He had Possum book two rooms. Manuel would meet them around dinner time to finalized the fake cleaning of the church in the morning. He gave Rick a bag of digging tools and three walkie-talkies. With a little handmade street sign, they'd be in business. No one would give them a second glance.

CHAPTER SEVEN

*J*ules, *we are in Merida. How is everything going?* Rick texted her at 8:15 p.m.

> All good, Rick. It's almost go time! Merida?

> I'll explain later. Go time?

> I'll explain that later too, Rick. Love you.

> Love you too, Jules.

Rick checked into the hotel and left a key at the front desk for Manuel. He was antsy to get started, but they needed to wait until sunup. He placed Chief on the desk in the room, and Rick scrolled through his phone to search for a good restaurant nearby.

Jules pushed her way to the front of the line at the Tequila Barrel. Once inside, she grabbed a margarita and picked a spot where she could see the curtain leading to the hidden back room where she'd had her encounter with Miguel the day before. She could also clearly see the entrance. It was the perfect vantage point. Her disguise was perfect, too. She looked so much like a man, in fact, that she had to continually shoo away call girls trying to get her to buy them a drink.

She was on her third margarita by four a.m., and there was no sign of Miguel or the potential diamond thief. Once the lights came on indicating the club was closing, she paid her tab, slid a fresh fifty-dollar bill toward him, and asked the bartender if Miguel was around.

"Miguel is in jail, señor."

"Why?"

"Murder, didn't you hear about it? It happened yesterday right outside."

"Oh, I wasn't here yesterday," she lied.

She made her way out of the club and into the back entrance of her hotel. She was exhausted and tired of wearing a suit, so she filled the tub with warm water and soaked for while, contemplating what to do next. She didn't realize she'd dozed off until she was awakened by her nose hitting the water.

Once in bed, she decided she'd find out in the morning who the dead guys were and when Miguel would be released on bond. As the sun crept up, breaking the darkness a little, she fell off to sleep in bed.

Rick placed the orange sign of a man pushing a shovel on the sidewalk in front of the St. Paul statue. Manuel and Possum were in the courtyard by the three large bells. The front of the bells faced a statue of Christ, and behind them was the statue of Paul. The way the letters of the bell were shaped, they created a small triangle design that looked more like an arrow just below the book pointing toward it. Rick placed the ladder beside the statue and climbed up. Possum came over and held the ladder as Manuel swept the sidewalk and placed a Do Not Cross barrier on both sides of the statue. They looked official. A local police officer walked by, glanced up, and continued walking and sipping his coffee. Rick reached below the book and felt a small crack. It was too small to get his fingers into.

"Hand me a prybar," yelled down Rick.

Manuel reached into the bag, climbed partway up the ladder, and handed it to Rick. Rick shoved the short end of the prybar into the crack and pushed down on it with all his might. The limestone dust fell as the crack opened a quarter inch more.

Rick climbed down the ladder, grabbed the long end of the prybar, and hung on it. It wouldn't budge. Manuel grabbed a long, fat pipe and passed it to Rick. He placed it over the end of the prybar then grabbed the far end of it and pulled down. His foot slipped and he fell forward. With a large crack, the bottom of the book busted open, and Rick fell to the street mostly uninjured, save for a small scrape and an imminent bruise.

Manuel quickly climbed the ladder and stuck his hand under the book. With a few tugs, he pulled out a flat leather pouch. As quickly as they had arrived, they were gone and no one was any the wiser.

Back at the hotel, they all went to Rick's room. Carefully, Rick opened the ancient leather pouch. A dusty brown piece of paper slowly appeared from inside the pouch. It was all in Spanish. Manuel read it as Possum printed out in translation what he read.

> *Una tormenta apareció cerca de Sisal.*
> *El poderoso barco fue empujado hacia el arrecife.*
> *El dios serpiente de oro se salvó y se había movido.*
> *Fue depositado en lo profundo del banco cerca de Nuan.*

> *A storm appeared near Sisal.*
> *The mighty ship was pushed onto the reef.*
> *The gold snake God was saved and had been moved.*
> *It was deposited deep in the bank near Nuan.*

Rick pulled out his phone and opened a map and typed "Nuan banks." The only thing that popped up was the Cenote Encantado Nuan, but no banks in the area.

"Damn, there are no banks near Nuan, only an ATM in a Circle K," said Rick with a sigh.

"Rick, Rick, Rick. I'm disappointed in you. I'll give you time to rethink what you just said as I open these three beers," replied Possum.

Rick thought about what he'd said and jumped up.

"Damn you, Possum, and your damn intelligence! It's not a bank as in Chase Bank, it's a bank as in the bank of a river! You freaking genius."

Rick ran up and gave Possum a huge bear hug. Manuel looked perplexed. Rick grabbed his MacBook and pulled up the Cenote Encantado Nuan near Tulum. It was a large sinkhole that was crystal clear and fed by an underground spring. It flowed parallel to the Caribbean. A large river disappeared into the jungle.

"We need help. It's a large area and we'll need manpower. Time to bring Gary and Carson up to speed."

Rick pulled up a website of wrecks near Sisal. There were several Dutch frigates that had succumbed to the brutal north winds and were pushed onto the reef. One ship was saved and the crewmen rescued. The other broke apart and was supposedly carrying Mayan slaves and contraband. The lost ship's manifest included fifty-five Mayan souls, eighteen crew, silver, coins, and something called divinidad de oro.

Possum translated it. "It means gold divinity. Think about it, a *gold god!* It could be a large solid gold statue of the Mayan god Kukulcán—the Feathered Serpent god. The Feathered Serpent deity. It is the most well-known and prominent god of the Mayan people. Holy shit, dude. That is priceless, if it's real."

Manuel pulled an ancient-looking bottle of tequila out of his backpack. He poured three shots into old Mexican shot glasses he had in a carry case.

"Here is to Kukulcán. May he be returned to my people."

"Cheers!" said Rick and Possum as they clinked glasses and downed the smooth, warm gold liquor.

"We're gonna need a few small boats and several metal detectors and scuba gear. We need to do a complete survey of the river flowing from the cenote. Can you assist in securing some local boats, Manuel?"

"Yes, I can secure four boats from a friend I have in Tulum. He will need cash payment as he uses them for local tours. We can just rent them for a week or so. I can get a good price from him."

"Okay, let's meet at Cenote Nuan in two days," said Rick."

"Bueno," replied Manuel.

Rick and Possum loaded up the rental car and headed back to Tulum. Rick texted Carson to see if there had been any updates on the DNA sample sent to Quantico.

Hi Rick, not yet but we are expecting them anytime now. Rendezvous soon?

Yes, let's meet at my room around 5:00 p.m.

See ya then.

Rick dozed a little as Possum drove down the lonely road to Tulum. He dreamed of Mayan treasure and snakes. One was his favorite and one he hated. He was awakened by his phone vibrating.

> DNA test in. Have a match.
> Talk soon.

Possum pulled in and dropped Rick at the front desk and pulled back around and parked. It was 4:20 when they arrived, and Rick went to his room and showered. He texted Jules before he hopped in the shower with Chief but didn't get a response. One he was done, he checked his phone.

> All good here, Rick. Need a
> couple more days. XXOO
> Jules.

Rick frowned. He was proud of Jules but was really missing her. Chief was on his perch shaking like a dog trying to dry off. Rick gave him a small piece of mango from the fridge and he went to town on it. There was a knock on the door.

"Come in!" hollered Rick.

Gary, Possum, and Carson stepped through the door.

"Hey, y'all. Update me," said Rick.

"Okay, we have a match. On a hunch, I sent Maxx's toothbrush to Quantico with the rape kit sample. Unsurprisingly, it was his DNA in Ava. They were a couple after all and she did claim she was raped in the past. I know she said she was the night you found her at the ruins, but to be honest, I'm not so sure that actually happened. I did some research and it turns out Ava has made false allegations against every one of her exes over the years. It is a common trait of BPD to bring false allegations against a loved one. Every single case was dropped because she refused to testify. Also, super common. She would go into a BPD rage, attack her boyfriend, then spin the story that the boyfriend was indeed the abuser. Once she cooled down, she would back down from her claims, as she knew she needed her care-taker or supply, as they call them. A person with BPD needs a supply. Someone to love and someone to hate at the same time. It's a sad illness," said Carson.

"Hm," said Rick, thinking hard. "Although, even if she lied about him raping her before, he still could've done it this time. Maybe he just finally snapped. Either way, he still could've killed her. We don't have enough evidence to prove he did or he didn't. So...we're back to square one?"

"Seems that way," replied Carson.

"Son of a bitch! We need to find Maxx and fast. He is the key to this."

"I did a trace on his credit and debit cards, and there has been no activity. I also checked with the airport and he has not flown anywhere, at least not out of Mexico. We aren't that far from Belize. I can expand the search," said Carson.

"Yeah, do that and I'll print some photos of him and place them around town," said Rick.

Jules checked with the Cereso Cancun and found out Miguel had been released from custody. The two eyewitnesses of the murders on the street were found decapitated in a taxi cab near Playa Azul. All charges had been dropped already.

Damn corrupt jail!

Jules returned to her boutique hotel and planned to repeat her performance from the night before. She took a nap and set her alarm for six p.m. She was still groggy from the lack of sleep from the night before. She dressed in her disguise and arrived at the Tequila Barrel around 8:40 p.m. The same bartender was working the opposite side of the bar, and she hid behind a small Mexican statue at a high-top table and watched the entrance.

Around 9:15 p.m., Miguel walked in and the bar cheered his release. He continued to the back of the bar and behind the curtains into his hidden office. No one matching Maxx's description came through the front door. To Jules, he was the most likely suspect to fence the diamonds.

Lots of young tourists and local prostitutes mingled. Jules kept eyeballing the curtain, and soon a blonde woman carrying an empty backpack pushed the curtain back and disappeared behind it.

Jules moved closer to the area and sat at a booth. She held up her phone and pretended to be taking a selfie. Once the woman stepped back out of the office, Jules snapped pics as fast as she could. Her backpack was bulging, and she was wearing a Boston Red Sox baseball cap pulled down low. All that could be seen in the photos was her nose, mouth, and chin. She never looked up so Jules could get a good look at her eyes. Shortly after, Miguel strolled out from behind the curtain. Feeling emboldened, Jules moved toward him, looking down at her phone, and bumped into him hard.

"¡Cuida tu paso pendejo!" exclaimed Miguel.

"Mi malo," said Jules in her lowest voice.

Miguel continued to walk, curse in Spanish, and shook his head as Jules put the key to his hidden office in her pocket. He walked out of the club and got in his car.

Jules also exited the club and headed back to her hotel. She opened Google Earth on her laptop and zoomed in on the Tequila Barrel. On the roof, she spotted a large vent above what was probably the kitchen. The kitchen closed at ten p.m, so the vent should be cool by the time she tried to make an entrance. Now she had to wait for the club to close. She only had a small window of time, and needed to get inside after the club closed but before the morning prep crew came in to open the restaurant. She might have an hour, she thought, since they served breakfast at six a.m. She set her alarm from 4:15 and closed her eyes.

Her mind was racing and she couldn't fall asleep. She sat up in the bed before her alarm went off and put on her dark jogging suit, rolled her hair up, and tucked it into a base-ball cap. Since it was a little chilly, she used a fishing mask to cover her face. She walked out of the front of the hotel and jogged north a little then back around to the back of the Tequila Barrel. On the south end of the building was a large tree. Once she scaled it, she hopped onto the roof and headed toward the kitchen exhaust vent. It was rusty; she kicked it one time and it fell right over. After donning gloves, she climbed down the narrow opening, then pushed the hood filters with her sneaker and they fell and banged loudly on the floor. She held her breath and waited. No one came in to check the noise. The building was empty. Quickly, she made her way to the curtain, pulled it back, and unlocked the door. On the back wall was a new painting of Pancho Villa, Mexico's most infamous bandit.

Really?

She removed the painting. Behind it was a wall safe. It was a heavy safe, and pulling it out of the wall was out of the question. The top drawer of Miguel's desk was partly opened, so she pulled it out and searched for the combination. She searched in all the notebooks in the desk and found nothing. She had been inside nearly twenty minutes already. In frustration, she slammed the handle of the safe. To her surprise, the handle went all the way down and the safe opened.

What an idiot! Miguel forgot to spin the combo.

She slowly opened it. She was sweating inside the mask and didn't see any cameras, so she removed her mask. It didn't matter anyway. She planned to leave Miguel the perv a note. Inside were several stacks of cash. Mostly US currency and some pesos. Behind the money was a small black felt bag. She grabbed it and opened it.

"Jackpot!"

The bag was full of uncut diamonds. She shoved it in her front pocket and took the cash too. It was all either drug money or money from stolen goods. Either way, it was hers now. She laughed and considered it her per diem. As a final gesture to Miguel, she placed a shiny penny inside the empty safe. She put the painting back on the wall and noticed a little hole in it. As she aligned it with the wall, she noticed a small, shiny reflection. She touched it. It was a pinhole camera. She smiled and gave a little wave to it.

On his desk, with a black permanent marker she found in the drawer, she wrote:

¡Cuida tu paso pendejo!

JC

Once outside of the office, she made her way back toward the kitchen. As she moved toward the hood, she could hear someone using keys to unlock the back door. She backed up and out of view as the door opened. Getting out that way was impossible now as the man came in and fired up the flat top grill. Back inside the club, she looked for an exit. There was only one, the front door. It was locked. She slowly turned the deadbolt and pulled open the door.

Beep, Beep, Beep!

"Damn alarm!"

The man in the kitchen ran into the club and threw on the lights. Jules tucked behind the end of the bar. The man ran toward the door. Jules held her breath and tried not to move. She was bent down to her knees, and her foot slipped and bumped into the Mexican mannequin holding a fake margarita. The margarita glass fell and crashed on the ground.

The man spun around and spotted Jules. He ran toward her. She hopped up as he swung at her. He missed as she ducked then hit him hard in the stomach with her elbow. He gasped for air and hit her with the back of his hand. She flew across the floor and into a table. He grabbed her and pulled her up to hit her in the face. She slammed her knee hard into his groin. Bending over in pain, he released his grip. With her hands cupped, she hit both his ears simultaneously. He screamed In pain and fell to the floor holding his ears.

With the speed of a gazelle, she bolted through the back door of the kitchen then onto the main street. Once she was a block away, she slowed down, removed her jogging top, and threw it in a culvert. She slowly jogged around the block and into the rear entrance of her hotel.

Back in her room, she plopped down on the bed and pulled the diamonds and cash from inside her waistband. Her adrenaline faded and the pain in her face became apparent. She looked in the mirror and saw blood trickling from her nose and the beginning of two black eyes. Blood had filled the inside of both eyes.

Rick's gonna freak out!

She quickly packed her bags and hopped in the dune buggy. Driving at night was dangerous, but nowhere near as dangerous as Miguel once he realized he had been robbed. She slowly drove out of Playa Del Carmen toward Tulum. She was gonna text Rick but knew he'd be sawing wood. The sun had not come up yet.

Once she got to the outskirts of Playa Del Carmen, she pulled into a Pemex gas station and waited for the sun to come up. She sipped on some coffee after filling up the dune buggy. The sun was creeping up, so she continued toward Tulum. She was so proud of herself, but her hands were still shaking and her anxiety was high. Using the techniques she had learned in therapy, she breathed deep and focused. After a few minutes of zoned-out driving, her nerves had settled some.

In what seemed like no time at all, she pulled into Dreams Resort. She donned her shades and walked through the lobby toward her room.

Rick stirred to a hand gently shaking him.

"Rick, are you awake?" whispered a familiar voice. Jules.

He rolled over to look at her. "Hi, baby, you're back? How'd it go?"

She slowly removed her sunglasses, revealing her two black eyes. Rick bolted up in bed.

"Oh my God, what happened?"

"You should see the other guy!" She laughed.

Rick hugged her tight and pulled her into bed. She reached into her purse and pulled out the bag of diamonds, and dumped them onto the bed. Rick's mouth fell open.

"You got them? How?"

"Long story. Coffee?"

Rick made two cups of coffee with the Keurig, and they sat in the kitchen. Jules told him everything that had happened as Rick listened in disbelief. He was angry at the chances she'd taken, but knew he would've done the same thing in her shoes. He didn't let her know he was upset and worried about her. He just showed her support and held her hand as she told the tale. Adventure and danger were in her blood, and there was no stopping her now.

CHAPTER EIGHT

Rick called the crew over to tell them that Jules had recovered the diamonds. They all agreed to keep it under wraps for now. It was highly likely the diamond heist was connected to the murder of Ava, and they hoped whoever did it might show their hand. Rick contemplated telling Paul about the diamonds, but was afraid he wouldn't be able to keep it a secret from his wife, in case Maxx was cleared and removed as a suspect. Paul was on a need-to-know basis, as anything he shared with his wife or anyone else could taint the investigation. It was easier to just keep him in the dark at the moment.

Manuel called Rick to let him know that the boats were available the next day for up to a week if they wanted them. He had also arranged for several scuba rigs and metal detectors for everyone. Rick brought Jules up to speed on the lost treasure, and she was itching to get involved. Rick decided to divide the crew up to work on certain projects. He and Jules would focus on the Ava case, while Possum,

Carson, and Gary would do the initial survey of Cenote Encantado Nuan.

Rick and Jules split up and put up photos of Maxx on opposite sides of the street in Tulum with a reward of ten thousand dollars for any info leading to his whereabouts. Jules put up the flyers on every pole she could find, then decided to check with some of the bartenders in town. She had used concealer to cover her black eyes and looked stunning in her sundress. She used her good looks and charm to get the attention of the male bartenders. Speaking perfect Spanish didn't hurt as well. The first bar she went into was the Asian Bodega Restaurant and Bar on the south end of town.

"Hola, mi has visto a este hombre?" asked Jules.

"No. ¿Quién es él?" replied the husky bartender.

She handed him the flyer, and he posted it behind the bar. As she walked out, she spotted a little café with internet called the Digital Jungle. She stepped inside and asked if anyone had seen Maxx. At first, they all said no—until she brought out the flyer and they saw the reward. Then one of the baristas approached Jules.

"Habla Ingles?" asked the barista.

"Yes, I speak English. Have you seen this man?"

Jules shook her hand and told her she was a private investigator. The barista took the flyer from Jules and studied it.

"Yes, I think I have. I believe he was in here two days ago. He used that computer."

She pointed to a computer in the back of the café. It was facing the entrance but separated from the rest.

"I spoke to him. He said his name was Mark though," said the barista. "I saw he was wearing a University of San Diego t-shirt. It's where I went to school, so I introduced myself. I came here on spring break three years ago and never left. He seemed like he was nervous and didn't wanna be bothered, so I left him alone."

Jules looked behind the computer and saw a surveillance camera. She immediately texted Rick to meet her there. Within minutes, Rick arrived out of breath from jogging over. Jules told him about the possible Maxx sighting.

"Can you remember anything else about him other than him being nervous?" Jules asked the barista.

She thought for a moment then said, "Oh yes, he was wearing a beanie pulled down over his eyebrows. I thought it was weird since it's so hot. He also kept his head down and kept looking at the front door as if he was sort of hiding from someone."

"Are there any other cameras, and can we look at the tape from the day he was here?"

"Sure, but it's a DVD. Wait, I'll just make you a copy. Hang on."

She returned from the back room a few minutes later with a DVD and handed it to Jules.

"May we use that computer?" asked Rick.

"Sure, let me log in for you."

Rick sat down at the desk. He texted Carson and asked him if it was possible to find an IP address from an email. He said it was but it wasn't his expertise. He texted Rick a number to call. Rick called it and it was one of the computer forensic guys from Quantico. After a long conversation, they agreed that the best way was to get a clone of the hard drive and send to him. But so many people used the computers in this café, he needed to know what email he was looking for. He had an idea. He paid the owner to block use of that computer for the day, and said he'd return with his laptop to clone the hard drive. The man didn't seem to care once Rick thumbed out a few hundred-dollar bills.

They returned to the resort, and Rick popped the DVD into his MacBook. He texted Paul to come over. The three of them scanned the surveillance video. When the guy wearing the San Diego t-shirt walked in, Rick froze the video. It was too dark to make out the man's face, and he was looking at his feet. Once he sat down at the computer, he was lit better but his back was to the camera.

"Is it him?" asked Rick.

"I can't tell," said Paul, squinting at the screen. "Can you go in slow-mo or frame by frame?"

"Sure."

Rick slowly moved the video forward. It was impossible to make out who the man was. Then he reached back to scratch his neck.

"Stop! Right there. Can you zoom in?" asked Paul.

Rick zoomed closer to the man's hand.

"That's him! Well, that's his ring anyway. Ava gave that to him. I remember it. She asked me if I thought he'd like it before she gave it to him. I thought it was an odd choice since tiger's eye was not too popular these days, but he loved it."

As the man typed, Rick saw Gmail pop up on the screen. He couldn't see who the man was typing to and he was taking notes. He dropped his pencil and when he bent down, Rick zoomed in on the email address: *rippgurl88@gmail.com*

"Does that email mean anything to you?" asked Rick.

"Not a thing."

Rick wrote down the email address. Now he had verified who the man was emailing. He just needed to crack the account and find the IP address. He thanked Paul, and he and Jules returned to the internet café.

Rick hooked up his laptop to the computer the man had used and opened a program called Ninja One Backup. After an hour, he had completely cloned the hard drive of the computer. They returned to the resort, and Rick plugged in his laptop and went online. He then used another program called Fire FTP to transfer the contents of the drive to the forensics team in Quantico. It would take a few hours to upload it, so they decided to head to lunch.

After they returned, Rick checked his MacBook and the file had sent. Now he just needed to wait. Rick's phone pinged and it was Possum.

Yo hombre. We did the initial survey of the cenote. The bottom is mostly sand. Nothing found but some old bottle caps and a piece of a wire fence so far. We could really use a magnetometer.

Gotcha, I'll have Johnie FedEx ours from the boat in Destin.

> *Great idea. Ok back to work.*

Rick called Johnie in Destin and he picked up on the third ring.

"Nine-Tenths Charters, Johnie McDonald speaking, how can I help you?"

"Hi Johnie, Rick here. Can you do me favor?"

"Sure, Rick. How's Mexico?"

"It's going well. I have a lot to tell you, but we can catch up later. Can you FedEx the magnetometer here? I know it's pretty heavy, but we need it. Oh, and can you also send the underwater drone?"

"Boss, that's gonna cost a fortune and might take a while. I doubt I can FedEx it. I'll probably have to use DHL, which will be slower."

Rick could hear Johnie typing on his laptop in the background.

"Listen, Rick, from Key West to Cancun it's only three hundred and fifty or so nautical miles. I can leave Destin today, top up the tanks in Key West, and be there by tomorrow. Cheaper and faster than DHL or FedEx."

"I love the way you think, Johnie. What about the charters?"

"We have nasty weather predicted for the next five days. All of the charters have been rebooked. The boat is free. I want a margarita!"

"Okay, Johnie. Come on over! See ya soon."

Rick hung up and shook his head, laughing at Johnie. He knew it made sense and it would be nice to have the big boat there anyway. He missed the lapping of water on a hull. A text from Paul startled Rick as he was reminiscing of past charters: *Rick, please come to my room.*

Rick quickly made his way over to Paul's room.

"What's up?" asked Rick.

Paul looked distraught as he rubbed his hands though his hair.

"I found this note on the bed after I returned from the pool. It's from Kirsten."

Rick took it from him and read it quickly.

Paul,

I had to leave. I feel responsible for Ava's death on my watch. Even though I had nothing to do with it, the guilt of not keeping a better eye on her is too much. I'm going back to South Africa. I just can't be here any longer. I know you would've talked me out of it, so I left without telling you. I hope you understand. I just need some time alone to reflect and I can't be in that villa anymore where she died. Please take care of what you need to do and meet me back home as soon as you can. I'm sorry I'm not strong like you.

Love, Kirsten

"Wow, I'm so sorry, Paul. Has she ever acted like this before? I mean so impulsively," asked Rick.

"No, but our daughter hasn't died before. I guess it was just too much for her to take."

"You mean your daughter, right? Kirsten was her stepmom, correct?"

"Well, yeah. It's just a figure of speech."

"So, what are you gonna do?" asked Rick.

"I guess I'll get Ava's body flown home and begin arrangements for a funeral. I'll probably be leaving in a couple of days."

"What about Maxx?"

"He hasn't been seen or heard of since the night Ava died. For all we know, he's in another country now. In my mind, the most likely scenario is that they had consensual sex, then after too many drinks, Ava had a split and went into one of her BPD rages. Maybe they went to the ruins 'cause he was trying to help distract her and cool her down, but it didn't work and she got even angrier. Maxx may have overreacted and hit back, causing her to fall over the cliff. Maxx knew she was capable of anything. Even lying that the sex they'd had wasn't consensual. She could easily say it was rape. It's a he said, she said thing, and we know how many times she made false allegations against her past exes. Maxx probably took off because he didn't want to face a potential rape charge in Mexico—who would? If she hadn't died, I'm almost positive she would've recanted her story and they would've have gotten back together. That damn BPD!"

Rick nodded along, though he wasn't as sure as Paul was about Maxx not raping Ava. Maxx still seemed like the likeliest suspect to have killed her, and he was determined to track him down. "Do you want me to continue to search for her and Ava's killer?"

"Maybe just a little longer. At least until I head back to South Africa."

"Okay, listen. There's something I have to tell you. I was trying to keep it on the down-low for now because I was afraid you would tell Kirsten, and we really need that to be on a need-to-know basis. Jules recovered your diamonds."

Paul's jaw dropped. "What? How?"

"She cased the most well-known fence in Playa Del Carmen, and she was there right after the exchange."

"Did Maxx make the drop?"

"No, a woman did. Jules couldn't get a good look at her, but it was definitely a woman."

"Damn, where are the diamonds now?"

"In my safe in my room. Don't worry, I'll be giving them to you before you leave."

"I'll contact the insurance company and let them know. They still haven't cut me a check, so I'll go ahead with the sale to Diamonds International. I'll pay Jules the finder's fee of $400,000 as we agreed," replied Paul.

"It's her first case alone. She'll be thrilled. I'll let her know as soon as I return to my room. Please don't tell anyone you recovered the diamonds other than the insurance company. Promise me."

"Okay, I promise."

They shook hands and Rick returned to his villa. He told Jules she would be getting her first paycheck as a private eye, and she nearly jumped through the roof.

"So, what are you gonna buy, Jules?"

"Mmmm, maybe a new camera to start. I've always wanted a spy camera, and those Ray-Ban Stories sunglasses will come in handy on stakeouts."

"Well, you can get whatever you want, baby. I'm so proud of you."

Rick hugged Jules tightly. Rick told Jules about Kirsten returning home early.

"Do you think it's suspicious for her to leave so suddenly?" asked Rick.

"I can't blame her for leaving. As a woman, I can understand better why she would want to leave. Kirsten must've been full of anxiety and dread after Ava's death."

Even though Kirsten had likely had nothing to do with it, just being close to her in the same villa when it happened would've made anyone uncomfortable. Both Rick and Jules knew Ava's murderer might never be found, but they were both committed to keep working the case.

The buffet was huge. Rick and Jules loaded up their plates and joined the rest of the crew at a large table. Everyone was there, including Paul. They all chatted about the treasure hunt and tried to keep it light, but inevitably the conversation switched to Ava.

"Rick, do you think raising the reward would help find Maxx and help us figure this whole thing out? What else can we do?" asked Paul.

"I've been thinking about that a lot. Dropping off all those flyers at local bars and restaurants with Maxx's picture and the $10k reward took a lot of time and effort, and I'm sure half of them were thrown in the garbage. What we need is to get that info to more people. How much are you willing to pay for info?"

"I can comfortably raise it to $50,000."

"I have an idea. How about we rent a couple of billboards with Maxx's photo and the $50k for any info leading to him and/or solving the murder? We can put one on each end of Tulum and one in Cancun at the exit of the airport."

"That's a great idea, Rick! Let's do it."

"Jules, can you make the arrangements? You speak the best Spanish. It'll save us some time."

"I'm on it!"

After dinner, Jules made a bunch of calls and set up a meeting with a man who owned several billboards on México 307. She worked out a package deal for four billboards. Two near Tulum, one at the Cancun airport, and one more at the entrance to Belize at the bottom of the highway.

Once that was settled, Rick and Jules sat on the veranda for an after-dinner drink. They could hear whimpering coming from the room next to theirs. It was Paul. Ava's death had taken its toll on him and with his wife gone back home, it must've all been too much. They both could hear his anguish though the walls.

They settled off to bed around midnight and could still hear Paul asking God why and slamming his fist on the table. Jules covered her ears with a pillow to block out the painful sounds.

The next morning, Rick's phone vibrated as a text came in from Johnie.

> *Rick, I'm here! I'm at Marina Puerto Aventuras. It's the closest I can get to Tulum.*

That was fast! We'll be over
soon.

Rick texted the crew and they all met in the lobby. Including Paul. The man who owned the billboards lived near Puerto Aventura, so they planned to meet him and do the contract. Jules purchased a local Mexican cell phone. That would be the number they'd put on the billboard. After they met the man and Paul made the payment, they all proceeded to *Nine-Tenths*. They were in separate cars, as Paul had brought his own with plans to drop the diamonds in Playa Del Carmen. Rick gave them to him in the lobby. He figured they'd have safety in numbers.

"You have a beautiful boat, Rick. I wish I could stay for a boat ride, but I need to get to Playa Del Carmen by two p.m."

Rick looked over at Johnie, and he winked. "Let's take the boat, Paul. The transient marina in Playa Del Carmen is a short walk to Diamonds International, and you really shouldn't be alone carrying those around."

Jules pulled up her blouse, revealing the .9 millimeter she had swiped from Miguel. Knowing he'd be safer with the crew, Paul opted in on the boat ride north.

It was about a thirty-minute boat ride to the dock at Muelle and less than a minute's walk to Diamonds International. The rumble of the MAN diesels pulsated through Rick's chest, drowning out the seabirds as Johnie brought the Viking 55 up on plane. Rick could tell Paul was impressed as he glanced down at the speed indicator that read 58 knots.

Once at the dock, Jules thought it best to stay on the boat with Johnie and Chief. She passed the handgun to Rick. He tucked it in the back of his waistband, and the gang escorted Paul to the exchange.

Paul was only inside Diamonds International for about eight minutes as Rick, Carson, Carson, Gary, and Possum stayed in eyeball's distance of the building, trying to blend in. He returned without incident.

"Lunch is on me!" exclaimed Paul.

"That sounds great. Let's go somewhere else other than Playa Del Carmen. I think Jules is nervous she may be spotted. After her run-in with Miguel, I'm sure he has goons looking for her," replied Rick.

"Since you have a boat, let's go there!"

Paul pointed directly down the dock to an island just on the horizon: Cozumel. They all climbed aboard, and Johnie slammed the throttled down. The mighty sportfisher's bow raised up, then settled down on plane.

Within ten minutes, they pulled up to Marina Fonatur. Johnie wanted to stay on the boat to make sure no one would come aboard and steal anything, but Possum offered to stay instead, since Johnie had been on the boat for days. He could use that time to search the local maps of the cenotes back in Tulum and spend some time with his buddy Chief. There was plenty of food on board anyway.

"Where shall we eat?" asked Rick.

"I know the perfect place. Chile Tequila. They have great fish tacos and a nice selection of fine tequila. I know the bartender Flacco there," replied Paul.

"Chile Tequila it is!" exclaimed Rick.

They all hopped in a van taxi and arrived in minutes. Just as Paul had said, Flacco was behind the bar. He gave Paul a big hug. Paul had been going there for years and was almost considered a local. They all munched on chips and salsa and did a couple of shots of Flacco's recommended tequila. Soon, a salesman named Luis Cervantes, angel of tequila, as he was self-described, stepped up to the bar with a man. It was the same Luis that the guy at the airport had mentioned to Rick when he first arrived in Tulum.

"Hola, amigos! I am Luis and this is my buddy, Gary McNamara. We call him Mac."

They all waved him over and Flacco poured him a shot. Luis brought over several expensive bottles of tequila and let them have a few tastes. Mac explained how he originally came to Cozumel as a young guy and would return often. At first for a week, then two, until finally nearing retirement, he spent six months here and six months back in the states. He knew everyone and Chile Tequila was his hangout. He was a likeable guy, and Rick pulled up a bar stool for him beside him and Jules.

Jules set her backpack on the bar and pulled out some papers and photos from the case, looking for her lip gloss. On top was the photo she'd used of Maxx for the billboards. Mac glanced over at it.

"You know Jake?" he asked.

"Jake?" replied Jules.

"Yeah, Jake. I see him here from time to time," said Mac as he pointed at the photo of Maxx.

"That's not Jake, that's Maxx. You've seen him?"

"Yeah, I saw him yesterday, as a matter of fact. He told me his name was Jake. Is that a nickname?"

"No, that's a cover name," responded Jules. "Where did you see him?"

"Here, right where you're sitting actually. He usually stops by here for happy hour." Mac glanced at his watch. "It just started. Maybe he'll show up."

Jules shared an astonished look with Rick. What were the odds that they'd find Maxx at this very restaurant? They quickly paid their tab and moved to a table farther back in the restaurant and not right on the street. Rick filled everyone in about Maxx. Mac asked if he could help, and Rick instructed him to sit at the edge of the bar facing the street. If Maxx showed up, he would tip his hat and give them a heads-up.

Patiently, they waited. An hour went buy with no sign of Maxx. Suddenly, Mac tipped his hat, and there he was, strolling toward the bar without a care in the world.

As Maxx approached the end of the bar, he looked up and saw Paul. His eyes popped and his mouth dropped. He immediately bolted for the exit.

Rick ran after him as he turned the corner. Maxx turned and fired at Rick, who ducked as a bullet whizzed over his head. He dove into a corner and waved at everyone behind him to stop. There was no doubt in anyone's mind now that Maxx had something to do with Ava's death.

CHAPTER NINE

Once back at the boat, they talked it over and decided to split up. Johnie would return to the marina on the mainland with Gary, Carson, and Paul, while Jules, Rick, and Possum would stay in Cozumel and try to locate Maxx. As dangerous as it was to carry concealed weapons in Mexico, it was far more dangerous to confront Maxx without a weapon. They all took pistols from the boat and plenty of ammo.

They checked into the Cozumel Palace on the edge of town. Rick got two rooms. They knew Maxx wouldn't return to Chile Tequila anytime soon and would most likely try to leave the island. Possum volunteered to stake out the airport, and Rick would take the ferry terminal. Jules would go around town and pass out photos of Maxx, since she spoke the best Spanish. They planned to meet up at Chile Tequila at eight p.m.

"Be careful, Jules. He shot at me already, so keep eyes in the back of your head!"

"I will. You both be safe too," she responded.

At the ferry terminal, Rick positioned himself on a bench chair near the entrance and exit of the Ultramar ferry. There was only one way on or off the dock. He grabbed a magazine and hid behind it. His pistol was tucked in the front of his waist, and he wore a floppy sombrero and sunglasses he'd picked up at a shop.

"¿Has visto a este hombre?" asked Jules over and over to every bar restaurant and tourist shop she went to in the Centro.

One man said he'd seen him but it had been a while. She pulled out several twenty-dollar bills, and the man said he thought he was staying at a hostel called Amigos. Jules grabbed a taxi and went straight to Amigos. She showed the lady at the front desk Maxx's photo.

"¿Has visto a este hombre?"

"Si," she said.

"¿Cuándo?"

"Cinco minutos antes. Solo subió a su habitación," replied the lady.

He's here now!

Jules slid a twenty to the lady and got his room number.

There was no time for her to wait for Rick or Possum, so she went directly to his room. When she arrived, the door was ajar. With her gun drawn, she pushed open the door with her foot.

"Don't shoot! Don't shoot!" yelled a young man sitting on his bed.

The girl on the bed next to him raised her arms in the air. They looked like college students.

"We'll give you whatever you want," she said.

"Relax, I'm not here to rob you," said Jules as she lowered her pistol.

The two of them were still shaking as Jules pulled out the photo of Maxx and passed it to the guy on his bed.

"Have you seen this guy?"

"Yeah, that's Jake, He just left. He was super in a hurry and he grabbed his stuff and hauled ass. That's his bed there."

"His name is not Jake. It's Maxx, and he's wanted for questioning about a murder in Tulum."

The guy's eyes widened. "Murder?"

"Yes, murder. Did he say where he was going?"

"No, but he had written a note on that notebook, and folded it up and stuck it under his pillow. He said to make sure his girlfriend got it. But when he left just a few minutes ago, he took the note with him. He was sweating and seemed very nervous when he left. He threw all his crap in a bag and didn't even bother folding it."

"He wrote the note on that notebook?" said Jules as she pointed at a blank notepad sitting on a nightstand beside the bed.

The guy nodded.

Jules picked up the notepad and looked under the bed and pillows for any clues. She texted Rick.

Just missed him at a hostel.
I'm coming to you. Stay put.

Okay, Jules, see you soon.

Jules took a cab directly to the ferry terminal, where she found Rick trying to look Mexican.

"Nice outfit, Paco," she said with a laugh.

"What happened?"

"I just missed him at a hostel he was hiding out at. All he left behind was a blank notebook."

"Let me see it."

Rick held it up to the sun and opened the first page. Small indentations were visible on it.

"I need a pencil."

Without a word, Jules ran into the gift shop a few yards away and returned with a pencil.

"Cost me five dollars! What a rip-off!" she exclaimed.

They moved to a metal high-top table next to a beer cart. Rick carefully turned the pencil sideways and lightly rubbed the paper with the side of the lead. When he was done, it could be easily read.

Dear Stan,

I can't wait to see you. I hope your business in Playa went as expected. I will rendezvous with you Thursday and start our new life together on the Caye. Once I get to the river Stann, I will call you.

Love, Maxx

"Is he gay?" asked Rick.

"I guess so." Jules shrugged. "Love is love."

"I'm gonna text a photo of this to Possum and let him know what's up. We should stay here until the last ferry leaves, I think."

"I agree," said Jules.

Possum texted Rick back.

> Who's Stan and why did he spell it Stan and Stann? Weird.

> I don't know. I wonder what Caye he's referring to? They don't call little island Cayes in Mexico like they do in the BVI and Bahamas.

> Or Belize!

> You freaking genius.

"I think he's headed to Belize, Jules," exclaimed Rick. "There's only one airport and ferry terminal here, so he can't get off the island without us seeing him."

"Actually, there are two airports, sort of," replied Jules.

"Huh?"

"There's the Base Aerea Militar 4."

"What's that?"

"It's a small runway for the military close to the international airport. It's mostly a museum now, but some small planes with dignitaries use it from time to time, according to Google."

"I'm going there now. Can you stand guard here?" asked Rick.

"I should go, Rick. I speak Spanish, remember? And I have the good looks and charm," she said with a wink.

"You're right, baby. You go but keep me posted. Don't get shot!"

"Yes, sir." Jules saluted Rick and ran toward a taxi.

Rick texted Possum what was happening and told him to stay put at the airport. About fifteen minutes later, Jules called.

"Rick, I think he was here. There are a dozen police cars here and the main gate is crashed open. Someone stole a De Havilland Twin Otter, and a stolen car was found near the tarmac.

"Son of a bitch! Hang on."

Rick texted Paul as Jules waited on the line.

> *Paul, does Maxx have his pilot's license?*

Yes, Ava bought him lessons two years ago for a Christmas present. He has his single engine rating. Why?

Too much to text. Meet you at the resort in Tulum.

Rick then texted Possum and told him to meet Jules and himself at the military base.

When Rick arrived, Possum was already there. Jules showed the photo of Maxx to the security guard, and he said the car just smashed through the gates and he didn't get a good look. The plane that was stolen was a De Havilland Twin Otter 172 and had just arrived that day with the Secretary of the Civil Service, who had come over from Cancun on official business in Cozumel. After they bribed the guard to show them the security footage, they could clearly see Maxx driving the stolen Mazda. Not even the local police had bothered to see the footage yet.

"He definitely didn't file a flight plan, but I'll bet my last dollar he's bound for Belize," said Rick.

"How will he land in Belize without getting caught?"

"Easy. Money! Belize is one of the most corrupt places down here. We need to see what airports are closest to his route. I doubt he'd land in Belize International."

Jules flipped her phone over for Rick to see. On her screen was a list of several small airports. They decided he probably landed on Ambergris Caye or at Caye Chapel Airport. Either way, the fastest way to find out was by boat. Instead of taking the ferry back to Cancun, Rick texted Johnie to pick them up and return to Belize. Since Gary and Carson were still doing a survey of Cenote Encantado Nuan' there was no time to involve them. Rick just texted them to stay put and keep the survey going. He didn't get a response from Gary and figured they were underwater.

"Let's go back to the dock," said Rick.

Johnie was just pulling up when they got to the dock. Without even tying up the boat, he spun around bound for Belize. First stop was Ambergris Caye. Once they arrived, they took a taxi to the airport. There were no De Havilland Twin Otters parked there. Only a couple of Piper Cubs and a biplane. Rick spoke to the man inside and there had been no arrivals that day so far. They returned to the boat, and Johnie slammed down the throttle for Caye Chapel Airport.

When they arrived, red lights were flashing on the tarmac. As they got off the boat and got closer, Rick spotted an ambulance and, off in the distance, a crashed plane covered in foam. It was a De Havilland Twin Otter. Jules ran up to the EMT.

"Busco a mi novio. Creo que estaba en ese avión," said Jules.

"La única persona a bordo era un hombre joven y murió. Está dentro pero está muy quemado. te pones; quiero ver," replied the man.

"¿Sobrevivió su equipaje?"

"Solo esto," said the man, as he pulled out a partially burnt passport and opened it to the photo page.

Jules looked down at it. It was Maxx's photo but the name read: *Jake Smithe*. She bribed the man to see the body. She slowly pulled back the sheet covering him. The man was wearing the same bright red Nike's Maxx was wearing when he took a shot at Rick. Without DNA, they couldn't be sure, but they were 99 percent sure it was Maxx.

"Son of a bitch!" exclaimed Rick in frustration.

Their lead suspect was now dead, and they were no closer to closing the case. They needed proof, but everything at this point led them to believe Maxx had killed Ava.

When the EMT turned away as Rick got his attention, Jules rubbed a handkerchief on the only part of Maxx's leg that wasn't burnt to a crisp. A few strands of hair and skin attached to the handkerchief. She folded it up and stuck it in her pocket. They had to be sure. They would get it to Carson, and he would have the DNA processed for them.

They headed back to the boat and returned to Puerto Aventuras Marina. Jules gave the handkerchief to Carson, and he immediately FedEx'd it to his buddies in the FBI. It would take a day or two to get the results. Luckily, they already had a sample from Maxx from before for comparison.

They all returned to their rooms. It had been an insanely long day. They planned to meet for breakfast and Rick would bring everyone up to speed.

Rick was up early and brewed a single cup of coffee in the Keurig in the room. The sound awakened Jules, and she rolled over with a smile.

"Coffee, baby?" he asked.

"No, I'm gonna have a tea."

She made her tea then they got dressed and ready to meet everyone at the grand buffet. At a large round table, they all sat and drank coffee, while Rick began to speak.

"I wanted everyone here so I don't have to say this twice. I'm extremely upset and frustrated, but we have to accept where the evidence sends us. We believe that Maxx is responsible for Ava's death and he crashed a stolen plane at Caye Chapel Airport. His body was burned beyond recognition, but Carson has sent a sample of his DNA to Quantico to get the results. At this point, it's merely a technicality. I think we can call this case closed. Paul?"

"Yes, I think so. As sad as the circumstances are, at least I'm glad we know the truth. Thank you all for everything you have done. I will prepare a check for each of you. I don't want any arguments! I know I never officially hired you, but you all have done so much for me. I sort of feel I have closure for Ava. She's in a much better place now and will no longer have to fight her BPD illness of inner demons. For that I am grateful. That scumbag Maxx can burn in hell though, as far as I am concerned. So, what exactly do you think happened, Rick?"

"I thought about it all night long as I attempted to sleep. What I think happened is Ava and Maxx got into a huge fight over at the ruins. They probably had sex prior to that, and something set off Ava and her BPD rage took over. I'm still not certain if Maxx raped her. Maybe he did, but there was no vaginal bruising and they were a couple after all. You told me Ava had a history of making false allegations. Maxx probably got scared of going to a Mexican prison, and he was the one we saw in the surveillance video who returned to your room once we went to the front desk to wait for the EMTs. I think he found Ava in the bathroom throwing up. Realizing she had attempted suicide, he strangled her, thinking the local police would close the case as suicide. He then stole the diamonds so he'd have money to be on the lam with. He was apparently living a double life and had a gay lover named Stan. Unfortunately for him, he was better at taking off than landing. He tragically crashed and died and closed this case in one fell swoop. You have the diamonds back, so I guess there's nothing else to do. I assume you will be reaching out to Kirsten?"

"Yes, Rick. I'll call her in the morning. She will be relieved that we figured it out and won't have to carry any unnecessary guilt around. Again, I can't thank all of you enough."

Jules stood up and went over to hug Paul. Tears were running down his face. He was better than before. Closure helped.

Carson told them he'd decided to head back to Virginia in the morning. He would let Rick know the results of the DNA test later. There was no doubt it would end up being Maxx.

After breakfast, they all returned to their rooms. Paul gave Rick an extra key to his villa, since he had rented it for another week but planned to leave for South Africa the next day. He told him he could let his crew stay there.

Manuel knocked on Rick's door the next morning at 7:30 a.m. He was eager to find out what progress had been made on finding the treasure. Rick let him in and ordered some coffee and pastries from room service. They all sat on the veranda.

"Do you have a place to stay here in Tulum?" asked Rick.

"Not yet," replied Manuel.

"Now you do."

Rick handed the key to Manuel and pointed to the wall next door.

"Gracias!"

They all got up and knocked on Paul's door. He had already left. Manuel opened the door and on the kitchen counter was a note.

Thanks again, Rick. I got an early start this morning. I still haven't gotten a hold of Kirsten, but she's probably asleep and jet-lagged from the long flight. She'll be so relieved when I finally let her know. I'll call her from London. I have to make a quick stop there to visit one of my diamond dealers then I'll dead head to Bloemfontein. Please write down my number below. I hope you can all come visit sometime. I'd love to show you my country and take you on a safari.

Your friend, Paul
021 555 0876

"Well, that's that, folks. Case solved. Time to move forward," said Rick.

Rick put Paul's South African cell number in his phone and returned to his villa. Since his Mexican number would no longer work.

They all planned to go down to the cenote after breakfast. Rick texted the crew to join him in his villa. They all arrived. Even Johnie, who had left the boat and paid a kid to watch it. He had taken a taxi to Dreams Resort and brought his snorkel gear in a dive bag. The magnetometer and underwater drone were sitting in a box by the front desk. The magnetometer was too big to carry all the way to the villas. After a few cups of coffee and some bagels, they all headed to the Cenote Encantado Nuan. In three separate Panga boats, they went upriver. The middle boat would tow the magnetometer, and the two outside boats would mark the areas on a map they had already searched.

They ran over the entire river area four times and didn't get any hits. They decided to go into the cenote itself with metal detectors. They found lots of treasure, if you could count bottle caps and old beer cans as treasure. Rick dove deep into the cenote and found a vent that seemed to lead somewhere, but the opening was far too small for any man to fit through. Not even a drone would be able to get inside it.

He kept on exploring and came to another area that had a bigger opening, but it would still be far too dangerous to try and squeeze through, plus it was pitch black in there.

"I've found an area we should explore," Rick said when he surfaced. "Let's use the drone."

He had just recently upgraded the lights to highly intense LEDs. Once the camera was started, Possum steered the drone inside from the boat above, while Rick helped get it through the small opening underwater.

The drone traveled deep inside and the cavern turned toward the sea. It opened into a large room with thousands of silversides and small white crawfish. At the very end of the cave, a small light shined through. Possum steered the drone toward the light, but every time he got close, the props kicked up the silt and he couldn't see a thing. He got as close as he could then pinned the area on the GPS. The water was a mix of clear and hazy. Not from silt but from differing water temperatures. It must have been the area where the cenote dumped into the Caribbean. There was literally nowhere else left to search.

He frowned. *Maybe we're at the wrong cenote?* he thought.

He returned to the boat, frustrated and cold. The water in the cenote was frigid. It didn't take long for Rick to warm up in the Mexican sun.

"Let's call it a day. Time to regroup."

They all returned to the resort and planned to have dinner in a private room at Bordeaux, the French restaurant in the resort.

Rick and Jules arrived first and ordered four bottles of cabernet and a few appetizers to get everyone started. The escargot arrived at the same time the crew did. Possum sat next to Rick and Johnie beside him. Gary was late as usual and walked in just in time to have the last escargot. It was so good he ordered another plate for himself.

Halfway through dinner, Rick's cell vibrated. It was Carson.

> Got DNA back. No match!

"What?!" exclaimed Rick.

"What's happening, Rick?" asked Gary.

"Y'all aren't gonna believe this, but the DNA Jules got from what she thought was Maxx's dead body was not Maxx."

"Whose DNA is it?" asked Possum.

"My guess is that it's from the pilot who flew the Secretary of the Civil Service over to Cozumel. I bet you anything he's missing."

Rick called the police in Cozumel, handed the phone to Jules, and she spoke in Spanish as he wrote down what to ask.

Where is the pilot from the stolen De Havilland Twin Otter? What's his name?

After a lot of fast Spanish, she covered the phone.

"Yes, the pilot who flew the secretary over is missing. His name is Diego Pérez. He was last seen checking the plane by a worker at the airport. He logged in but never logged out."

Jules thanked the man on the phone. Rick watched over her shoulder as she did a Google search for Diego Pérez. There were several. She added "pilot" to the search and only one popped up. Diego Miguel Pérez of Cancun. She quickly found him on Facebook. His photo showed him standing beside a De Havilland Twin Otter 172 with a huge smile on his face. When she scrolled to his About page, it showed that he was a government employee. His DNA would most definitely be on file. Rick quickly forwarded the info to Carson.

"Son of a bitch! This case isn't over," exclaimed Rick.

"If Diego was on the plane when it crashed, where is Maxx? Better yet, how did he escape the plane?" asked Gary.

"Hold that thought, Gary!"

Rick texted Paul.

> Paul, did Maxx know how to
> skydive?

> Yes, he was an avid skydiver.
> After he got his pilot's
> license, he started jumping
> on a regular basis. He joked
> that he'd always take a
> parachute with him when he
> flew in case his engine died.
> I guess he didn't on his
> last flight.

> Paul. Call me.

Rick's phone rang in less than a minute.

"Hey, Rick, what's up?"

"I know it's hard to believe, but the DNA we took from the body of the crashed De Havilland Twin Otter was not Maxx's. We think it belongs to the pilot of the plane. He's missing."

"You've got to be kidding me."

"I wish I was."

"I'm still in London, but I'm flying home tonight. I haven't been able to get in touch with Kirsten yet. I'm getting worried."

"Damn, man. Okay, well call me when you get home. I'm sure she's fine. Maybe her cell phone died and she forgot a charger or something."

"You're probably right. I'll keep you posted."

Rick slammed his phone down on the table in frustration.

"We need to reopen the case. And go over every single detail. Maxx ain't gonna get away with this. That fucker's still alive. He parachuted out of the plane."

CHAPTER TEN

A day had passed since they got the news that the body on the plane was not Maxx's. The treasure hunt had gone nowhere. They had surveyed the entire cenote and the river flowing from it. It was time to rethink it.

Carson called Rick just as he returned from lunch with Jules.

"Rick, we ran the DNA through CODIS and the government's database. With the assistance of the Quintana Roo, we got a match. It indeed belonged to Diego Pérez. I had the local authorities send me the red Nikes you mentioned and I swabbed them. I found trace DNA on them belonging to Maxx. The cause of death was murder. A small incision in the back of the head was found. It was determined that a knife was jammed into his brain from behind. We theorize that as Diego was flying, probably with a knife to his back, and got close to Belize, Maxx shoved the knife into his skull, killing him instantly. He swapped shoes with Diego. They wore roughly the same size. He must've hopped into the second seat and taken over controls. He was only rated for a single-engine Cessna-type aircraft, so the twin props were probably too much for him to deal with. Guess what Diego did when he wasn't flying dignitaries around?"

"What?"

"He ran a jump school. His plane was full of parachutes. I don't know if Maxx intentionally crashed the plane or jumped out when he realized he didn't know how to land a twin-engine aircraft. There was no smoke found in Diego's lungs, so he was dead before the plane hit the ground. That we are 100 percent sure of. An APB has been put out for Maxx in both Mexico and Belize. Since Diego subcontracted for the government, Interpol has been brought in. They'll find him. It may take a while, but they'll get him."

"If I don't get him first! Thanks, Carson. We're getting together shortly and going to start from scratch going over every clue we have."

"Okay, if I can assist anymore, just call me. Oh, wait. There's one more thing. Remember that email address you asked me about? Well, we ran a search and the IP address came from Dreams Resort."

"What?! So, whoever Maxx was emailing from that internet café was staying here at Dreams? Either staying there or working there?"

"We can only pinpoint it to the resort."

"Okay, well that sure puts a spin on it. Thanks, Carson."

"My pleasure."

Rick and Jules gathered all the clues they had collected and called the gang over to their villa. Rick spread everything out over the bed and turned on every damn light in the villa. It was still a little dim in there. The resort only used forty-watt bulbs in everything. Rick texted Johnie to bring over one of the LED lights he used while working in the engine room on *Nine-Tenths*. Once the light was hung in the villa, it was much easier to see everything. Each person on the team took a piece of evidence and made notes.

Possum focused on the imprint note found in Maxx's hostel. It bothered him that the name Stan was spelled Stan and Stann. He wasn't sure why, but it did. The only thing he could come up with was that Stan must've been Maxx's boyfriend and he'd misspelled the name because he was writing the note in haste. He read it under his breath over and over.

> *Dear Stan,*
>
> *I can't wait to see you. I hope your business in Playa went as expected. I will rendezvous with you Thursday and start our new life together on the Caye. Once I get to the river Stann, I will call you.*
>
> *Love, Maxx*

Also, why wasn't there a comma after "river"? There was one after Stann. What river was he referring to?

Maybe I'm just being a grammar Nazi!

He decided to focus his energy on finding out who Stan was. He pulled up all of Maxx's social media accounts and cross-referenced it with his friends and friends of friends and only came up with one Stan. It was a guy who lived in Oregon. After clicking his profile and scrolling down, he realized that Stan had passed away two years ago. There was no reference anywhere he could find that Maxx was gay or bisexual. The only thing remotely close as a clue was a gay pride flag that he had used on his profile, but it was more about the Orlando gay murders perpetrated by a terrorist a few years prior, and many people used that flag. It just said "Orlando Strong" and had a small gay pride flag flying under it. If Maxx was gay or bi, he kept it close to the vest and hadn't come out publicly at least.

He did a Google search of first Stan then Stann. It pretty much went nowhere. He brushed it aside as an accidental misspelling and continued his search for anyone named Stan in Maxx's life.

Rick went back to the surveillance videos taken from the villa the night of the murder, and also the one they got from the internet café, to try and find any obvious connections. He watched each one side by side, frame by frame, trying to make sense of it. On the video taken outside the door of Paul's villa, he could clearly see a man walk in after he and Paul went to the front desk to wait for the EMTs. He was only inside a few minutes and he came running out carrying a small baggy. It had to be the diamonds. It was impossible to see the man's face in either of the videos, but they were certain it was Maxx at the internet café.

He needed something that would match in the video to prove it was Maxx who entered Paul's villa. He meticulously went through each video, freezing the frames and trying to find something, anything. He decided to focus on the internet café video and look for anything that stood out. Then he remembered the ring. In the café, he wore a tiger's eye ring that Ava had given him. He quickly switched over to the villa video, looking for the ring. The man moved so fast that the video was blurry and he couldn't make out the ring. He went back to the beginning.

As the man reached for the door, Rick paused the video and zoomed in. There it was: the tiger's eye ring, clear as a bell. There was no doubt now that Maxx was the man who'd entered Paul's villa.

Meanwhile, Jules looked into Ava's past run-ins with police. She found records of nine domestic violence charges she had filed against ex-boyfriends. Every single one had been dropped because she'd refused to testify. Her false allegations had certainly affected many men's lives in a negative way. Jules asked Rick if it was okay for her to contact Vebjørn in Norway, the leading expert on Borderline Personality Disorder that Rick had chatted up before. Rick forwarded Vebjørn's messenger link to her.

> Juliana: Hello Vebjørn.
> I got your info from my
> partner Rick Waters. My
> name is Juliana Castro
> and I'm assisting Rick in
> the investigation of Ava
> Giovanni's death. Can you
> please answer some questions
> for me?

A little time went by then Jules's computer pinged. It was Vebjørn.

Vebjørn: Yes, I'll be happy to share my knowledge, or lead you to another source if it's out of my sphere of knowledge. Go ahead!

Juliana: How common is it for a person with BPD to make false allegations against a loved one, or anyone for that matter?

Vebjørn: How common it is, that I can't tell you, but I can give you a little more background. BPD or borderline personality disorder, which is its full name, has an interesting history to it. The term "borderline" was used because the people with this diagnosis are bordering on neurosis and psychosis. That's how that name came to be. Neurosis and psychosis are both referring to "loss of touch with reality." Neurosis is the "mild" loss of touch of reality, and psychosis is radically out of touch with reality. We all can have a mild neurosis at times, when we are scared or somewhat elevated emotionally, but then we correct ourselves and align with reality once that heightened emotional state is over pretty quickly. Due to a number of reasons, this can be much much harder for someone with BPD.

Juliana: How often do they recant their stories? Common or not?

Vebjørn: This is not uncommon. By the way, their symptoms usually get triggered in intimate relationships, but they also can be triggered immensely if their shames get activated. This can also happen outside of intimate relationships, depending on a lot of things, of course. So, if they are accused of something that will be shame inducing, that might trigger them to recant. Or get more stuck in their false belief, or delusion, to use a more colloquial term.

> Juliana: Well, thank you so much. I appreciate your help. If I have any other questions, I'll message you. Have a great day.

> Vebjørn: Bye for now.

Gary tried to help but was too busy making phone calls and having business meetings about his new investment in Mississippi. When he and Rick and the rest of the crew had worked on a case in Mississippi, he had befriended a guy named Tungsten in northern Mississippi. Tungsten had been so helpful to the crew that Gary had gone into a partnership with him to build a giant covered coffee bean facility on the farm Tungsten owned.

Gary had flown to Costa Rica and purchased the rights to a hybrid coffee bean that had been planted there. It had only one had harvest so far and the beans were so rich, they were unlike anything he'd ever tasted. He'd bought out the farm in Costa Rica and had hundreds of the coffee bean plants and soil brought to Mississippi. In the year-round climate-controlled facility in Mississippi, he could grow more organic plants and completely control the harvest times. His facility would be able to harvest four times a year, unlike the two they did in Costa Rica.

He would keep the facility running in Costa Rica and label those beans as imports and charge a much higher price. His plan was to use the mother beans in Mississippi and pump out a massive amount of boutique coffee that would have the same quality standards every single time. He called the coffee Una Vida, or One Life. Each bag would have positive affirmations written on it about living your best life. Gary always said, "Life isn't a trial run. We only get one chance at it."

Rick was soon getting frustrated with the case and the fact they weren't finding any new leads. He asked everyone if they wanted to take a boat trip over to the Tulum ruins. He thought they could do a little fishing and hug the coast, maybe even some snorkeling or diving. Manuel said he had to return to Sisal for some personal business, so he would catch up with them again in a day or two.

The rest of them changed into their swimming attire and met in the lobby for the short drive over to the boat in Puerto Aventuras. Johnie had been onboard for a day and changed all the fuel filters and done the routine maintenance. The boat was purring like a kitten when they arrived.

"Johnie, can you hug the coast as close as possible without hitting a reef or running aground?" asked Rick.

"Not a problem. I have the entire Yucatán coast on my new Navionics app. I even added Belize to the subscription, since it's so close. The app is amazing. It links to my chart plotter via the Plotter Sync. It's amazeballs!" replied Johnie.

Johnie motored at six knots, a rock's skip away from the coast. Possum set up two trolling rods, and within minutes, they had pulled in a Spanish mackerel and a nice little wahoo. He immediately released the mackerel and filleted the wahoo. He put it in a large bowl with some chopped up onions, peppers, and fresh lime juice. He reset the rods and put the fresh ceviche in the fridge to marinate. There were two larger fillets left, so he turned on the grill and soaked some applewood chips in water.

Once the chips were adequately moist, he grilled the fillets. He set them on a plate with some mango dipping sauce he had gotten in Tulum at a gift shop. Everyone ate with their fingers. The fish was delectable.

As Johnie continued their slow journey south, Rick pointed out the Dreams Resort they were staying at. The grounds were lovely and looked even more inviting from the view off of the boat.

Chief was perched high up on top of his cage on the fly-bridge beside Johnie at the helm. He was flapping his wings and squawking emphatically at the frigates closely following the boat. He was cock of the walk and he made sure everyone knew it.

Jules was using this time to catch some rays up on the bow. She was stretched out on a soft mat, with a Corona in one hand and a Wayne Stinnett novel in the other. She looked like an angel as Rick looked down at her from the flybridge. He loved that girl so much.

"Check this out, Rick," said Johnie.

Johnie handed his iPhone to Rick and told him to look at the iPhone then on his charter plotter. The images matched perfectly in real time. As they approached the area of the Cenote Encantado Nuan, he could see it pop up on the iPhone. It was only about thirty feet inland from the beach. Rick could clearly see the river that was fed from the cenote as it wandered into the thick rainforest and disappeared. As he looked at the image, he noticed a dark blue line underwater that started about twenty-five feet from the beach and went about ten yards before dissolving into the white sand. It almost looked like a ditch in the sand. At first, Rick thought it could be a trough caused by a rip current off of the beach, but as he scanned the water lapping on the shore, he saw no signs of any rip current.

"Can you get me closer to that, Johnie? Let's snorkel a little."

Johnie anchored *Nine-Tenths* at the end of the underwater trough, and everyone grabbed snorkel gear. Rick threw on his scuba gear and snatched his Pulse 8X from his dive bag. He almost never went in the water without a metal detector. Everyone but Johnie snorkeled. Jules even took Chief on an innertube and let him play in the water.

Rick dove down to the trough, which sat in about thirty-five feet of water. He scanned the area back and forth with his Pulse 8X and followed it as it continued toward the shore. About ten feet from the edge of it, he got a ping on his detector. He grabbed his pointer and narrowed the area. With a sand claw, he dug down in the soft sand until he felt something. He tugged at it and a wad of sand, rocks, and mud popped out. It was concretion, a hard, compact mass of matter formed by the precipitation of mineral cement within the spaces between particles. Basically, a lump of sand that had hardened. He waved his detector over it in his hand and it went off like the fourth of July. It was too hard to break into, so he put it in his dive vest pocket.

He moved closer to what was the beginning of the trough and spotted a halocline. An area where cold fresh water mixed with warmer salt water, creating a haze. He moved closer and felt a blast of cold water hit him.

Fuck me!

He moved closer. He was at the beginning of the trough. He stuck his hand in and felt cold water rushing over it. It was the cenote dumping into the Caribbean. He marked it on his handheld GPS and tried to stick his hand farther into the hole. When he did, the edge of it crumbled and two round brown objects sank into the water. He caught one in his hand and rubbed it with his thumb. He picked up the other one and stuck it in his pocket. They were both pieces of eight—small, pure silver coins from a time long ago. He almost spit out his regulator in excitement. He made his way to the surface and started yelling like a man who'd lost his mind. Everyone swam over and he showed them the coins. They made their way back to the boat. Rick was almost hyperventilating.

"Where'd you find that? On the bottom under the boat?" asked Possum.

"Nope, in a vent from a small hole coming from our cenote! It's gushing cold spring water. It's far too small for anyone to get inside. We can try to excavate it and widen the hole, but we'll need gear. Apparently, the river that ended in the jungle is just one of the exit points. This vent must lead directly to the cenote underground. I ran into a small vent at the bottom deep in the cenote when I dove it, but there's no man who could fit through that hole. Not even a small woman. Even our drone is too big. It would have to be a midget."

"Or a young Mayan," interjected Gary.

"You could be right, Gary. We need to get inside that vent somehow. The golden god could be inside there."

Once back onboard, Rick pulled out a plastic bucket from the engine room and mixed some white vinegar and water into the bucket. He placed the concretion in the solution and watched it bubble, occasionally stirring the mix with a screwdriver. Once most of the bubbling stopped, he reached down, wearing gloves, and started to crush the hardened minerals in his hands. A large piece fell to the deck, revealing something shiny. He tugged at it and it broke loose. It was a pristine piece of a gold snake about two inches long. It was curled up, but the tail had broken off and it looked like it was part of a bigger piece.

"Quick, give me the tester!" exclaimed Rick.

Johnie handed him the portable digital tester.

"Boom!" shouted Rick. "Pure gold!"

Possum pulled out a book of drawings of ancient Mayan gods and spun the book over to Rick. The snake closely resembled a snake that sat in the head of the famous Mayan god, Kukulcán—the Feathered Serpent god. It may have been part of a necklace or pendant, but it was definitely Mayan. The Mayans made many different-size trinkets and jewelry in honor of their snake god. This one was small, but there had to be more. Many more and much bigger!

Upon Rick's command, Johnie spun the boat around and headed back to Puerto Aventuras. At the dock, Rick instructed Johnie to get a portable hydraulic flange spreader and other various digging tools. He would have to go into Playa Del Carmen or Cancun to find one, but he was all over it. They planned to meet at sunup the next day and excavate that vent hole.

Rick and Jules woke up to the sound of Chief making long-tailed grackle noises. He had picked up several bird sounds from the local fauna. It was still dark outside, and Rick shot Chief the stank eye. Chief continued his rant of different birds, including seagulls, killdeer, and even the guttural drumming sounds of the mighty frigate. Rick had to admit he was impressed.

He reluctantly crawled out of bed and ordered two pots of coffee and some assorted fruit and pastries from room service. He made sure there would be some grapes for Chief. Even though he was perturbed that Chief had awakened him at 5:20 a.m., he still loved the bird dearly.

All the breakfast treats arrived around six a.m., and Rick called the crew's phones and invited them all over. Before they had gone to sleep, Johnie had texted Rick that he had indeed scored a manual spreader. It had two long handles that could be pumped by hand to create massive pressure to open a car door or a doorframe to get inside a house. He had to pay twice what it was valued at, as he'd bought it from a fire station in Playa Del Carmen.

Gary decided to pass on the boat trip and stay behind. He had to deal with lawyers in both Mississippi and Costa Rica and would be in Zoom calls all day.

The rest of them hopped into Possum's rental and headed to the boat. Johnie was on board and had all the tanks filled the night before. Rick was still groggy when they boarded the boat. Dozens of frigate birds floated lazily above on the morning's up drafts. It was a glorious day.

They arrived at the site of the vent as Rick and Possum geared up. Johnie and Jules would operate the underwater drone and record the entire search for posterity. Rick did a giant stride off of the stern just as Possum rolled off the starboard side backward. Once in position, Rick placed the spreader inside the vent. He pumped and pumped the handles. The sides of the vent busted opened and sediment fell. The hole was long, and with each use of the spreader, they only got about four inches closer. Rick estimated that the small part of the vent hole was at least thirty yards long before it opened up any. It was useless. They needed a way to get a camera deep inside.

They decided to call it a day after burning through a couple of scuba tanks. A different approach was needed. They ascended and dried off on the deck.

Without warning, Possum yelled, "Eureka!"

CHAPTER ELEVEN

On the boat ride back to Puerto Aventuras, Possum showed Rick his phone. On his Amazon app, he had clicked on a palm-sized drone called CHASING Dory. It came with a forty-nine-foot tether. They would have to add an additional tether to reach the opening. It had GPS and dead reckoning guidance technology. It was their best bet to get through the vent and view the cave opening. The drone they now had was nearly three feet wide and far too big to fit into the vent hole. Rick ordered the Dory drone and paid extra to have it arrive from Mexico City overnight. Rick called Manuel.

"Hello, Manuel. Que paso amigo?"

"Hi, Rick. I'm just finishing up here. Gonna head back to Tulum this afternoon. Any update on the search?"

"Yes, we found an exhaust vent coming from the cenote. I ordered a palm-sized drone to get inside so we can see the cavern."

"Cancel that. I have one. I have two actually. How big is the vent hole?"

"I'd say about eight inches around."

"Okay, I have a tethered camera that we can guide inside. It's not as handy as the drones, but it shoots in 6K and has super strong LED lighting. The image is amazing. I'll see you all later today. Oh, wait. I also have a grabber. I can attach it to the tether of the camera, and if anything small and interesting comes into view, we can hook onto it and pull it out."

"Sweet!" exclaimed Rick.

They arrived back at the dock just after ten a.m. Back at the villa, they shifted their focus back to the case, since there was nothing they could do until Manuel returned with the camera. Rick's phone rang.

"Rick, it's Paul. I've arrived home and Kirsten is not here! She hasn't been here either. I called her several times and her phone just goes directly to voicemail."

"Did you call the airline?"

"Yes, she never checked in and so her ticket was counted as a no-show. I'm freaking out, mate. Something's wrong."

"It's okay, calm down. There's got to be a logical explanation. Maybe she booked a different flight or decided to go somewhere else first before heading straight home. I'll do what I can to help locate her. I'll call you if I have any questions or updates. What's her cell number and what carrier?"

"It's +27 555 1696, we are both on Vodacom."

"Okay, try and relax and I'll see if I can get any info on her cell."

Rick hung up and called Carson.

"Hey, buddy, I need another favor. Imagine that."

"Shoot, Rick."

"Can you run a trace on a cell number and tell me what towers it has most recently pinged off of?"

"Sure, what's the number?"

"It's +27 555 1696 and its on Vodacom."

"Okay, give me an hour or so and let me see what I can come up with."

"Thanks, man."

Rick got everyone up to speed on Kirsten's disappearance.

"Dude, before you know it, this entire family is gonna be missing!" said Possum sarcastically.

"Let's hope not," said Rick grimly.

As he waited, he scrolled though all the photos he had taken of the villa. He had several shots of shoes that belonged to Kirsten. He zoomed in and started writing down the name brands. He then googled each one. Some were super expensive. They were a wealthy family, so it was no surprise. He got to the high heels, which were from a brand called Passion Luxe. He went to the website, passionfootwear.com, and watched the video on the home page. The high heels Kirsten wore often were convertible. With the push of a button and a spin of the heel, she could turn high heels into flats.

"Check this out, Jules!"

Jules looked at Rick's computer and watched the video.

"That's amazing. I can't tell you how many times that would've come in handy for me. I could've just gone to my meeting in high heels, then afterward, pulled the flat caps out of my purse and saved my poor feet. So smart."

"Yeah, they're pretty cool. Pricy too. Her pair is about two hundred and fifty dollars."

"Yikes!" exclaimed Jules.

He continued to go over the crime scene photos. He zoomed into the table where the Effexor pill bottle was found. There was a small glass beside them with a light film around the bottom edge. He remembered Paul saying that he had asked Kirsten to mix up Ava some BC powder. He figured that was the film he was seeing on the glass. He then remembered Jason telling him that he didn't find any partially dissolved capsules in her stomach, and it gave him an idea. He did a Google search.e did a s

Is Effexor caustic?

He scrolled down and found a page about Effexor side effects on WebMD. It said the capsules needed to be administered orally, by swallowing the capsule whole. If patients had difficulty with this, the capsule could be opened and the entire contents could be sprinkled on a spoonful of something soft like applesauce or yogurt, and swallowed immediately without chewing, followed by a glass of water to ensure complete swallowing of the pellets.

He immediately texted Jason.

> Jason, did you test the contents of the glass on the table beside Ava's bed?

> No, you said her mom gave her some BC powder. Why?

> Can you just test it and get back to me ASAP?

> Yes, I'm home but it's still in evidence in the lab. I'll head over there now. I'll call you back with the results.

> Thanks, Jason. Standing by.

Rick knew he was onto something. If his hunch was right, it would break this case wide open. Suddenly, there was a knock on the door. It was one of the bellmen from the resort. He had a small package for Rick. Rick opened it and it was a miniature tequila barrel addressed to JC.

Juliana Castro?

"Jules, look at this. What the hell is this about?"

Her face looked rather pale all of a sudden. "I think I know."

There was a little red ribbon coming from the round, flat part of the front of the barrel. She pulled it and the end opened. Inside was the note she had left for Miguel.

¡Cuida tu paso pendejo!

JC

She slowly flipped the note over. A crude drawing of a stick woman with long black hair was lying on the ground with a hole in her head and blood all over. She gasped, putting a hand over her mouth.

"He knows who I am and where we are!" exclaimed Jules. "Who?"

"Miguel! We need to get out of here and find a new place fast. God, I'm so stupid—I shouldn't have left my initials on the note."

Rick texted the crew to come over immediately. Johnie was on the boat, so he left him off the list. Gary and Possum knocked on the door within minutes.

"We need to find a safe house. As you know, Jules had a run-in with Miguel, the diamond fence in Playa Del Carmen. He knows where she is and just sent her this as a warning."

"Why would he send a warning?" asked Gary.

"That's a good question. Maybe it's so personal now that a woman bested him. Regardless, we need to leave immediately. We also need protection. Weapons. All we have is the .9-millimeter Jules lifted from Miguel. Carrying a gun in Mexico is dangerous. But not having guns against a group of thugs with guns is even more dangerous."

"Where can we get some?" asked Possum.

"I have an idea," replied Rick.

Rick texted Manuel and asked him to download the Signal app. It was a centralized encrypted instant messaging service that would enable them to chat undetected and untraceable from any authorities. Rick gave him his handle and waited. A few minutes went by and then his phone pinged.

TreasureMan43: I'm here. Que Paso?

> Boatguy66: We need weapons. Handguns, shotguns, whatever you can muster.

> TreasureMan43: How soon?

> Boatguy66: Yesterday!

> TreasureMan43: Meet me at the marina in two hours. I'm in Valladolid.

> Boatguy66: Done!

Rick then called Johnie.

"Johnie, I need you to fill the tanks to the brim. We'll be there soon."

"10-4, boss, I'm on it!" replied Johnie.

They all hastily packed and hopped into Possum's rental van. Rick and Possum sat up front, while Jules crouched down in between them behind their seats. As they drove out of the resort, a car coming in passed them. Jules ducked.

"It's Miguel!"

In the side mirrors, Rick could see a total of five men in the car. Two up front and three in the backseat. Possum calmly drove to the end of the resort driveway and headed north to Puerto Aventuras.

"They didn't see you, Jules," said Possum. "They kept going."

Once they arrived at the boat, they put all their gear on the deck and waited for Manuel. Rick placed Chief in his cage on the flybridge.

About an hour later, Manuel arrived carrying two large black duffel bags. He handed them to Johnie, who placed them on the settee in the main lounge. Rick and Jules both unzipped each bag and began to place the weapons on the dining table. Two Mossberg 12-gauge shotguns, three 9-millimeter and two .45-caliber semi-automatic pistols. There was a sleek wooden case at the bottom of one of the bags. Manuel shot a glance at Rick and used his fingers to say, *I'm watching you.* Rick knew that case was for him. He opened it and inside were two pearl-handled Colt 45 long-barrel handguns, and a gun belt and leather bandolero full of bullets.

"Go big or go home, hombre," said Manuel.

"I guess so, Manuel."

Inside the bottom of the other duffel was a plastic hard case. Rick unlatched it and inside were matching FX-05 Xiuhcoatl assault rifles chambered with standard NATO 5.56x45 mm ammunition. In another box were a dozen full magazines.

"Where the hell did you get these?" asked Rick.

"Don't ask, don't tell," responded Manuel with a wink.

"Jesus!" exclaimed Rick.

"No, Xiuhcoatl is not Jesus. It's the 'Fire Snake' in the language of the Aztec civilization. Kinda works, considering you found a gold snake the other day."

Rick shook Manuel's hand and told him to only communicate via Signal from now on. They all needed to lie low for a few days. The hunt for Kukulcán would have to wait for now.

"Where we heading, boss?" asked Johnie.

"Don't call me boss, you know I hate that."

"My bad. Where we heading, Rick? Better?"

"Yes. Isla Mujeres. I'll explain on the way."

Rick spun *Nine-Tenths* around, ignored the No Wake signs, and gunned it. The mighty hull lifted up high, and soon they were up on plane doping fifty-eight knots.

"I think I found a place, Rick."

"What's it called? I'll pull it up on the chart plotter."

"Puerto Isla Mujeres Resort and Yacht Club. It butts up to the World Mark Hotel, and the marina and hotel share the grounds and amenities. I'm gonna call and see if I can book two adjoining rooms. I looked up the resort and it's built with cement walls and has large heavy wooden doors. Plus, that perv Miguel won't be looking for us there."

They all calmed down on the ride to Isla Mujeres. Some dolphin came to the bow as they turned into the marina. Rick didn't call ahead on the radio. He just found the transient slip and grabbed one of his fake passports. Today he'd be Greg, Greg Wilder. Once they secured the boat, he and Possum went to the office to check in.

It was better for everyone involved if Jules stayed out of sight as much as possible. She donned a baseball cap and tucked her hair inside. Once she saw the expansive gorgeous pool, she knew she couldn't stay hidden forever. There was sun tanning to do. She grabbed her disguise bag she kept in her stateroom and threw on a bright red wig and reading glasses. She barely recognized herself in the mirror.

After Rick passed out the keys to the room, Gary and Possum took number six, and Jules and Rick took number seven. Johnie opted to stay on the boat. He was gonna be at the swim-up pool bar mostly anyway. Jules brought Chief to their room and set him up on his travel cage on the dining room table. She gave him a grape and he was super chill. Rick turned on the TV, and a news flash came on the screen.

"Come here, come here." He waved to Jules. "Look."

A shot of Dreams Resort came on the screen with police tape wrapped around Rick and Jules's room.

"Hoy en el resort Dreams en Tulum, un presunto negocio de drogas que salió mal dejó a algunos turistas luchando por sus vidas. Varios hombres armados dispararon contra una de las habitaciones del resort con rifles automáticos de alto poder. No se han realizado arrestos, pero si ve a alguno de estos hombres, considérelo armado y peligroso y llame a las autoridades," said the reporter.

"What's he saying, Jules? It's too fast!"

"¡Ay, Dios mío!" exclaimed Jules as she covered her mouth in fear. "He said several men shot up the Dreams Resort in Tulum."

"No shit? That's our room. Look at all the bullet holes!"

"He said the men are to be considered armed and dangerous, and if they are spotted to call authorities. They think it's a drug deal gone bad," she continued.

Several photos popped up on the screen, and she recognized one of the men as Miguel.

"That's him," she said, pointing at him. "Rick, we got out of there just in time."

"I'm sure he's not done. If he's willing to shoot up a resort in broad daylight, he's willing to do anything. Keep your eyes peeled at all times."

Jules shivered a little bit and really regretted waving so obnoxiously at Miguel's hidden camera. What's done was done though. Rick walked over and hugged her.

"It's be all right. We have the Fire Snakes, remember?" said Rick as he patted the duffel bag.

Jules looked up at him and smiled.

"I'm sorry I caused all this, Rick. We need this like a hole in the heart."

"It's a hole in the head," replied Rick.

"It's a catch 20/20 that he's the one who fenced the jewels, I guess. We needed to get them back, but he's a terrible man. I just wish I wasn't so cavalier on the hidden camera."

Rick started laughing. "It's a catch 22. Hindsight is 20/20. You were close though."

She playfully hit his arm. "Stop it, mister! Your American sayings are stupid anyway," she said with a pouty look on her face.

"I love you anyway, baby!"

Jules unpacked all their luggage and put it in the dressers like she always did. Rick placed all the guns on the bed and made sure they were all operational. Some of them were quite old. Beggars couldn't be choosers, though, and they were both grateful that Manuel had come through. Jules hoped there would be no reason to ever fire a single one.

They spent the next two days lounging at the pool, soaking up the sun, and going over the case files. It had been five days since Kirsten vanished. Rick contacted Paul every day. He was beside himself. First his daughter died, now his wife was missing.

On the third day, Rick arranged for two golf carts they could use to explore the little island. They'd had enough of the room service and wanted something different.

Possum, Gary, and Johnie followed Rick and the now redheaded Jules into town. They went into a place called Jax Bar & Grill. Henry the bartender suggested ceviche. It was a large bowl of mixed conch shrimp and octopus with no fish. They met a nice American lady from California named Linda who said she was friends with the members of the Grateful Dead.

After their third round of Tecates, they decided to go into the shopping area. Jules wanted to get a new pair of custom Mexican shoes. A young guy brought over a bottle of tequila with a dead scorpion in it.

"Hola, I'm Julian, and this is my gay uncle."

"¡Callarse pendejo! He always says that," replied the older man.

"Would you like a free shot of scorpion tequila?" asked Julian.

"We didn't come here for a haircut," replied Rick.

Rick egged Jules on to try a sip and walked around flapping his arms like a chicken. She made a frown and downed the shot glass.

"Smooth!"

They all tasted the tequila, and Rick bought a bottle. Jules found a pair of shoes she liked, but when she picked them up, the heel of one of them fell off. She turned it over and looked at the bottom.

"I guess these aren't the convertible kind you showed me on your computer, Rick."

Rick looked down at the shoes, and his mouth dropped open. He just stood there and stared.

"What is it, Rick?"

"We gotta go. Now."

He rushed them all to the golf carts and they sped back to the resort. Rick ran into their room and started scattering the photos all over the bed. He came to the one of the high heels he had taken in Paul's room. He then opened his laptop and searched for the shoe company, Passion Footwear.

"That's it!"

"What's it, Rick?"

"I think I figured it out. I need a pair of these shoes. Better yet, I want those shoes."

He called Paul.

"Paul, this is gonna sound weird, but can you mail me some of those convertible high heel shoes Kirsten had? Oh, wait, I assume her luggage is with her?"

"Yes, Rick, she is still missing as you know. Why her shoes?"

"I think I'm onto something, but I need a pair of those shoes."

"That sounds crazy. She has some others here. She loves that company. Do they have to be the same exact pair?"

"No, but they have to be the ones that you can change the high heel for flats."

"Oh, she's got plenty of those. I can FedEx one to you. Wait, better yet, I'll bring one with me. I'm heading back to Cancun to search for Kirsten. I'm afraid something bad has happened to her."

"Okay, download the app Signal and only message me through there starting now."

Rick hung up and waited. A few minutes passed and his phone pinged.

AfricaPaul55: I'm here.

Boatguy66: When you get to Cancun, message me, we'll come across in the boat.

AfricaPaul55: Will do. I'll send you an ETA soon.

Boatguy66: We'll be waiting.

CHAPTER TWELVE

Rick called Jason, who was back in Quantico.

"Jason, during the autopsy and in the crime scene photos, are there any photos with a ruler for size reference? Especially the back of Ava's neck. I need copies emailed to me ASAP if possible."

"Yes, no problem, I'll send you the entire case file. It's encrypted and the password is 'Mexico.' I have to go back to the office though, so give me an hour or so."

"Okay, I'll be on the lookout for them."

"What are you onto, Rick?" asked Jules.

"I don't wanna say now. It might be stupid but I may be right."

The sun was going down, so they took the golf carts to the end of the resort to a little restaurant called Seso-loco. Rick ordered a couple of pizzas and they had a round of special margaritas made by Erik the owner. Erik was a likeable guy and a hard worker. Rick noticed him passing pizzas to delivery drivers, making change, washing dishes, and making drinks.

"Erik, can you come here for a second?"

"Yessir, what can I do for you?"

"Call me Rick. I was wondering, what's the most expensive part of doing business in Isla Mujeres?"

"Supply costs, as everything has to be brought over by ferry from the mainland. Plus, well, I can't say. Let's call it overhead."

"Overhead, as in protection?"

"Si, I mean yes. Protection."

"From crooked cops? Look, don't worry, I'm a private eye. Our conversation goes no further than this table."

"I understand. I really can't talk about it. All I can say is every Thursday, I have to pay a guy or he will shut me down."

"What time does he come?"

"At two p.m. like clockwork. It's my slow time."

He looked at his watch.

"That's tomorrow actually."

"Would you mind if I met him and tried to negotiate a better deal for you?"

Erik frowned, shaking his head. "That would be dangerous for everyone. I don't think it's a good idea."

"You leave that to me, Erik. I promise no one will get hurt."

The look on his face showed he was still opposed to the idea, but he eventually relented and shrugged his shoulders in agreement. Rick had no intention of having a meeting with the guy. He figured the man must work for the Mexican mafia as a collector. Rick planned to wait for the guy in the back of the restaurant, then follow him back to his drop. He needed to find out where they were based. He knew Miguel was high up in the organization and had to be involved. It was a lucky break they'd decided to have dinner at Erik's place. Everyone was keyed in on Rick and Erik's conversation and knew what to do. Back at the resort, Rick handed each person a job.

The next day, Rick, Gary and Possum all arrived at Secoloco's at separate times and situated themselves in different locations as if they didn't know each other. At 1:29 p.m., a short, stocky Mexican guy with a teardrop tattoo under his eye arrived at the restaurant. Erik handed him a paper sack and he was on his way. He headed up the street on the island driving a 50-cc scooter, as Rick followed him on his golf cart. Not far behind Rick was Possum and Gary. Rick had asked Jules to stay behind with Johnie and take care of Chief and have a relaxing day by the pool. Even with her red wig, he preferred to keep her out of harm's way if Miguel was indeed connected to the protection ring.

After several stops, the man on the moped headed to the central part of town, parked his scooter, locked it up, and made for the ferry terminal. The gang followed him in as nonchalant a manner as possible and took their seats behind the man. He constantly looked around, casing his surroundings, but never made eye contact with the crew. Once at the ferry terminal, he hopped in a car.

"Dammit," said Rick. Without transportation, they would lose him. Rick scrambled to find a taxi. He finally got one's attention.

"You speak English?"

"Si, ah yes."

"Follow that car, it's my uncle and I forgot to get his address."

"No problemo."

With Rick in the passenger seat and Possum and Gary in the back, the man drove from the terminal to Playa Del Carmen. The car in front of them stopped at a pharmacy. Rick had the taxi driver stop a few car lengths back in traffic.

"This is good," said Rick.

"Cash or charge? It's eight hundred and forty pesos."

That came to about forty-three dollars, so Rick handed him a fifty-dollar bill and they all exited the taxi. They were all armed with pistols but didn't have the big rifles or shotguns. They watched the man knock on the door beside the pharmacy. A small metal window opened on the door, and then shortly after, the door opened. The man handed a large bag he was carrying in a backpack to the man and turned and left.

They followed him a few blocks, and he walked to a small house on a side street and used his key to let himself in. Rick figured that was where he lived. From across the street, they watched the house, and eventually he opened the curtains a little and Rick could see a TV on inside. The man sat on a recliner and drank a beer, staring at the TV.

"Okay, he definitely lives here. What we need to do is case this house. I'm sure he does collections every day. So, we can go pick up a rental van and take shifts waiting for him to leave."

"I'll take the first shift, Rick. I can't stay up too late. I had way too many margaritas at Secoloco last night," said Gary with a chuckle.

Possum pointed up the street and spotted a Mexi-rent sign.

"I'll run up and get us a van. Just chill here in case he leaves."

Rick messaged Jules on Signal and let her know what was happening, so she wouldn't worry.

Gary's shift ended at midnight; Rick took over. At four a.m., Possum's alarm went off and he took Rick's spot. At 7:30, the front door opened and the man stepped out carrying his backpack.

"Go time!" said Possum as he nudged his mates snoozing in the captain's seats behind him.

Rick put on the full bandolero and both Colt 45s in their holsters, and climbed up to the passenger seat. He put on a light Cozumel windbreaker Jules had gotten him, covering up the weapons, just as the man backed up and turned the corner. He never once looked up at the white van.

They followed him but not too closely. He focused his collections in the Villas Del Sol area of Playa Del Carmen. Every stop was the same. He'd go into a restaurant or bar and be handed a small paper sack, which he'd shove in his backpack. Rick spotted the telltale signs of a handgun tucked in his back, creating a small bulge under his shirt. After a dozen or so pickups, he headed back to town. Rick passed him this time and parked the van on a side street past the pharmacy. His plan was to position himself at the pharmacy and have Possum bump into him while looking down at his phone. Gary would wait across the street as backup in case it went sideways.

Rick posted up next to a sunglass stand and kept one eye on the shades and one on the street up ahead of him. He spotted the collector getting out of his car in a parking spot about three businesses down from the pharmacy. When the man was one building away, Rick placed a pair of sunglasses on his head, the signal he had arranged ahead of time to let Possum know to start walking. Rick wished his Spanish were as good as Jules. He'd let Possum do the talking.

As soon as the man was even with Rick, Possum bumped into him hard while pretending to look at his phone. His pistol was covered in a newspaper laying over his arm. He moved around him, which put his back toward Rick.

"Perdóneme," said Possum.

"¡Mira hacia donde vas, pendejo!"

"Eso no es muy agradable."

As Possum was apologizing, Rick reached over and pulled the pistol from the man's back. He spun around and Possum jammed his own gun into the man's ribs. He raised his arms, and Rick motioned to him to lower them. Rick and Possum guided him to the door and kneeled down on each side of him with their pistols pointing up at him but hidden from the street by the inside of their thighs.

"Ahora toca la puerta y actúa normal," whispered Possum, instructing him to be cool.

The little window on the door slid open and then the man behind the door opened it. In one move, Rick kicked the door open as Possum slammed his elbow into the collections man, sending him backward into a parked car. Possum slammed the back of his head with the side of the heavy pistol, knocking him unconscious. Rick shoved his pistol under the man's chin and moved him slowly backward. Possum was right behind him.

"Ask him who his boss is," said Rick.

"¿Quién es tu jefe?

The man didn't say. Possum asked him again as Rick cocked the Colt 45 under the man's chin.

"Miguel!" shouted the man.

He was answering Possum as well as warning Miguel with his shout. Rick punched him in the gut and he bent over. With the butt of his Colt, he slammed the man in the back of the head, slinging him to the ground like a sack of potatoes. Rick rushed the inside door to a room and kicked it open with Possum flanking him. As the door flew open, gunshots hailed across the room, whizzing just past Rick's head. With both pistols drawn, he fired at the men. Three men fell dead in their tracks and one hiding behind the desk began shouting. Possum changed clips and kept his gun pointed toward the desk. Rick had both guns aimed there as well.

"Stand up! ¡Ponerse de pie!" shouted Possum, looking behind him every other second to make sure they wouldn't be ambushed from the street.

Gary stepped in the doorway and yelled, "Clear, I got your six!"

The man behind the desk slowly raised one of his hands in surrender. As he slowly stood up, Rick motioned to him to move slower. It was Miguel and he was bleeding from his left shoulder. Miguel's right arm was in the air and it appeared he couldn't lift his left arm.

"Did you try to kill Juliana Castro?"

"No se—"

"Speak English, motherfucker. I know you can!"

Rick fired a shot off just over his head.

"Okay, okay, yes. She stole from me!"

"How'd you find her?!"

"¡Cameras essa!"

He motioned to the wall to the right of Rick, and pinned on the wall was a photo of Jules clearly taken from the surveillance camera in his office at the Tequila Barrel. Just as Rick glanced over, Miguel whipped his left arm up from under the desk and, as if in slow motion, revealed a sawed-off shotgun with a pistol handle. As he pulled the trigger, Rick rolled to his right and fired both Colts. One bullet hit Miguel in the torso, and the other hit him right between the eyes, hurling him backward against the back wall. His body balanced there for a split second, then slid down the wall, leaving in his wake a red trail of blood and brain matter on the dusty concrete whitewashed wall.

Rick snatched the photo of Jules from the wall then grabbed as many papers from Miguel's desk as he could. Shoving them under his shirt and zipping up the windbreaker. On the desk was a pile of paper sacks full of protection money. Rick picked them all up and handed them to Possum. With the back of his hand, he smashed a large pile of cocaine that Miguel had been weighing, scattering it all over the desk and floor in a cloud of white dust. He quickly looked for cameras and there were three. They were hardwired and led to a closet. Inside the closet was the hard drive. He ripped it from the wall and tossed it to Gary.

"Let's get the fuck out of here."

"Wait, Rick!" yelled Possum.

Using a fat permanent marker, Possum wrote on the wall, *La Barredora estuvo aquí!*

"I read that The Barredora gang is a rival gang from up north looking to move into the Cancun turf. Now the police will think this was a gang vs. gang shooting."

"Nice touch, Possum. Smart thinking," said Rick. That should keep the police from looking into this mess any further. Gang vs. gang shootings were common now that there was no area in the Mexican Riviera immune to the violence.

Before they walked back to the street, each one of them pulled their t-shirts up over their face. A crowd had gathered. It wasn't safe to return to the van with all these people. Gary and Rick took off down a side alley, and Possum went the other direction.

Once far enough away, Rick purchased two Corona t-shirts, gawdy Cancun baseball caps, and a rolling carry-on bag. They went behind the store and changed and put all the weapons and drug money in the carry-on. He messaged Possum on Signal to do the same, casually return to the van, and pick them up on the corner of Calle 2 Nte. and 10 Avenida Nte. As Rick and Gary waited, they could hear sirens coming from every direction.

Possum pulled up and they hopped in. He slowly drove toward the main highway that led back to the ferry terminal in Cancun. On the way, dozens of Federale pickup trucks and local police sped past them in the opposite direction. Once they boarded the ferry, they knew they were in the clear. Rick sat down and let out a long sigh of relief.

"That got real, real fast! At least they won't be coming after Jules anymore."

"I'm not so sure, Rick. Look at this," said Possum as he handed Rick one of the papers form the pile they had swiped.

On the paper was the same photo of Jules and words in Spanish under it.

Se busca viva o muerta a Juliana Castro. Recompensa - cien mil pesos.

"What's it say?" asked Rick.

"Basically, it's a reward for the capture or death of Jules for the equivalent of five thousand dollars. Plus, there's more. It appears Miguel has some Federales in his back pocket. He's been paying dirty cops so he could run his operation. We aren't safe here at all," replied Possum.

"Dammit," said Rick.

He quickly messaged Jules to pack everything and take the boat with Johnie a half a mile offshore and leave the dinghy at the dock. Once the ferry arrived in Isla Mujeres, Rick and Possum hopped in one golf cart and Gary on the other.

"Wait, what about the van back at the ferry terminal?" asked Rick.

"Fuck it. I'll call them later," said Possum. "All they can do is charge me for a drop-off fee. Besides, I used an alias and a prepaid debit card with only three hundred on it. They can't even trace me."

They climbed on the dinghy and motored out of the slip. Off in the distance, they could see *Nine-Tenths*. Rick held the dinghy as Possum and Gary climbed on board. Rick got Jules and Johnie up to speed.

"What's that on your ear?" asked Jules.

"What?"

Rick reached up and rubbed his ear. A small speck of blood was on his finger.

"Holy shit! I didn't even feel it." When he'd felt a bullet whiz by his head, it must have just grazed his earlobe. "That was too close for comfort!"

"Where are we going, Rick?"

"We can't stay in Mexico. I guess Belize."

"Ambergris Caye?" asked Johnie.

"That's as good a place as any."

Rick pulled up his phone and did a search.

"Let's go to the Belize Yacht Club Marina in San Pedro."

"I'm on it," replied Johnie.

They all breathed a sigh of relief once they got into Belize waters. The Mexican Federales were crooked but nowhere near as crooked as the Belize police. The difference was that the Belize police didn't have a contract on Jules's life. When they arrived at the Marina, they found there wasn't a slip large enough to handle *Nine-Tenths*, and they were directed to visit the Marina at the Reserve. The nice English-speaking dockmaster at the Belize marina called ahead for them and reserved them a side tie slip.

Gary and Possum jumped off as the boat slowly inched toward the docks, and Jules and Rick threw them the dock lines. Once tied up, they all went inside the galley and Rick closed the sliding glass doors so they could go over their next moves.

"As much fun as it is to search for the Feathered Serpent god back in Tulum, we need to find Maxx and close this case. Mexico is too hot for us right now. I'll follow up with Manuel and see if he can make any progress on the treasure. It's been lost for thousands of years, it ain't going anywhere anytime soon," said Rick.

Rick looked over at Jules, who was going over the papers they had swiped from Miguel's hideout.

"Are you okay, Jules?" asked Rick.

"All I'm worth is five thousand dollars!" she exclaimed.

"Baby, if I ever put out a contract for your life, it'll be for a cool million." Rick winked at her.

She smiled and kept reading.

"Rick, what's the address here?" asked Possum.

"Hold on."

Rick picked up his iPhone, then laid it on the table and spun it around for Possum to see.

100 All Pines Road
Stann Creek, Belize

Possum stared at the phone and looked like he was in deep thought.

"Let me see that note that Maxx wrote to Stan. Remember how he spelled Stan's name with one n and later with two?" asked Possum.

Rick pulled out the pencil laten image and placed it on the table.

Dear Stan,

I can't wait to see you. I hope your business in Playa went as expected. I will rendezvous with you Thursday and start our new life together on the Caye. Once I get to the river Stann, I will call you.

Love, Maxx

"I don't think he misspelled Stan. I think he was referring to Stann Creek. Right where we are!"

He studied the note carefully, then pulled out a magnifying glass. "Rick, can you get Paul on the phone? I need to ask him a question."

Rick called Paul on one of his burner phones. "Paul, it's Rick. Can you talk?"

"Yeah, I just landed in Cancun. I'm waiting for my luggage."

"Possum needs to ask you a question, hang on."

Possum took the phone, and the crew could only hear his side of the conversation.

"Hi Paul, did Kirsten have any nicknames? No, not romantic ones you use. Any that her friends or family might use?" There was a short pause then Possum said, "Really, you don't say! Let me pass you back to Rick."

Rick took the phone back from him. "Hang on, Paul." He covered the phone. "Gary, where is your jet?"

"Oh shit, in all the excitement, I forgot. It's still sitting at Cancun International at the executive side. I put Clay up at the resort and told him to hang tight until I needed him."

"If I were you, I'd get that thing as far away from Cancun as possible. The Federales will confiscate that for sure if they find out we are involved in the shootout at Miguel's or running with Jules. Can you call Clay and have him bring Paul and the jet to Belize City?"

"I'm on it!"

"Paul, change of plans, too much to tell you on the phone. You just have to trust me. Go over to the executive side and look for a sign with your name on it. It's Gary's pilot, Clay.

Go with him. You're coming to Belize City. We'll send a car for you."

"Okay, Rick, I'll walk over as soon as my bag comes off the carousel."

Rick hung up and stared at Possum with a devious look.

"Spill it!" said Rick.

"Come look at this."

Possum held the magnifying glass over the note. They all gathered around trying to see.

"Okay yeah, so what? He can't spell," said Rick.

"Look closer."

Rick leaned in and looked frustrated.

"When I asked Paul if Kirsten had any nicknames, at first he said Angel and Darling. Then when I asked him for non-romantic nicknames, he said sometimes they called her Sten, short for Kirsten. Now look again."

Rick looked closer.

"Son of a bitch! It says Dear Sten, not Dear Stan. He ain't gay. He's having an affair with Kirsten. Oh my God! They are both involved in this!"

"Now read it out loud," said Possum.

"Dear *Sten*, I can't wait to see you. I hope your business in Playa went as expected. I will rendezvous with you Thursday and start our new life together on the Caye. Once I get to the river Stann, I will call you. Love, Maxx," read Rick.

"That's it! He didn't misspell Stan, he was referring to the river Stann or Stann Creek. Right where we are parked! You freaking genius you! You're getting a raise, Possum."

"Well, you don't pay me, you can't afford me," he said with a laugh.

Gary instructed his pilot Clay to fuel the jet once they got to Belize and hole up at the Bomboleo Inn, the closest hotel to the airport, and be on standby. Once Paul arrived, Rick told him about the note and Possum's revelation.

Paul ran a hand through his hair, his lips tight. "It all makes sense now. I always felt uncomfortable with Maxx when he was around Kirsten. He was overly friendly with her compared to me. They were only a few years apart, unlike her and me. So, you think Maxx killed Ava after all and stole the diamonds to get a fresh start with Kirsten?"

"It looks that way. But there could be more to the story, I'm afraid. I just don't know yet," replied Rick.

The sun was setting and the adrenaline had long since faded from them all. They all got an early night's sleep. Rick, Paul, and Possum would scour the area in the morning with a photo of Maxx and see if anyone had run into him.

CHAPTER THIRTEEN

"Cock-a-doodle-doo, cock-a-doodle-do!" squawked Chief, mimicking a rooster and waking everyone up just as the morning sun appeared on the horizon.

"Damn bird," mumbled Rick as Jules yawned beside him.

Possum beat everyone to the galley and had coffee brewing.

"Morning, hombre!" said Possum.

"Yes, it is," replied Rick with a grumpy look on his face.

Jules made chilaquiles for breakfast, and they all sat around the big table and ate in mostly silence. After breakfast, Rick made several copies of the most recent photo of Maxx and passed them out. Everyone except Jules would canvass the area. She protested, but Rick reminded her there might still be a bounty on her head, and they had no idea how far-reaching that contract went. She finally agreed after a small tantrum. Rick kissed her on the forehead and told her he loved her and that they wouldn't be gone too long.

"Let's roll, boys."

They each split up and went around with the photos. Around noon, they met back at the marina with no good news.

"If he was here, no one noticed him and he probably isn't here anymore," said Rick.

"Maybe he rented a boat and is hiding in one of the other cayes," said Johnie.

"Good thinking, Johnie. Can you round us up some lobsters for lunch? I'm gonna go speak to the dock master and see if any boats have been stolen or rented," replied Rick.

Gary and Possum returned to *Nine-Tenths*, and Johnie set off to score some lobsters.

"Good afternoon, sir. I'm Rick. Would you mind answering some questions I have?" asked Rick.

"No problem, amigo. My name is Pablo."

"Oh, good, you speak perfect English."

"Yes, I'm from Texas. I'm just another gringo in Belize."

"Cool, I'm from Texas too. Listen, have any boats been stolen from here in the past few weeks? Or did you rent any out that haven't been returned?"

He looked up toward the ceiling and thought for a minute.

"No boats have been stolen and we don't rent boats here."

"Okay, damn!" said Rick as he laid the photo of Maxx on the table in frustration.

Rick had already asked the deck boys if anyone matching Maxx's photo had been around, but they all said no. The office was hot. Even with the window open, Rick was sweating. He was about to pick up the photo and leave when the man looked down at it and pulled it closer.

"I did sell a boat, though. To that guy."

"Well, I'll be damned, you just made my day," said Rick, his shoulders relaxing. Finally, another lead. "Can you tell me anything else about him?"

"He came in here wearing a beanie. It was hot as usual, so he took it off after a while. That's definitely him in the photo. He was acting nervous. I didn't care—he paid cash. All hundred-dollar bills. As they say in Belize, you are either *wanted* here or *not wanted*," said Pablo.

He fumbled through his desk and found a sales contract. "He bought a little twenty-three-foot used Edgewater from me. I just had it painted light blue."

He pointed to the for-sale sign still up on the wall and ripped it down, tore the price and phone number off of it that were printed on the bottom, and handed the sign to Rick.

"Let me guess, his name was Jake."

Pablo looked down at the contract.

"That's exactly right. Jake Smithe."

"Do you know where he went?"

"No idea. He left and helped some blonde woman onto the boat, and they both headed out of the channel. I haven't seen them since. Is he in trouble?"

"You could say that. Thanks for your time."

As Rick walked out of the door, he glanced back to see Pablo burning the sales contract for the boat and throwing it in the waste basket.

He got back to the boat just as Johnie sprawled out a large gunny sack of spiny lobsters.

"Johnie, put them in the live well. We're leaving. We need to find a boat. This boat." He held up the sign with the boat's picture on it. "It could be on any caye around here. If we find that boat, we find Maxx."

Johnie had already topped the tanks. Rick passed out three pairs of stabilizing binoculars and laid out a chart of the area. Rick took the helm for a change and let Johnie have one of the binoculars. He idled around the island closest to the marina first—Placencia Caye. Several monohull sailboats and a couple of cats were moored in the lee of the island, but no sign of a blue Edgewater.

Rick continued on to Lark Caye. It was mostly uninhabited rainforest with a couple of small cinder block houses. There were so many cayes in the area, it would be a miracle if they found the boat. After searching ten more cayes, they decided to call it a day and anchored just outside Turneffe Atoll. Jules prepared all the lobster tails on the grill with a side of mashed potatoes and corn. They all sipped on Belikin beer that Johnie had picked up when he got the lobsters.

"Do you think we'll find him, Rick?"

"I think we'll find them both, together. Sorry, Paul, but that's where the evidence is pointing," replied Rick.

"I know, I know," said Paul as he shook his head in disgust.

The next morning, they continued north to Hick's Cayes, Long Caye, and Caye Caulker. They pulled into Caye Caulker to the ferry terminal for Belize City, and managed to coerce the dock boy for some fuel. Johnie topped off the tanks as Rick stepped onto the dock and showed several of the employees Maxx's photo and the picture of his boat.

"I see dat boat, he stop here for fuel last week then head south," one of them said. "He wif a white woman."

"Thank you, thank you!" exclaimed Rick.

He hurried back on board *Nine-Tenths*.

"He's been here. He can't be too far."

They spun the boat around and retraced their steps. The only islands they hadn't stopped at were the ones way out west, but they were small and mostly uninhabited. They made their way back to where they'd started and turned west. They motored around the Royal Belize on Ragged Caye then onto the Rockers Island, Coco Plum, Man O' War Caye, and Thatch Caye. *Nothing!* Rick slammed his hand on the boat's railing in frustration.

Johnie used his new app to check if there were any other small islands nearby. "There's Tobacco Caye, but it's just a three-acre spec," he said.

"We've come this far, we may as well check it out."

It had been a long day, and they had burned a lot of fuel. They finally arrived at Tobacco Caye after dark. They circled the tiny sand spit that had a few houses hidden by overgrown mangroves. No sign of the elusive blue boat. They decided to drop anchor and wait until sunup to continue.

"It'll be all right," said Jules as she and Rick lay in bed that night. She snuggled up closer to him. "We'll find him, I'm sure of it."

"I hope you're right," said Rick with a sigh, kissing her forehead.

At seven a.m., Johnie fired up the twin MAN diesels. Since it was dark when they arrived, Rick decided they should circle Tobacco Caye one more time before moving on to Columbus Caye. As they circled around, each one of them looked through the binoculars.

Jules suddenly shouted, "Look, a blue boat!"

Johnie pulled closer. It was tucked into some mangroves, so only the stern was visible. It had the same type of outboard engine and hull color as the boat Rick had a photo of, but he couldn't make out the brand.

He jumped in the dinghy and slowly motored over. As he approached it, he reached up and pulled it to the side from the mangroves.

Edgewater 2300cc!

"It's gotta be him," he said when he was back on *Nine-Tenths*. "Edgewaters are white from the factory, but this one has been repainted that ugly light blue. I bet anything, it's him. We need to case the area after dark."

Rick, Gary, and Possum put on black clothing and striped their faces with Dead Down Wind face paint.

"Rick, I'm coming too!" insisted Paul.

"It's too dangerous. We know what he's capable of," replied Rick.

"I don't care. If Kirsten is with him, I want to be there. Period. Hand me that paint."

Rick reluctantly passed it to him and grabbed him a black top from his stateroom.

"Just stay behind us. Here, take this. You know how to use it?"

"I was raised in South Africa, mate. Of course, I do."

They all climbed into the dinghy. They tied it off near the blue Edgewater and climbed onshore. It was pitch black with no moon, and the stars looked like you could touch them, they were so clear. There was a dock beside the boat that led to a little bungalow.

Rick put on his night-vision goggles and approached slowly, and hid behind a bougainvillea bush. As he looked toward the little house, he could see a flickering candle through the thin curtains. A figure walked by, then another. He gave the crew a sign that there were indeed two people inside. He needed to get a positive ID on Maxx, so he picked up a small pebble and threw it toward the window. He missed completely. He tried again.

This time, he hit the casing of the window, and the pebble bounced up and just barely pinged the glass. Rick could see the silhouette of a person coming toward the window with a gun in their right hand. He opened the curtain a little and peeked out. It was Maxx.

Rick motioned for Possum to take his position as he and Gary flanked the door of the building. He waved at Possum to throw another pebble. When he did, Maxx opened the front door. Rick was bent down and kicked it open, startling Maxx. Before Rick could get to him, he bolted back inside as they all followed.

"Don't move or I'll kill the fucking bitch!"

Maxx had his arm around Kirsten's neck and the gun pointed at her head.

"I fucking swear I'll kill her."

"What are you doing, Maxx? Let her go," pleaded Paul.

"Please help me, he's crazy!" shouted Kirsten.

Maxx looked at her with surprise. Without warning, she elbowed him in the gut and he released her for a split second. As he swung the gun around, Paul fired off a shot, hitting him in the neck. Maxx fell to the ground as blood pumped out of his neck. Paul had hit a major artery. Kirsten ran toward Paul and flung her arms around her.

"You saved me!"

"You went with him! Why are you here?!" asked Paul.

"No, you don't understand. Let me explain."

Rick moved over to Maxx and slid the gun away from him with his foot. A large pool of blood about two feet in diameter and growing covered the wooden floor. Rick kneeled down to Maxx and cupped the hole in his neck. There was no stopping the blood.

"Why'd you kill Ava, Maxx?"

Maxx looked up at Rick as the color ran from his face.

"I didn't."

His head slumped and his body went limp. Rick closed his eyes with both of his fingers.

"We have to go and we have to go now! Tie her up, and help me get Maxx to the dinghy."

Rick gagged Kirsten against Paul's wishes, but she was screaming and causing a scene. They needed to get out of there before any cops arrived. The small island had no authorities, but all the noise they'd made would draw attention.

Once everyone was on the dinghy, Rick grabbed a gas can from the Edgewater and returned to the bungalow. He poured gas all over the bed and floor and set the candle near the curtains, which caught fire immediately. He closed the door and ran back to the dinghy.

Boosh!

The sound of the gas catching fire was unmistakable as flames engulfed the living room. They were all back at *Nine-Tenths* as the fire raged. There would be nothing left of the little house or any proof that they were ever there. It had to be that way. Rick looked back at the house with binoculars. A fireball had risen higher than the mangroves.

"Put her down below and head to deep water," said Rick.

"Is this necessary, Rick?" asked Paul.

"Yes, until I sort this out. She needs to be down below. Possum, you watch her."

Johnie motored through the cut between Tobacco Caye and Water Caye as Rick and Gary weighted down Maxx. When they got to 1,500 feet, they dumped him over the starboard side and watched his body sink. He was dead and there was no way they could explain it to Belizean authorities. It was the only way.

Rick sprayed down the deck and removed any evidence of blood. He bleached the entire area, then washed it off aggressively. Scrubbing the deck with a stiff brush. He repeated the steps several times then brought out some luminol he had in his P.I. bag, and sprayed the deck and used his black light to shine down on it. They wrapped up all of the dark clothes they had worn, tied them up to a five-pound dive weight, and chucked them overboard too. They all jumped in the water, hoping no sharks would be attracted to them, and washed off with Dawn dish soap. Once they were satisfied there was no more evidence on them, they climbed back up onto the boat and rinsed off with the stern shower on the dive platform. They all changed into clean, warm clothes. It was a whirlwind and seemed surreal.

"Bring her up," instructed Rick. "This is gonna be uncomfortable, Paul, but it has to be done. I have to question her."

"I understand."

Rick sat directly across from Kirsten at the big table in the salon.

"Kirsten, I'm gonna ask you some questions. I need you to be honest or you'll end up with the fishes like Maxx. You understand?!"

"Maxx? What do you mean?"

"We had to bury him at sea. You don't want your husband to spend the rest of his life in a jail in Belize, do you?"

"No! Oh my God, I can't believe this."

"Did you have anything to do with Ava's death?"

"No, I swear. I can explain."

"Why were you with Maxx?"

She was almost hyperventilating as she tried to speak.

"After Ava's death, I felt so much guilt that I had been upstairs when she died. Not guilt from killing her—I'd never hurt her—but guilt from not protecting her from Maxx. I decided to fly back to South Africa. I was going insane and the anxiety was too much to handle. I had every intention of calling you, Paul, when I arrived. I swear. I just knew you'd try to stop me from leaving and I couldn't spend one more night in Mexico."

"So, you aren't having an affair with Maxx?"

"Are you crazy?! I love Paul. Maxx had an obsession with me. I know that now. When I arrived in Cancun to catch my flight, he called me at the airport as I was just about to check in. He said he had Paul and was going to kill him if I didn't meet him in Belize. He said if I called anyone or told the police, he would behead Paul and mail his head to our home in South Africa. I didn't know what to do. He instructed me to meet him at the marina in Stann Creek. I took a bus down to the Belize border, crossed there, then hired a car to take me there. When I arrived, he said he had Paul in a cabin on Tobacco Caye. He took me in the boat. When we got there, Paul wasn't there, of course. It was all a ruse. He raped me repeatedly, Rick. Look at my wrists and ankles. He tied me to the bed nude for days. It was a nightmare. I finally convinced him that I wasn't going to run and wanted to be with him. I was just biding my time until I could find a way to escape. I'm so sorry, Paul." said Kirsten as she cried almost uncontrollably.

Rick could see the look on Paul's face that he was in pain, and wanted to go comfort her.

"I feel so dirty. He did unthinkable things to me. He bragged about sodomizing Ava and throwing her off the cliff at the ruins. He's a sick person."

"How do you explain this?"

Rick slid the note he had found in Maxx's room at the hotel in the Centro. She picked it up and looked at it.

"I've never seen this before. I swear!"

"Why would he leave you a note and call you Sten?"

"He always called me Sten. I have no idea why he wrote that note. Maybe to throw you off? Maybe he was playing cat and mouse and thought the whole thing was a game? I never touched a hair on Ava's head. I loved Ava. Sure, we had our differences, mostly because of her BPD, and she was jealous that I am so young and with her father, but that's all. Maxx killed Ava. That's a fact. He bragged about sneaking in, stealing the diamonds, and finishing off Ava in the bathroom. He's pure evil. A psychopath. You can ask me a thousand times and I'll give you the same answer every time. I did *not* kill Ava. Maxx did, then he conned me into meeting him. So go ahead, ask me whatever you want."

Rick sat there in silence, looking at her and eyeing her wrists and ankles. She definitely had been tied up. He began to believe her. His gut instinct was telling him Maxx had indeed killed Ava. He had maintained his lies even with his last dying breath.

"Why did you go with him so willingly on the boat at the marina at Stann Creek?"

"Because he said he was going to take me to Paul. He said he knew who killed Ava and had proof. He said he'd trade Paul's life for me, if I'd go with him. I had no intention of being with that sick fuck. I just wanted to save my husband."

Tears were welling up in Paul's eyes, and Rick could see he believed her. He knew her better than anyone, so he nodded for him to go to her. Paul wrapped his arms around her. They both began to sob.

"I just wanna go home, Paul. Please take me home."

"We're going home, Angel, I promise."

Rick waved his finger in a circle, signaling Johnie to bring the boat back to the mainland.

"Gary's pilot will take y'all to Florida in his jet. You can fly back to South Africa from there," said Rick.

Johnie took the boat to Belize Dive Haven Marina, and Gary arranged for a taxi for them to the airport.

"Thanks again, Rick, for everything you have done. I'll wire you some money for your time," said Paul.

"Nonsense. You don't need to do that. I was on vacation, remember?"

"Some vacation. I think you need a vacation from your vacation."

"You may be right," said Rick with a grin.

They all shook hands, and the couple disappeared down the street in the taxi. Johnie topped off the fuel tanks at the marina.

"What now, boss?" asked Johnie.

"Well, first stop calling me boss!"

"Dammit! I'm sorry, Rick. Bad habit."

Jules had gone to the bathroom before they arrived at the marina. She stepped out, and everyone's jaw hit the floor.

"Let's go find the treasure!"

She had shortened her hair some and it was now hot pink. She looked completely different.

"Holy shit! What the?!" exclaimed Rick.

"I'm tired of being left out. Let's go back to Tulum and find that snake guy!" she said.

"You mean Kukulcán—the Feathered Serpent god."

"Yeah, that gold dude. I'm ready."

"Okay, but we stay on the boat except at night. Deal?"

"Deal!" she said as she crossed her fingers on one hand behind her back.

"Let's roll, boys," said Rick.

Rick took in Jules's new look.

"You're kinda sexy as a neon pink head."

"Don't get used to it, buster. Once we're back in Florida, I'm going back to my original color. It's just a temporary spray. Washes out."

CHAPTER FOURTEEN

After an hour of pounding through the seas, Rick took the helm. He wanted to drive the boat. It had been a dream of his to get the boat, but because of his schedule he rarely got the chance to actually steer.

It was still early morning as he neared Tulum and slowed down. He drove close to the coast, passing the ruins and the possible site of the treasure. Once back in Puerto Aventuras, they settled in and did some maintenance on the boat. Johnie changed all the fuel filters and topped off the water tanks. Gary took the scuba tanks into town and had them filled. Rick messaged Manuel on the Signal app, and he agreed to meet them later at the marina.

Around ten a.m., Manuel arrived. He had a small portable hard drive with him.

"Plug this into a laptop, Rick. I want you to see this."

Manuel clicked on a video file and it began to play. It was clear that it was from inside the vent hole. As the small camera was pushed farther and farther into the opening, it got darker and darker, then suddenly blindingly bright as Manuel turned on the LED floodlights. Large schools of silversides flashed in the light as it entered the cave opening. Judging from the video, the cavern room was about twenty feet wide and maybe thirty feet deep. The bottom was sand. Rick could see small crawfish on the floor.

Fresh water.

Manuel moved the camera all around the cave. It was impossible to see if the main source of the spring water started in the cave because every time it got to the edge of the cave, it kicked up limestone silt. At the end of the video, as Manuel was pulling the camera back out, he turned off the floodlights. It went pitch black. In the far-right corner, Rick spotted something.

"What's that? Can you back it up?"

"No problemo."

As Manuel backed up the video to where the lights were on, Rick told him to stop.

"Can you move it forward frame by frame?"

"Does a donkey shit in the street?"

"That's a new one," responded Rick.

When he got to the frame where the lights went out, he stopped it.

"Look, right there!" exclaimed Rick.

On the far right of the video, the faint image of light appeared.

"Bingo! It's coming from the top of the cave. It's an entrance from above. Maybe big enough to climb down into," said Rick.

"It's too faint. It must be a tiny hole to let in such little light," replied Manuel.

"Or, or...wait for it. It's overgrown with weeds blocking the sun."

Manuel thought for a second.

"You are right, Rick. It has to be. We have to find that opening. That must be how they got the treasure into the cavern. It won't be an easy task. The cavern is in a thick overgrown area of the jungle. We will have to literally use machetes to get even a foot inside. It's muy dense!"

"Can it be done?" asked Rick.

"Yes, but it will take time. We have to be careful too because this area is also known to be where the cartel has some grow fields."

"Weed?"

"No, poppy seeds. And they are ruthless."

"Shit, who isn't, in this county?"

"That's true, Rick, that's true."

"We'll need to use GPS to locate the corner of that cave."

"I don't think we can get that. The ceiling is solid limestone. All we can do is estimate based on how far the camera is from the boat. We can do that now if you want."

"Let's do it! As soon as Gary gets back, we can shove off," exclaimed Rick.

They left the dock at 11:15 a.m. Excitement hummed in the air. As they approached the vent hole, Possum was racking his brain, trying to come up with a way to get GPS coordinates of the opening on the surface. They anchored ten feet from the vent hole underwater. Gary, Rick, and Manuel all geared up for the dive. Jules fed the cable attached to the underwater camera to the boys off of the stern. She wanted to be underwater but was a new diver, and everyone had a part to play.

Johnie stayed up on the flybridge with his binoculars with Chief to keep a lookout for any approaching boats. Once down at the base by the hole, Manuel began to feed the camera inside. That gave Possum an idea. He fired up his Mavic Mini drone and hovered it directly above the guys below. He could see Jules letting out a foot of cable at a time as Manuel pushed the camera in. He could clearly see the guys under the gin-clear water on the screen of his iPhone. The drone was equipped with a 4k camera and he had it pointing straight down. As Jules fed a foot out, Possum moved the drone a foot in the same direction.

Rick was wearing a full-face mask and could communicate with Jules and Possum via a walkie-talkie on the deck.

"Okay, Jules, keep it coming."

"Yes, boss," she replied.

"Stop that!"

After fifteen minutes, Rick said, "Stop. That should be enough."

If Possum was right, the drone was exactly over the top of where the camera was in the cave below, but all he could see was heavy jungle. He snapped a screenshot of where the drone was hovering. Then he got an idea. He saved the route exactly and lowered the drone to the ground. It hit some branches on the way down and crashed but not too hard. It was sitting on its side, and on the screen all he could see was weeds. The DJI app had a lost drone setting. All they had to do was go to shore and use the app to find it. It should be relatively close to the opening of the cave.

The crew climbed back on board *Nine-Tenths* and rinsed off. Possum told Rick what he'd done, and Rick clapped him on the back in thanks. "Good thinking. That'll be a big help," he said.

There was still plenty of daylight, but they had forgotten one thing: machetes. They'd have to try again the next day. With the boat back at the dock, Jules prepared some fresh snapper they had caught recently. They all sat on the stern scarfing down the spicy fish and drinking Tecates.

Manuel left around five p.m. and planned to meet them back at the boat with every conceivable bush-cutting tool he could get his hands on.

"Hasta mañana, Manuel."

"Adios."

The sun couldn't rise fast enough for Rick. Manuel showed up at eight with several machetes and some curved hand saws. He had something to do in town and told them he'd meet them at the site a little later on in his own boat.

They hastily made their way to the vent hole site. Johnie would stay on board with Chief and keep watch while Gary, Rick, and Possum would cut their way through the heavy bush following Possum's route on the app. Rick passed out the walkie-talkies to everyone. Jules would stay behind and mind the dinghy. She wasn't happy about it but went along.

It took them over three hours to find the drone. It had a broken propellor, but other than that was still in good working order. They began to search the entire area, trying to find the opening to the cave below.

Jules was bored beyond belief sitting on the dinghy, plus she was getting sunburnt on the water. She decided to step ashore and get in the shade. She could clearly see the trail the boys had cut through the jungle. Curiosity got the best of her, and she knew Rick would be upset with her, but she wanted to be a part of it.

She walked slowly up the trail. If she got lost, she had her cell phone in her back pocket and her walkie-talkie. Rick might scold her for this later, but it wouldn't be too harsh. She got about three quarters of the way down the trail and had to pee. Glancing around, she didn't see anyone around, so she took a few steps into the bush to do her business.

As she took her third step, the ground got soft and then gave way. She screamed as she fell. She fell into darkness for what seemed like forever and then slammed into the water. She struggled to get her way to the surface. She wasn't hurt but freezing. The spring water was giving her chills.

She looked up at what must've been fifty feet, and she could see the small hole she'd fallen through. It couldn't be more than two and a half feet across.

"Rick, Rick!" she yelled. "Helllllllpppppp!"

Only the birds chirping in the jungle answered her.

It was useless. She swam to the side of the cave, grasping for the edge, and put her fingers in the limestone holes so she wouldn't have to tread water anymore. Terror crept over her. She feared she'd die of hypothermia if she didn't get out soon. The walls were steep and slick. Her walkie-talkie had sunk to the bottom when she dropped it in the fall.

She pulled her phone out of her back pocket. It was history. But it had a shiny silver case around it, and she used the light to cast its reflection on the wall. Mayan drawings covered the limestone wall, including one of the ancient serpent god they were searching for. He was well adorned and the largest pictograph of them all.

Her eyes widened in shock.

"Did you hear that?!" asked Rick.

"Hear what?" replied Possum.

"I don't know, I thought I heard someone scream. Maybe I'm hearing things or it could've been a bird or something."

The crew searched for another thirty minutes, trying to find the opening. It was miserably hot and they had run out of water. Possum offered to walk back to the dinghy, so he and Jules could go back to the boat and refill their insulated water bottles. He took both Rick and Gary's bottles with him. When Possum got to the dinghy, Jules wasn't there. He figured she might have taken a walk down the beach. He grabbed his walkie-talkie.

"Jules, this is Possum. Come back."

Silence.

He repeated it.

Silence.

"Hey, Rick, you might wanna come back here," Possum said over his walkie-talkie.

Rick and Gary came hurrying back to the dinghy. "What's wrong?"

"I can't find Jules."

"I told her to stay here!" said Rick in frustration.

Rick quickly tried to use his own walkie-talkie. "Jules, it's Rick. Please answer."

Silence.

"Johnie, come in."

"This is Johnie. What's happening?"

"Did you see Jules leave the dinghy?"

"No, Rick, I didn't. I was focused on the water mostly. I noticed a few minutes ago she was gone, but I thought she had joined y'all."

"When's the last time you saw her?"

"Ummm, maybe thirty or forty minutes ago. I looked over at the beach with my binocs and she was just sitting on the edge of the boat. Then I looked back right before you called me and she was gone."

"Okay, guys, she left the boat around forty minutes ago. Let's spread out and look for her. Keep calling on the radios, she may be out of range," said Rick.

Gary went south on the beach, Possum went north, and Rick went back up the trail.

"Jules! Jules!" yelled Rick.

He went back and forth between yelling and calling her on the radio. He could hear Gary and Possum doing the same. She never answered. Rick was freaking out. He began to look down at the trail, searching for any sign of her.

Maybe she dropped an earring or something.

He knew he was grasping at straws.

Jules was shivering. She knew the average temperature of cenotes was around seventy-seven degrees. Her body temperature was dropping rapidly. She was getting cramps in her arms from hanging onto the wall.

Suddenly, she heard Rick. His voice was faint, but she could hear him calling for her.

She yelled back, "Rick, I'm here! Help!"

Her voice echoed inside the big cave, but she knew he wouldn't hear her through the small opening. She listened intently. Her only chance was to find the walkie-talkie. They were searching for her above ground, not in a hole.

She looked down into the clear water, but it was pitch black. Her only option was to dive down and feel around the bottom of the cave. She'd start at the edge and work her way to the other side. It could be anywhere. Back and forth she swam, then she popped up to catch her breath. She was having no luck, but at least it took her mind off freezing. She searched the entire bottom, as best she could in the darkness, and came across something shiny. She picked it up and shoved it in her pocket. She was getting scared and didn't wanna die—then she heard Possum.

"Jules, Jules, where are you?!" he yelled.

Then she heard his voice again.

"Jules, this is Possum, are you reading this?"

That sounded like he was also talking into the walkie-talkie. It gave her an idea.

She waited for him to repeat, then ducked her head underwater and stared at the bottom. As Possum spoke, a tiny red light flashed on the walkie-talkie. She swam over to the area and waited again.

The red light flashed once more; someone else was speaking.

She was treading water directly above it. She dove down and as she got close to the bottom, the red light flashed again. She could just barely make out the muffled sound of

Rick's voice underwater. She reached down and snatched it. She swam up out of the water and gripped the edge of the wall.

"Rick, Rick, it's me. I'm in a hole. A cave. Help me!"

"Jules? Where are you? Please describe the area."

She was still trying to catch her breath. She was so thankful that Rick had ordered the fully waterproof walkie-talkies instead of the cheaper ones.

"I was walking halfway up the trail and turned left about three feet. I fell into the opening."

"You found it?!"

"Yes, Rick, I found it. Please get me out."

Rick called Possum and Gary and told them to meet him at the dinghy.

"Possum, go to the boat and get the dive lights, duct tape, and the long safety line we drag behind the boat when we are swimming. Oh, and grab the mylar survival blanket. Bring Johnie back with you."

"Will do," said Possum.

Possum hauled ass to *Nine-Tenths* and came back as fast as possible.

"Okay, the trail we cleared is about fifty yards. She thinks she might be halfway down the trail and to the left. So, let's walk slowly and focus on the edge of the trail. Maintain radio silence. I will speak to Jules only. We don't wanna talk over each other."

A boat was approaching. Rick grabbed the binoculars. It was Manuel. He waved him over to the beach, and he ran his Panga up on the sand.

"Jules fell into the cave. We need to spread out and find her."

"Oh no. She found it?" Manuel looked both excited and worried for her at the same time.

"We're coming, Jules," Rick told her over the walkie-talkie. "Hang in there."

"Thank you, Rick! I'm cold."

"Jules, please yell my name every twenty seconds. We will stop and listen."

They began walking up the trail and looking. The jungle was so thick that the side of the trail was all brush and hard to see through.

"Rick! Rick!" she yelled.

They walked slowly and searched every inch. She continued to yell his name as he instructed her. About fifteen minutes into their search, she screamed in desperation. She sounded like her entire body was shaking from the cold.

"I heard her. Over there," said Rick, pointing. "Jules, scream like a panther again, I heard you."

"Riiiiiiiiiiicccccccckkkkkkkkkkkkk! Heeeeelllllllll-ppppppppp!"

"There!"

Rick pointed to the side of the trail where some of the bushes looked stepped on. He ran to them. Just a few feet off of the trail, he saw the hole. It was still partially covered in vines and weeds. He ripped at them and stuck his head in the hold.

"Jules?!"

"Rick, thank God. Please get me out. I'm freezing."

"We got you, baby. Hang on."

"I ain't going anywhere," she blurted out with half a laugh.

Rick grabbed the three dive lights and taped them together facing outward. He took some of the twine he had that he planned to use to mark the search and tied it around the lights. He lowered it into the hole, and it lit the entire cavern up like daylight. Rick could see Jules looking up, shivering. He made a huge loop with the heavy rope and made a slide and grip knot, creating a makeshift rescue harness. He slowly lowered it down through the hole to Jules.

"Jules, slide this around your chest and hang on tight, baby."

She did as Rick told her. Once it was snug, she gave it three quick tugs.

"Wrap it around that tree, and all of you get a good grip," said Rick.

They pulled, walked backward, and Jules began to ascend. They continued to pull and soon were close to the top. Rick reached down and took her hand and helped her out the rest of the way.

Jules collapsed in his arms and began to cry. She continued to shiver. Her skin was cold. Rick rubbed her arms then wrapped the silver survival blanket around her. Her fingers were practically frozen in their grip on the walkie-talkie. Rick had to help her open her fingers to let it go.

"If I hadn't found this, Rick, I don't think you would've found me. I dropped it when I fell. I can't believe I found it. If it wasn't for the red flashing light when you speak, I doubt I would've seen it in the blackness. Oh, I found this too."

She reached into her shorts pocket and pulled out a gold coin and placed it in Rick's palm. He looked down at it and his eyes popped. The coin had a large cross on the back of it and was dated 1721. It was Spanish gold.

"The walls down there are covered in drawings. They look Mayan."

He shoved the coin into his pocket and hugged her.

"Let's get you in the sun. This can wait. This coin is yours, baby! I'm gonna get it mounted on a gold chain for you."

Jules smiled as tears rolled down her cheeks. She was so relieved to be on dry land. She always knew her man would save her. She never gave up hope.

Gary and Possum pulled up the dive lights, covered the hole with branches and shrubs, and Possum logged it on his portable GPS. They removed all traces that they had been there and followed Rick and Jules back to the dinghy. Once back on the boat, Rick boiled some water and made Jules some hot tea. He helped her out of her wet clothes, and she dried off and slipped into a robe and heavy socks. She was slowly warming up. Once she returned from the state-room and sipped on the tea, she was close to being back to her normal temp.

"Gather 'round," said Rick.

They all got closer, and Possum and Gary patted Jules softly on the shoulder, showing her they were happy she was back.

"I want to thank y'all for helping me find my Jules. I don't know what I'd do if we hadn't found her."

Rick's eyes were welling up and he was having a hard time talking. It made Jules tear up as well. She wrapped her arms around his legs as he spoke.

"We may have found Jules, but Jules found the cave. She also found this."

Rick pulled the gold coin out of his pocket and flipped it in the air.

"Heads or tails?!"

Out of habit, Possum exclaimed, "Tails!"

Rick caught the coin in his hand and slammed it down on his forearm, covering it with his palm. He slowly removed his hand, revealing the shiny gold coin.

"Tails it is! You win a beer, Possum!" They all leaned in to see it. Rick handed it to Possum. He held it up to the light and looked at both sides.

"It's Spanish gold. I thought we were looking for Mayan treasure?" he asked.

"Who the hell do you think stole it? The Spaniards! You know what this means?" asked Rick.

"It means there is a motherload in there. Spanish gold mixed with Mayan treasure. Oh my God," said Possum.

"Bingo!" exclaimed Rick.

"Let's go get it, Rick," said Jules.

"We will, baby, we will. Let's get you 100 percent first. We can start first thing in the morning."

CHAPTER FIFTEEN

Johnie fired up the huge diesel engines, and Manuel returned to his Panga and followed them back to the marina. He side-tied to *Nine-Tenths* and climbed onboard to go over the plans.

"Let's put our heads together. We know there are probably coins scattered all over the bottom and mostly under the sand. We're gonna need wetsuits. Jules can testify to how cold the water is. We can work in one-hour shifts then swap to surface jobs. I guess we can use nets to scoop up the coins then put them in a bag and pull them up. Any other ideas?" asked Rick.

"Too bad we can't just vacuum them up," said Gary.

"We can," replied Manuel.

"What do you mean?" asked Rick.

"I have a friend who runs a business of septic pumper trucks. We can remove the pump and run it from the diesels on the yacht," said Manuel.

"That's a great idea, Manuel. Why don't we just rent a pool sump pump?" asked Rick.

"For two reasons. My pump is free and it is far more powerful than the ones they use to drain pools. It sucks the caca!"

"Okay, you're right. Can you do me at least one favor though?"

"Que?"

"Please get new hoses. I don't wanna touch those nasty old hoses," said Rick with a wince.

"Okay, cobarde. I'll see if I can get new hoses. He has a shop just past Tulum."

Rick tried to translate in his head what "cobarde" meant and was staring up thinking.

"It means wuss, Rick. Ha-ha," whispered Jules.

Rick pursed his lips but agreed. Maybe he was a wuss, but he had no intention of touching shit-truck hoses.

"We need a filter or screen or something," injected Possum.

"I got you covered!" said Manuel.

He left and hopped in the car headed for Tulum. He returned a few hours later pulling a trailer. They all stepped off of *Nine-Tenths* to see what he'd brought. On the trailer was a V-twin Honda and a massive sump pump on another smaller trailer with small inflatable wheels, as well as a pile of brand-new hoses wrapped in plastic. It took four of them to get it off of the trailer and into Manuel's Panga. Rick threw the hoses onto the deck of *Nine-Tenths*.

"This will work better than trying to run the pump off of the yacht engine. My buddy just got two of them. He uses them for houses he can't get his trucks close enough to. It's never been used and as you can see, cobarde, the hoses are also new."

Rick shot Manuel the stank eye then smiled.

"Since the cave is pitch black, why don't we work under the cover of darkness? There's no sense in drawing any attention to us," said Rick.

"I agree," said Manuel. "I'll return around nine tonight with the strainer. I have to run to Valladolid to get one. We can head to site when I get back. That work?"

"Sounds great. We'll be ready. Jules, you up for it or do you need another day to recover?"

"Hell yeah, I'm ready!" she exclaimed.

Manuel left and Possum rode with him just to keep him company. The clock ticked slow as the rest of the crew waited. Jules made fish tacos for everyone, finishing off the last of the fresh snapper they had on board. Manuel and Possum returned a little early, and Johnie got the yacht ready to go. Possum rode in the panga with Manuel. He ran the panga high up on the beach. Gary, Rick, and Jules took the dinghy to the shore. They used night-vision goggles to see, and instructed Johnie to take the yacht five hundred feet past the site, drop anchor, and keep watch. They would maintain radio silence except for emergencies. It took all four of them to get the pump off the boat and up the trail. According to Google Earth, the closest house to them was well over eight miles away. No one would hear the Honda engines.

Rick brought three extra fuel cans with them and an electric winch and a handheld hoist, which he could also run off of the electric outlet built onto the trailer of the pump. Rick and Gary took the first shift.

"Let's get wet," said Rick.

They lowered the scuba gear into the hole first then climbed down the knotted rope Rick made on *Nine-Tenths*. In full wetsuits, the cold still hit them when they got in the water. They soon warmed up as the thin layer of water between their suits and skin warmed.

"Here we go," said Rick.

Manuel lowered the hose down to them. Once Rick gave him the signal, he started the pump. Jules watched as Manuel created a filter to catch anything larger than a dime out of the top of a pig roaster. He placed it on four large rocks and put the metal screen flat on top of them. The hose violently shook as sand, silt, and water rose from below. Jules and Possum grabbed the hose behind Manuel to help him hang on. At first, the sand and silt just began to pile up beneath the screen. Once it flowed fully, it was easier for Manuel to hold onto it.

Jules grabbed a shovel from Rick's dig bag and cut out a trough to let the water flow away from the screen. Possum shook the sand back and forth on the screen for it to sift better. Jules periodically pushed the sand along so the pile wouldn't rise to the screen. Suddenly, a loud ping rang out as a coin hit the screen. Then another and another. Jules grabbed each coin as they settled on the screen and put them in a mesh scuba goodie bag. The occasional ruby or emerald would hit the screen, and she kept them separate, including figurines or anything precious other than coins. She would occasionally grab a limestone or rock and toss it aside. The rocks and limestone would make the hose shake more, warning them that one was coming. It would slam the screen with a loud thud.

The hose began to shake, and she braced herself. With a boom, a solid gold bar smashed the screen. She set it aside. Then ten more came up the hose. Her excitement couldn't be contained as she hollered, "Woohoo!!"

A total of eleven sat in a pile beside the screen so far. Within forty minutes, she surmised there was at least ten pounds of pure gold Spanish coins in the goodie bag. An hour in, Rick gave Manuel the signal to stop the pump.

Working in pitch black would've been impossible if it wasn't for the night-vision goggles. Rick ascended and Manuel hauled up his empty tank.

"Do you want to dive?" Rick asked Jules. The water at the bottom of the cave was no deeper than thirty feet and it was less than an atmosphere of pressure, so they didn't have to fear getting the bends.

"I'll give it a shot," said Jules.

Gary climbed up the rope and Jules began to suit up. She moved to the edge of the hole as Gary steadied her and lowered her tank down into the cave. She hesitated as she looked into the hole with Rick looking up at her. Anxiety overcame her and she stepped back.

"I can't do it. I wanna stay up top," she said.

"I totally understand, Jules. You've barely had time to recover from falling into the hole. Let alone even process. I'll go back down."

Gary shimmied down the rope instead and flung his tank on and descended. Rick gave the signal, and Manuel started the pump again. They repeated this process for six hours and filled three carry bags. A sliver of light began to show on the horizon, so they called it.

Once on the surface, they covered everything with cut leaves and branches, and Rick messaged Johnie to return with *Nine-Tenths*. With the three coin bags and another filled with jewels, figurines, and bars, they loaded the dinghy. As they approached the yacht, Johnie came to the stern to help them pull the goodie bags onto the sport fisher. Johnie's eyes widened at the shimmering reflection of gold through the goodie bags, even in the dark.

"Holy shit!" exclaimed Johnie.

"I second that remark," replied Rick.

Once the bags were dragged into the salon, Rick spread a little of the treasure out on the table for everyone to admire. After a few minutes of taking it all in, he moved them to his stateroom. At the edge of his teak floor, he pushed down on a hidden button and opened a large section of the floor. He put all the bags under the floorboards and closed it up.

Johnie slowly idled about a mile from the site, then lit up the navigation lights and brought *Nine-Tenths* up on plane. As they approached the marina, the sun had peeked above the horizon. Rick and Gary tied up *Nine-Tenths* to the dock, while Possum made fresh coffee and his famous biscuits and gravy. He placed a pile of biscuits on the center of the dining table with a steaming bowl of sausage gravy. He knew exactly how to make it by heart with that pop of black pepper in each bite.

"Come eat!" yelled Possum.

They all sat around the table and made a plate. After a few bites in silence, Rick suddenly burst out into laughter. They all began to laugh. The reality of what they had just done sank in and they all felt the same thing. Manuel picked up his coffee to make a toast.

"Fuck that. Hang on, Manuel," said Possum.

He bolted to the fridge and took out a bottle of champagne and orange juice and made everyone a mimosa. He slid a glass toward Manuel.

"Now toast," said Possum.

Everyone raised their glasses. Manuel spoke:

> *"¡Por los aquí presentes!*
> *Algunos jóvenes y algunos viejos,*
> *Amo a mis amigos,*
> *Pero ama más el oro*
> *¡Salud!"*

They all clinked glasses. Rick and Johnie looked confused but clinked anyway.

"Let me translate, Rick," said Jules.

> *"To everyone here*
> *Some young and some old*
> *I love all my friends*
> *But more so the gold."*

"Wow, that rhymes in English," said Rick.

After breakfast, they began to discuss what to do with the treasure. Mexican law would not allow Rick and the crew to take the gold back to the states, but there was no way they were doing all this work for free.

"Manuel, I have proposal for you. Be honest and let me know how you feel. Since we are partners in this, but you are Mexican with Mayan blood, how about we take half of the coins and some of the loose jewels, you keep the other half and any figurines, encrusted jewelry, or anything else of significant historical value."

Manuel took a sip of his mimosa and considered it.

"I accept, Rick. On one condition."

"Shoot."

"If we do find the gold statue of Kukulcán, I want you and the crew to accompany me to present it to the Museo de San Roque in Valladolid. I've spent most of my life looking for it, and if we find it, I owe half of the find to you. Our names will be inscribed in history there."

"You have a deal, Manuel."

Rick shook his hand and they clinked glasses again. With full bellies, fatigue began to set in from being up all night. Rick and Jules showered and settled in their stateroom for a nap. Everyone else went to their cabins as well, while Manuel stretched out on the settee and dozed off.

Possum woke up first around three p.m. and put more coffee on. The smell of the fresh Volcanica organic Mexican coffee Manuel had given Rick as a gift wafted through into the cabins slowly, waking everyone. One at a time, they all staggered into the main salon like zombies. Manuel offered to get food and fill the empty scuba tanks. He drove into town and returned an hour later with two aluminum trays of piping hot food.

"My friend Kiki makes this at her restaurant in Tulum. It's her specialty," said Manuel.

He peeled the aluminum foil back on one container, revealing Chicken Mole, refried beans, Spanish rice, pineapple pico de gallo, and a stack of handmade corn tortillas. The other aluminum container had Mexican corn on the cob covered in cojita cheese and crema. In a separate cooler, he had a six-pack of Jarritos Mandarin sodas and some plastic baggies with a white liquid inside, plus a plate of flan.

"What's in the baggies, Manuel?"

Before he could answer, Jules interrupted. "It's horchata! You'll love it, Rick."

"Today we are all brothers and ahem, sister, and we are all Mexican."

They scarfed down the amazing meal and discussed the night's dig. As soon as the sun settled below the horizon, Johnie fired up the motors and they proceeded to the site. They repeated the process from the night before.

Hours turned into days and days into a week. They continued to load the goodie bags on *Nine-Tenths* every night. By the fifth night, only a few coins occasionally came up the hose. They still hadn't found the serpent god they desperately wanted to find. Every so often, the end of the suction hose would hit solid limestone and the hose would violently shake, and Rick would need Possum or Gary's help to get it unstuck. Just as they did every other night, they covered everything up with leaves and branches before daylight. It had become like clockwork for them, as if going to a regular job. The gold booty had almost become mundane and taken for granted after all the days of work, yet the mysterious Kukulcán still eluded them.

"It's gotta be here somewhere," said Rick to Jules in bed that night, as he stroked her hair. "I just know it."

"We'll find it, Rick. I have faith. Why do you want it so badly?" asked Jules.

"I guess because it's Manuel's lifelong dream, and I want to see that come true for him, plus it's a challenge. I'm a treasure finder, not a treasure hunter!"

The next night, they vacuumed the silt floor and only found one coin in three hours. The entire floor of the cavern had been covered. The suction hose hit solid limestone more and more often, as they had already sucked the majority of the loose sand and silt to the surface. Every time it hit bottom, they'd pull as hard as they could for it to release.

Rick was getting frustrated and beginning to think maybe he was wrong and the serpent god wasn't actually there. They all did. Rick went to the far-left corner in an area that still had a little sand remaining and shoved the hose down. Again, within minutes, it hit bottom.

Gary swam over to help Rick pull it loose, then dropped his regulator out of his mouth. He began yelling indistinguishable gibberish as bubbles flowed from his mouth. He shoved his regulator back in his mouth and motioned for Rick to look.

From his back pocket, he pulled out a small dive light and shined it at the edge of the hose on the bottom. The reflection of gold shone back in their eyes. Rick vacuumed around the area, and a face with a snake on its head came into view. He dropped the hose, and both he and Gary hugged and yelled underwater. They had found it. It was wedged into the limestone. They dug around with their fingers and were able to get all the way around the base of it and touch fingers. They ascended and started yelling in unison.

"We found it! We found it!"

Jules, Manuel, and Possum began to dance in a circle hooting and hollering. The only way to get the statue out was to use the electric winch. Manuel slowly lowered the cable down to Rick, and he carefully wrapped it around the widest part of the statue. From Rick's estimation, it was four feet tall and about two feet in circumference. It was heavy but had to be hollow. If it was solid, they would never have been able to lift it.

He gave three tugs on the cable, signaling Manuel to start bringing it up. It spun around in the air as Manuel drew it closer to the surface, and created a disco ball effect on the walls of the cave from the shine of the three dive lights hanging above it. At the surface, it took all of them to get it through the opening and onto solid ground. They all stared at it, sitting in the center of the trail looking ancient and mystical. Tears rolled down Manuel's cheeks. His life work was complete. They all gathered in a circle around the golden god and put their heads together in prayer. The sheer joy and excitement were palpable as Manuel began to speak. He first said it in Spanish and repeated it in English.

"Gracias, Dios, por permitirnos el honor de encontrar este valioso tesoro y regresar a mis ancestros Mayas. Thank you, God, for allowing us the honor of finding this valuable treasure and returning it to my Mayan ancestors. Amen."

"Amen," they all repeated.

Manuel wrapped the statue in soft cloth, and they carefully carried it to the dinghy. Back at *Nine-Tenths*, they loaded it on the swim platform and then onto the deck. Once inside the salon, Rick unwrapped it for Johnie to see. Chief flew off of his perch in fear to get away from it, and Jules picked him up and pulled him to her chest to calm him down.

The red ruby eyes of the statue and snake headdress had scared Chief. He got used to it after a few minutes.

They hid it under the sole of the boat and returned to the marina after Manuel snapped several photos of it with his phone. The plan was to go to the museum in Valladolid and set up a date for a grand ceremony for its return. He would not give away its location for fear of being robbed and planned to return it along with other historical finds in an armored truck with lots of firepower. He didn't trust the Federales or local police to escort them, so he hired a private security firm from Texas to come in.

A few days later, the trip was complete and they'd delivered the statue to the museum. Once it was verified as authentic, the find would be announced to the press. A few days later would be the grand unveiling. The entire crew would be on hand for the ceremony. Johnie took Nine-Tenths to Cozumel and hired armed guards to watch the boat. He took the ferry back to the mainland and met the rest of the crew in Valladolid.

Rick took everyone to a store called Sastrería El Amigo Juan in Valladolid to get custom tailor suits made and a fine dress for Jules. The ceremony was extravagant. Many dignitaries from all over Mexico attended. The highest-ranking official was the Secretary of the Interior from Mexico City. Everyone gathered around in a circle at the center of the museum. The museum curator pulled a string on a red velvet cover revealing the golden serpent god. Oohs and ahhs filled the echoing hall, followed by massive applause.

Manuel and the entire crew posed for a photo with the statue and answered questions from the press. Champagne and hors d'oeuvres were passed out as Rick and the gang made their way around the museum sharing pleasantries. It was a day to remember, and the curator handed them a plaque with their names on it, matching the one below Kukulcán—the Feathered Serpent god.

CHAPTER SIXTEEN

They wasted no time after the ceremony. After saying their goodbyes to Manuel, they proceeded back to Puerto Aventuras Marina. Manuel had arranged for a fast boat to take them to Cozumel, where *Nine-Tenths* was docked. Gary's jet would be waiting at Cozumel International. He and Jules would fly back to Destin, while Rick, Possum, and Johnie would bring *Nine-Tenths* back to the panhandle. There was no way they could get the treasure through customs at the airport, and Rick didn't want Jules to be in the boat in case they were ambushed.

As soon as the sun disappeared, Rick hugged and kissed Jules and reassured her they'd be safe out on the water. She tried to hold back her tears, but she couldn't. She and Gary took a taxi to the airport as Johnie backed the yacht off of the dock.

Everyone on the boat was packing. Rick tucked a .45 in his back and hid the FX-05 Xiuhcoatl assault rifles under some fishing netting with all the ammo. They were taking no chances. Once they got offshore, Johnie went dark and ran full bore north. It was 688 miles due north to Destin. *Nine-Tenths* had a range of close to five hundred miles. They couldn't make it without refueling, but it was too dangerous to refuel in Key West, so Manuel had arranged ten jerry cans of diesel for them and strapped them to the rails. They could do the trip in around thirteen hours if they ran at top speed. Chief sat on his cage on the flybridge and stayed awake the entire trip.

About two hours into the trip, Johnie called Rick up to the flybridge.

"Look, Rick," said Johnie, pointing at the radar.

Off the portside of *Nine-Tenths* was a blip coming from the direction of Veracruz.

"They are coming fast," said Johnie.

"Reverse course!" yelled Rick.

Johnie spun the yacht around, heading directly back to Cozumel. They continued to watch. The blip also changed course and continue to follow them and gain on them.

"Suit up!" yelled Rick.

He ran to the bow and opened a hatch, pulled out three ballistic vests, and passed them around. He also handed them some foul weather jackets to conceal the vests. It was apparent from radar that they couldn't outrun them. Rick instructed Johnie to lower the speed to six knots, and Rick and Possum tied trolling skirts to the lines and fed the line out. It was drizzling a little, so the foul weather gear wouldn't look out of place. They had no idea who was coming up on them. If it was Mexican Coast Guard or other authorities, they would try to play the part of fishermen. Johnie turned on the running lights and the deck lights as

Rick laid out some frozen ballyhoo on the fillet table with some rigging.

The boat pulled up to their starboard side, and began shouting orders in Spanish over a P.A. system.

"¡Apague sus motores y prepárese para abordar!"

Possum translated for everyone.

"Kill the engines, Johnie. They want to board."

"Ask them who they are, Possum," said Rick.

"¿Quién eres?"

"Búsqueda y Rescate Marítimo," responded the man in fatigues, now within shouting distance.

"They claim to be Mexican Coast Guard. They're lying," whispered Possum.

It was obvious they were lying, considering they were driving a sixty-foot Midnight Express. They may have been wearing fatigues and sporting machine guns, but they were no Coast Guard. They were pirates: scumbags from the mainland of Mexico.

"Tell them they have no jurisdiction here," said Rick.

"No tienes jurisdicción aquí," yelled Possum.

It was a good thing he had honed up on his Spanish with Manuel back in the Yucatán.

"¡Cállate, estamos subiendo a bordo!"

"They insist on coming aboard."

Rick assessed the situation. He knew if they came aboard, it was all over.

"Start the engines in ten seconds, Johnie. Possum, tell them they can come aboard, but we have to run our engines to keep our freezers going. Tell them we will turn around and back up so they can board on the stern."

"Tenemos que arrancar o motores, uelta pescado en el congelador. Daremos la uelta y podrá abordar desde la popa," said Possum.

"Bueno, gira lentamente," said the man angrily.

"He said go slow, Johnie."

Rick looked up at Johnie and smashed his fist into his palm slowly. He counted four men aboard. Two on the bow and one on a .50 cal mounted turret at the top of the boat, plus the driver. Johnie started the engines and began to spin the boat around. He pretended he was having difficulty with the twin props. At first, he spun slowly away from the fast boat, then he reversed the throttles and began to come back the other way as if he was going to do a 360 and back up to their port side. Johnie waited for Rick's signal. Rick knew they were no match for that .50 cal machine gun, but he also knew the fiberglass on the Midnight Express was far thinner than his Viking.

As soon as the bow was pointed directly toward their port, he yelled, "Now!" and ducked.

Johnie slammed the throttles forward, and the Viking slammed into the fast boat. The man on the turret fell off and onto the bow of *Nine-Tenths*. Before he could get to his feet, Rick fired a single bullet directly into his face. The other men all fell forward as well, and Gary and Johnie unloaded their pistols toward the boat.

The bow of *Nine-Tenths* had smashed halfway through the Midnight Express and was wedged into it as if they were one boat. Rick pulled up the fishing net and grabbed the FX-05 Xiuhcoatl assault rifles and tossed one to Gary. Before the two men on the bow could get a shot off, Rick and Gary opened fire on the pirate boat. Sparks and fiberglass exploded as the bullets ripped through the boat. The driver slumped over the wheel, knocking his throttles fore-word. The fast boat moved forward, spinning *Nine-Tenths*. They spun in a circle, connected like two maritime dancers.

"Reverse, Johnie! Reverse!"

The boats continued to spin in a circle. Seawater gushed into the Midnight Express, and it got lower in the water as they continued to spin.

Rick climbed onto the hull to try and separate the two boats. The anchor of *Nine-Tenths* was wrapped in the fiber-glass of the t-top. He climbed into the wheelhouse, shoved the dead driver aside, and pulled the kill switch, instantly turning off the six four-hundred horsepower outboards of the fast boat. It settled more into the waters and was going down fast. If Rick couldn't get the bow loose, it was going to drag them down with it.

"Release the anchor, Possum!" screamed Rick.

Possum stepped on the anchor button, and Rick unhooked the anchor safety strap. The outboards gushed steam as they fell below the surface. Only the t-top remained above water. The weight of the engines sank faster, and the bow of the boat started to rise.

"Full reverse!" yelled Rick.

He kicked the anchor over and tried to bust it loose. Anchor chain spilled on the deck of the Midnight Express in a pile. The boat had 150 feet of chain and 300 feet of rode. Johnie hit full throttle on *Nine-Tenths*, and it pulled the fast boat sideways through the water.

With a loud crack, the fiberglass bow released from the other boat, and Rick fell forward and banged his head on some broken fiberglass. Blood gushed from his forehead.

He was stunned and off balance. The anchor was still stuck deep in the fiberglass of the Midnight Express. The bow of the fast boat rose straight up then with a loud woosh, the boat sank under the water stern first.

The anchor chain ran out fast as Possum screamed at Johnie to bring him a knife. Johnie threw the engines into neutral and slid down the ladder of the flybridge. He grabbed the fillet knife Rick had placed on the cutting station. The whole chain was in the water and the rode was flying out of the anchor locker. If Possum couldn't cut the rode, the sinking boat would pull them down to the depths with it. He was sawing through the line as fast as he could but needed a serrated knife. There was no time. Only about fifty feet of rode was left. It was fastened tightly to the boat with a heavy shackle. It wouldn't budge.

Possum grabbed his .45 and placed it against the rode and fired as fast as he could. Bullets ripped through the rode and the fiberglass of the anchor locker. The entire line flew out, and with a loud snap, it broke where he had fired his gun and flew out of the anchor locker. The part left of the rode attached to the shackle slapped back against Possum's face, busting his nose wide open. Blood spewed everywhere. He grabbed his face and looked at the blood in his hand. He struggled to climb out of the anchor locker as blood flowed down his shirt.

"Where's Rick?" yelled Possum.

Johnie ran to the railing. All he could see were pieces of fiberglass, other boat pieces, and the two dead bodies of the pirates floating face down. He ran to the ladder and climbed up to the flybridge. He shined the spotlights in the water. Possum was on one knee with his hand on the railing. Coolers, life jackets, and other buoyant parts of the fast boat popped to the surface.

"Rick, Rick!" he yelled.

Possum seemed dizzy from the smash to his nose. His eyes watered, and he blinked like he could barely see. A huge bubble exploded on the surface. They both yelled and yelled. Chief was squawking loudly from all the excitement. Possum buried his head in his hands. If Rick was stuck on the fast boat, he was gone. They stared at the water in silence.

"A little help, please?!" yelled Rick.

Possum and Johnie spun around to see Rick kneeling on the swim platform with blood dripping down his face. Johnie got to him first and helped him over the transom. Possum stumbled clumsily toward the bow. It looked like a bloodbath on the deck. After catching their breath, they all rejoiced to be alive.

Johnie was the first one to notice the bow leaning lower than normal. Water was gushing into the cabin from the giant hole on the bow. The center of the bow was cracked below the water line.

"Johnie, get the boat moving. Go to five knots."

There was no time to patch their wounds. If they didn't stop the water, the boat was going to sink. Rick ran to the bow and shined a flashlight over the edge. The entire bow was smashed in and the center was cracked.

"Hurry—grab the fire hose, a knife, some self-tapping screws, and my cordless. I'll get the ditch bag. Johnie, send out a mayday. We have no choice," said Rick.

"I'm on it," responded Possum.

Rick climbed below and could see water creeping into his stateroom. If it got as high as their engines, they were doomed. He threw his ditch bag on the deck as Johnie put a flight suit on Chief and tied a tether to his wrist. He met Possum on the bow.

"Cut five pieces of the fire hose, about three feet long."

Rick wrapped a nylon line under his thighs in a v-knot and ran a few wraps around the empty anchor winch. He shoved some screws into his mouth and put the cut firehose over his shoulder, and climbed over the demolished rail.

"Okay, lower me down. Tell Johnie to hold it steady at this speed."

The crack on the deep v was just above the waterline at five knots. Rick had to reinforce it to keep it from opening up anymore. Just below the lowest part of the crack, he drilled one side of the fire hose to the hull. With all his might, he stretched it across the hull and screwed the other side to the starboard side. He repeated the process every three inches. Possum handed him down more screws, and he put several on each piece.

"Go to the workroom. In the back of the cabinet is a tub of Stay Afloat. Get it and bring it here fast," said Rick as he hung a few feet above the water.

Possum ran into the salon and climbed into the workroom. Water was still flowing into the boat but not as fast. In the very bottom back of the cabinet, he found the tub and ripped the lid off. He ran as fast as he could toward the bow and grabbed a huge handful of the goop and passed it to Rick. Rick shoved it into the crack, starting at the bottom, and moved his way up as Possum handed it to him.

"Okay, pull me up."

Possum helped Rick to the deck, and they both went below to see if the patch had worked. The floor of Rick's stateroom had about two inches of water in it. The automatic bilge pumps and were going full blast, but the yacht was still sluggish and rolling heavy in the slow swells.

"I have an idea."

Rick grabbed the shop vac and attached half of the cut firehose to the suction side and the other half to the exhaust. He plugged in and climbed into the engine room. The water was only about three inches from the bottom of the oil pans. He shoved the suction side of the hose to the bottom of the engine room and water began to flow. Possum held it over the rail. Within twenty minutes, most of the water was expelled. Rick turned off the shop vac and watched. The water wasn't rising.

Both Possum and Rick let out loud exhales of relief. The immediate crisis had been averted, for now.

"Mayday, mayday, mayday. This is vessel *Nine-Tenths, Nine-Tenths, Nine-Tenths.*"

Johnie released the button and listened.

"Mayday, this is vessel *Nine-Tenths* and we are located at 23.399520 North, -86.701921 West at a speed of five knots."

He repeated his calls over and over. Their location was almost dead center of either Cancun, Cuba, or Key West. They had to make a decision. They decided to try for Key West. They were out of VHF range, so Rick grabbed the SSB and repeated the calls asking for US Coast Guard. After a few minutes, he got a response.

"US Coast Guard sector Key West, are you reading?"

"Yes, this is vessel *Nine-Tenths*, we are partially disabled and we took on water. Can you send assistance?"

"Please repeat your position, vessel *Nine-Tenths*."

Johnie took the SBB back and continued talking. "We are located at 23.399520 North, -86.701921 West at a speed of five knots."

"Do you need helicopter rescue?"

"No, repeat no, we need assistance or maybe a tow. We are not abandoning ship."

"10-4 *Nine-Tenths*, we are scrambling cutter *Thetis*, maintain speed and direction. We're on our way, over."

"10-4 Coast Guard, we will maintain speed and direction. *Nine-Tenths* out."

Rick let out a big sigh. "That's great news."

He was still bleeding from his head, as was Possum from his nose.

"Before we get these injuries cleaned up, we need to toss those illegal weapons off the boat," said Rick.

"Not to mention that dead Mexican on the back deck," replied Possum as he pointed at the guy lying by the fighting chair.

"Agreed."

Rick and Possum took his arms and feet and swung him off the port side. Possum gathered up all of the weapons Manuel had given them and threw them overboard too. They still had a few weapons onboard, but they were all Rick's and legally registered. They cleaned the blood off the decks as best they could.

"When we get closer to Key West, we need to toss the treasure," said Rick. "We can use the heavy mess bags and mark the spot with GPS. We can come back and get them later. With an accident of this magnitude, the Coast Guard will do a thorough investigation and search of the boat. We are in thousands of feet of water now. We need to get to shallower water or it's lost again, maybe forever. Johnie, take it up to twenty knots. I don't care what the Coast Guard said."

Johnie moved the throttles forward. He prayed that Rick's makeshift patch job on the deep v would hold. Luckily, the seas were rolling and not too big. Johnie kept watching the depth finder, his heart still beating fast.

Rick and Possum had loaded the treasure into the heavy mesh bags and doubled them up. He tied a large hoop knot to the top of the bags. Once they got close to the straits of Florida, the depth went from over 6,000 feet to suddenly a little over 300 feet. With the Coast Guard still far away, they dropped the bag overboard and Possum marked it in the GPS. It was still too deep for scuba but they could retrieve it with an R.O.V.

Two hours later, the cutter came into view. Rick called them on the VHF, and two Coast Guardsmen motored over in an inflatable and boarded *Nine-Tenths*.

"I'm Petty Officer Anderson, who is the captain?"

"I am. I'm Rick Waters. This is the crew, Johnie McDonald and Poss....Mike Jackson."

"What happened?"

They had all gone over their story so they'd be on the same page.

"We were enroute to Destin Florida and we hit something. I think it was an abandoned sinking vessel. We saw some fiberglass in the water after the crash. We searched the water for survivors, but I'm positive it was abandoned. Some of the fiberglass and wood had large barnacle growth on it," said Rick.

"How bad is the damage?"

"Let me show you."

Rick showed the coasties to the bow, and they leaned over and saw the patch job Rick had done. It appeared to be holding up well.

"Do you require medical treatment?"

"No, we both banged our faces when we hit the object. We'll be okay."

"We will escort you to Key West Coast Guard station and you can tie up at pier D2. I will send a medic to check you regardless. Can you move faster than five knots?"

"Yeah, I think we can comfortably cruise at around twenty knots in these seas."

After several hours, Key West came into view. They were also in cell range, so Rick called Gary.

"Hey Gary, Rick here."

"Hey, Rick. Are y'all getting close?"

"Sort of. We are almost to Key West. Can you fly here with Jules? I'll explain when you get here. I don't wanna freak her out. You understand?"

"Gotcha, we'll head out ASAP. You okay?"

"Yeah, we're all good. I'll fill you in when you arrive."

"Got it!"

CHAPTER SEVENTEEN

Once at the dock in Key West, the Coast Guard took an incident report and questioned Rick, Possum, and Johnie separately. Their stories were rock solid. After an extensive search of the boat and many photographs, they released the boat to Rick, and he motored around to 3D Boat Yard on Stock Island. *Nine-Tenths* would need extensive repairs before it could return to the water.

Rick made a deal with the boatyard to have the repairs done. He would empty the boat of all their possessions, as it would be there for a few months. Jules and Gary met Rick at the boatyard the next day near sunset.

Jules gasped as soon as she saw him. "What happened to your head, Rick?"

"It's no big deal. I'll tell you the whole thing over dinner. Come with me."

Rick walked with them to where the boat was dry-docked. When they got to *Nine-Tenths*, Jules covered her mouth with her hand in shock.

"What the hell happened?! You tell me right now, Rick Waters!"

"It's okay, Jules. Let's go to the condo and I'll explain."

She wrapped her arms around Rick, and they walked to Gary's rental car. Rick had rented a three-bedroom Airbnb in Key West for a few days so he could deal with the boatyard. They stepped into the condo, and Jules gasped again when she saw Possum. He had a bandage across his nose and jet-black bruises under his eyes. They were worse than the ones she had, which were now fading. They all sat down at the kitchen table, and Rick told them the entire sordid affair. They listened and soaked it all in. Chief sat on his perch on the desk and appeared to listen as well.

"Where's the treasure now?"

Possum slid his portable GPS over to Gary.

He pulled up his own nav app and plugged in the coordinates.

"Three hundred and fifty feet down? How the...?"

"Three letters: R.O.V." replied Rick.

"Ahhh okay. I'll work on getting us one," replied Gary.

"I knew you would. It ain't going anywhere, so there's no hurry. We can tow one out with *Nine-Tenths* once she's repaired."

"I have a better idea. Leave it to me," said Gary.

Over the next few days, Rick and Jules boxed up all their stuff from *Nine-Tenths*. They would fly it back to Destin in Gary's jet once they were done. Rick was astonished at how much crap had accumulated on the boat. He had to throw away a lot of frozen bait that had gone bad as well as any food left in the fridge. Jules took it upon herself to clean out all of the cabinets in each stateroom, while Rick focused on the workroom, galley, and salon. Anything that they used on the boat on a regular basis stayed, such as tackle boxes, tools, and dive gear. But all their clothes and personal items would be removed, so mold wouldn't set in. Jules also stripped the sheets off all the beds.

Rick was under the sink when Jules yelled, and he hit the back of his head on the cabinet opening.

"Dammit! What is it, Jules?" he said as he rubbed his head.

She opened a plastic bag she'd found in one of the drawers.

"Check this out. It's the shoes Paul brought from Kirsten."

Rick looked down into the bag. "I think those are the same exact shoes she had in Tulum. You know, the convertible ones. I had forgotten all about that."

Rick took the bag from Jules and texted Carson.

> Carson, can you run a DNA test on something for me?

> Send it. You know the address.

> 10-4. Wait until you hear what happened to us! I'll tell you in person, next time I see you.

Sounds good.

Rick put on some gloves and pulled one of the shoes out of the bag. He had to see how these shoes worked. Curiosity had gotten the best of him. He grabbed the heel of the shoe, pushed the button, twisted the heel, and pulled it off. He flipped it over and looked at the bottom. It stopped him in his tracks. He opened the photos on his iPhone of the crime scene back in Tulum and scrolled until he got to the picture of the back of Ava's neck. He zoomed in then held the shoe next to the photo. It was a perfect match.

Oh my God! Kirsten killed Ava.

"Jules, we have to go to South Africa."

"When?"

"As soon as possible. Probably tomorrow."

Rick called Gary and told him to hang tight at the condo.

"Gary, wanna go on a road trip? Well, an air trip?" asked Rick.

"Sure, where to?"

"To Quantico, then South Africa."

"Okaaaaaaay," he said, scratching his head.

Rick texted Carson back.

Carson, change of plans, I'm coming to you tonight. What airport?

> *Fly into DCA, text me your info, and I'll send a car for you.*

> *Will do. Thanks.*

Rick called Paul. He kept it friendly and didn't give him any info he didn't need.

"Hey, Paul. Rick Waters. How are you doing?"

"Hi, Rick. We're getting on here. We had a memorial for Ava. Many folks from town came. Ava was well liked. Very few people knew she had BPD. She could be the kindest, nicest person in the world to strangers. It's the loved ones she abused. They call the folk who support people with BPD 'flying monkeys.'"

"I didn't know that. I'm glad you're moving forward. I have to have some work done on my yacht, and I was wondering if you'd like a visit? Is it too early? I kinda wanna check out the wildlife park. I've never been on a safari."

Rick kept his suspicions about Kirsten close to the vest. He needed to be sure before sharing something so powerful with Paul.

"Of course, Rick. Kirsten will be thrilled you are coming. She has taken Ava's death incredibly hard. Just message me your ETA and I'll pick you up. I'll arrange a safari for you when you arrive. I know all the guides."

"Will do, Paul. See you in a few days."

Johnie and Possum decided to stay in Key West to take care of Chief and make sure the work on *Nine-Tenths* was being done properly. Possum dropped Gary, Rick, and Jules off at the Key West airport and then went back to the condo. Gary's pilot Clay made his flight announcements, and soon they were wheels up.

When they landed at the airport, they were met by a driver. He took them directly to the Courtyard by Marriot, which was the closest hotel to the FBI lab. Carson was sitting in the lobby when they arrived.

"I took the liberty of booking a couple of rooms for you. What do you have?"

Rick handed him the bag of shoes. He showed him how to remove the heel.

"How fast can you get a DNA test done?" asked Rick.

"In less than forty-eight hours, but it can take a long time to get a match through CODIS," he replied.

"We won't need CODIS. You will find two DNA matches on these shoes: Ava and Kirsten Giovanni. I can almost guarantee it. I just need 100 percent proof. We will stay the night then fly to South Africa in the morning. Can you email me the results?"

"Sure, Rick. No problem. I'll drop it off now. Y'all just check in and I'll have the car bring you to my favorite steakhouse, and we can discuss what you wanted to tell me."

They all changed clothes and met the driver in the lobby.

"Where we headin'?" asked Gary.

"Carson's house. He's grilling steaks. He refuses to eat steaks anywhere else. Says no one does them as well as him. You'll see."

Gary poured half a glass of Glenlivet from the bar in the town car, while Rick and Jules kicked back and chatted with the driver. It was a short trip to Carson's house. He pulled up to a large golden gate, punched in a code, and the gate opened. He stopped right in front of the house on the circular driveway. Carson met them at the front door.

"Welcome to Chez Carson. The best steakhouse in Virginia."

They laughed as he let them in. Carson's house was spectacular. He gave them the grand tour, then opened the French doors, revealing a beautiful courtyard with a built-in grill and smoker. The grill was already lit and Carson had set up plates on the outdoor table and opened a bottle of red wine. He poured them all one and placed the steaks on the grill.

"How's everyone want them?"

"Medium rare," chirped Gary.

"Mooing," said Jules.

"Rick?"

"Medium, please."

"I like mine rare too, Jules. Y'all just chill and I'll have them ready shortly."

During dinner, Rick caught Carson up on the treasure find and the pirate attack. He also told him of his suspicions about Kirsten. He was convinced she had done it.

They ended dinner early and waved off after-dinner cocktails. They had to be up super early to begin their trip to South Africa. It would take them a little over seventeen hours to fly to Bloemfontein, South Africa, with a stop in Cape Verde for refueling. It was so comfortable flying in Gary's new jet that Rick didn't wanna fly commercial ever again.

Paul and Kirsten were waiting for them with a car when they landed. Rick still hadn't gotten the DNA results from Carson.

"How was your flight, Rick?" asked Paul.

"Luxurious! You know Jules and Gary, right?"

"Of course. Welcome to my country. Let us escort you to my home."

Paul helped Jules with her bag, not because it was heavy but because he was just a gentleman. He loaded their bags into his Range Rover. It was the most opulent SUV Rick had ever sat in. The leather seats had warmers in them and the stitching was exquisite. It had a Harmon Kardon sound system and front and rear cameras.

"This is some kind of ride," said Rick.

"The diamond business has been very good to me. I had it equipped with multiple cameras. Over the years, I have created some enemies. I can't be too careful."

"I understand that. The screen is so large and clear."

"Yeah, it records in 4k front and rear, even audio. It records to this little flash drive in the navigation center. I have the same one in my safari version."

"Safari version?"

"Yeah, I had Range Rover of Cape Town build me one that seats six with a retractable roof and a raised center observation seat. So, I can have someone sitting high above the roof line scouting for game. I'll show you at the house.

I had the staff prepare us a great meal, and we can visit my hunting lodge tomorrow if you wish."

They pulled into Paul's property. The large steel gate opened automatically when he pulled up. His entire property was surrounded by an eight-foot cement and cinder block fence with barbed wire across the top. It was a fortress. He had armed guards at the entrance and several on the grounds, with a pack of trained Doberman pinschers and two Irish wolfhounds. Paul parked the SUV in front of the main house. There were several other outbuildings near the house.

"Welcome to our home," said Kirsten with a smile that didn't quite reach her eyes.

"Damn, those are massive dogs!" said Rick, pointing at the wolfhounds.

"Yes, tallest dogs on earth. I had them imported here. We do have lions nearby." Paul grinned.

Rick wanted to catch Kirsten in a lie or something, so he asked her couple of random questions, hoping it would make her throw her off her guard. He'd have to wait for the DNA test results to finally expose her. His plan was to get the results and, with the help of the local authorities, try to get a confession out of her.

"How are you doing, Kirsten? I know we haven't had a chance to talk much but how are you dealing with Ava's passing," said Rick.

"I'm still dealing with a lot of guilt."

I bet you are, thought Rick as he gritted his teeth.

"I just feel responsible because I was there and it happened to her. I know it's not my fault, but I wish I could have done something."

Paul interrupted. "Rick and Jules, you can stay in the main house in the only spare bedroom not being renovated. Gary, I'll give you the guest quarters. It has everything you could possibly want. If anyone wants a nap, feel free. I'm sure you must be jet-lagged."

With the time change and long flight, it was almost six p.m. They all needed to adjust to the time zone, so they opted to try and stay awake until at least midnight. After everyone showered and changed, they met Paul and Kirsten in the massive great room for pre-dinner drinks. Rick had never seen so many animal heads in one house before. Paul even had a full-size elephant mounted as a centerpiece of the massive room. He told them he was an avid hunter and philanthropist and had given millions to the nature park to protect against poachers.

"I'd like to introduce you to my favorite South African liquor. It's called Witblits. Have a sip."

One of Paul's servants passed around glasses to each of them on a silver platter. Rick took a sip and nearly choked as he coughed. It burned his throat going down.

"I get it from the Western Cape. It's a grape-fermented brandy. It's not sold in stores; you have to know where and who to get it from." He winked. "I guess the closest thing to it in the states would be called white lightning."

"You could say that," said Rick, still coughing.

Jules and Gary took smaller sips after seeing Rick nearly lose his lunch.

"Come, let's eat. You all must be famished."

Paul led them to the grand dining room. It too was adorned with wild game mountings, and the mahogany table was covered in a full lion skin. The meal set out for them was fit for a king. Paul had his staff prepare some local delicacies, including braais, which was several types of local game barbequed. There was ostrich, impala, kudu, crocodile, giraffe, zebra, and springbok. A dish he called bobotie was a blend of tender meats and crunchy nuts, then topped with a layer of milk and egg. There were several desserts Rick couldn't even pronounce and some of the best wine he'd ever tasted.

After dinner, they settled on the fully screened-in back porch. Kirsten didn't join them, though; she said she was tired and going to bed early. Rick tried to act natural as he wished her a good night.

"Khat?" asked Paul.

"What?"

"No, khat. It's a type of leaf you chew on that makes you feel euphoric. It's similar to what you Americans call ecstasy, but it's all natural and much weaker. Even so, it's illegal here but rarely enforced. I have it brought here fresh. I got into the habit of chewing it from some local guides while hunting in Mozambique. It can also tend to keep you up, similar to drinking too much coffee too late in the day."

"I'll pass," said Rick.

"Me too, maybe tomorrow for some energy," said Jules.

Gary, of course, grabbed a huge wad of it and started chewing. Rick and Jules settled for some local cigars Paul had custom rolled. It was a lovely evening and they were all yawning.

"I have no commitments for a few days, so what would you like to do tomorrow? You can sleep in a bit and I'll show you Bloemfontein. We can visit the Zanchieta Wildlife Rescue Centre & Lodge. You can get up close and even pet some of the smaller local indigenous animals. Or we can get up early and go to my hunting lodge for a short hunt. We can go on a full safari in a couple days, if you wish."

They were all so tired they opted to do the city first and the hunt the next day when their bodies would be more acclimated to the time zone. Rick didn't really care. All he wanted to do was expose Kirsten and make her pay for murdering Ava. The rest was just gravy.

"You ready for bed, baby?" asked Rick.

"Yes, please."

They all said their goodnights, went to their bedrooms, and fell fast asleep within minutes. Except for Gary, that is.

Gary had chewed so much khat that he was wide awake and amorous. It was one of the side effects of khat. Gary stood on the front porch of his guest room pacing. Paul stepped outside and noticed Gary was still awake and walked over.

"Can't sleep, huh?" asked Paul.

"Nope, and I wish I'd brought a girl with me. I don't know what the hell is in that stuff, but I feel like I ate a bottle of Spanish fly."

"Yeah, the khat can do that to you."

Paul pulled his cell phone out of his pocket and spoke in a language that sounded Dutch.

"You speak Dutch?" asked Gary.

"No, it's Afrikaans. It's similar and I can understand Dutch well, but it's different."

Within minutes, a stunning, dark-skinned local girl approached Paul.

"Amahle, this is Gary. Gary, Amahle. Please make sure Gary is comfortable tonight and has anything he desires."

"Yes, Mr. Giovanni."

Amahle took Gary by the hand and led him to the bedroom. He smiled hungrily at her.

"Have a good night, Gary," said Paul with a laugh.

The next morning, Rick and Jules munched on local pastries and coffee with Paul on the back porch. Gary stumbled in looking like he'd been hit by a Mack truck, but he had a devilish grin on his face. His neck had a hickey on it, and Jules noticed right away. She shot Gary a look. He just grinned more.

"Kirsten won't be joining us today," said Paul. "She has plans with her friends. But she'll tag along for the hunt tomorrow."

Rick did his best to hide his disappointment. There would be time to get her talking tomorrow.

After breakfast, they piled into Paul's Range Rover and headed into town. Rick checked his phone and still hadn't gotten the DNA results from Carson. He was really starting to get impatient.

What's the ETA on the test?

Sorry for the delay, Rick.
We got one. It's Ava, still
waiting on the second. I'll

*send as soon as it arrives.
Running through CODIS just
in case.*

Standing by.

"How long have you lived here, Paul?" asked Rick.

"At the house or in South Africa?"

"Both, I guess. I thought you were born here."

"Oh, no, no, no. I'm a New Yorker. Full-blooded Italian. I grew up in Queens. I was sort of a bad boy when I was younger. I'm embarrassed to say, but I got three to five for a drug bust. I only served two years at Rikers. I was only eighteen then. After my felony charge and release, I decided I needed a fresh start. I had read about diamond mining in a magazine and saved my money to come over and work. After a few years, I bought my own mine. The rest is history."

"But your accent?"

"I've lived here twice as long as I did in New York. It's an easy thing to pick up."

"That makes sense."

After a short drive, Paul pulled up to the animal rescue lodge.

"Here we are," he said.

Paul bought everyone tickets, and they started the tour. Jules was wide-eyed and giddy like a kid in a candy store. Rick took pictures of her holding a baby serval. The goal of the lodge was to rescue, rehab, rewild, release, and repeat.

Besides small animals, they had one albino lion and several other large cats that were injured and would never survive in the wild. At the end of the tour, Gary gave them a substantial donation. They thought he was joking when he handed them a handwritten check with many zeros on it. He just smiled and told them to deposit it and it would clear. That was Gary. Always giving.

Next, Paul took them to the Langenhoven Park Farmers Market. They all got some homemade fudge, and Jules picked up a couple of bracelets a local woman crafted from tribal beads. Paul picked up some produce and they decided to head back to his estate for an early dinner. They wanted to get to bed early so they would be fresh for the hunt the next morning.

Gary chewed more kaht, met up again with Amahle, and disappeared shortly after dinner. Rick and Jules made it to nine p.m. before having to call it. They set their alarms for six a.m.

"Wake up, Jules, time to get ready," whispered Rick in Jules's ear.

She had slept right through the alarm. The jet lag had really affected her. Rick put on the hunting vest Paul had set aside for him, and they met him in the great room. Gary was already having coffee with Paul when they joined.

"Good morning, everyone," said Paul.

"Morning, Paul," said Rick with a yawn. "Morning, Kirsten."

"Time to gear up. Follow me," said Paul as Kirsten passed out coffees.

They all walked behind Paul as he stepped into the library. His desk had several scales and magnifying devices sitting on it that he used to inspect diamonds. He walked to a solid steel door, and with a key around his neck, he unlocked it. When he opened it, the light automatically came on, revealing a massive gun room. There was a long stainless-steel table with a soft mat covering most of it in the center of the room. A large assortment of handguns and rifles were placed side by side on the table.

"Okay, everyone choose at least one handgun and rifle. Every rifle is a .30–06 caliber and the side arms are all .45s."

Rick picked up twin Taurus handguns with a belt holster. His rifle of choice was a Browning X-Bolt with a Monte Carlo stock. Gary chose a SIG Sauer automatic pistol and a Winchester Bolt Action long rifle. Jules picked up a single-action Colt revolver and a Tikka T3x Lite RoughTech rifle made by Springfield. All the rifles had precision optics and leather shoulder straps.

"Good choice of handgun, Jules. Just be careful with that one. It has a hair trigger."

"I'll be safe. I took a gun safety course and I'm comfortable around all firearms. Thanks for letting me know about the trigger though," replied Jules.

Paul drove them in his custom-built Range Rover past the Soetdoring Nature Reserve to the north. He opened a single gate over a cattle crossing and locked it behind him. His property butted up to the reserve. Jules and Kirsten sat in the third-row seats in the back and had time to talk.

"Do you like safaris, Kirsten?"

"I love animals." She smiled. "That's one thing Ava and I had in common. We used to talk a lot about the plains animals and how she loved to take photos of them. It seemed to be the only thing we could ever talk about that wouldn't turn into an argument." Kirsten sighed. "That damn BPD made conversing with her difficult. She always tried to twist what I said into something it wasn't. I won't miss those circular conversations."

Rick overheard Kirsten's last comment; it set the back of his neck tingling. *There's her motive, then. She was sick of dealing with her.* Gary was gazing out the window as Jules and Kirsten talked, while Rick sat up front with Paul.

"How big is your property?" Rick asked Paul to keep the mood light.

"I bought it in 1982 for pennies on the dollar, and it is approximately five thousand acres," said Paul. "It heads north and is almost indistinguishable from the reserve next to it. You can hunt on my property but not the reserve, so I'm always checking my location with GPS to make sure I don't accidentally cross over. I can literally shoot a lion just feet from the reserve as long as it's on my side. There are no fences between the two."

As they drove, Jules popped up in the high chair looking for wildlife. She spotted a herd of zebras in a field to their right.

"Look, look, zebras!"

Paul stopped the SUV for her to get a better look.

"Just wait, Jules. When we get closer to my camp, you'll see many animals, including most likely the big five.

"The big five?" she asked.

"Yes, lion, leopard, rhino, elephant, and water buffalo. They are all here. Plus, several snakes we want to avoid, especially the Boomslang. They are plentiful here and love the tall grass. Before we go on the hike, we need to all put on our anti-bite leg covers. I have plenty of pairs in the back of the Range Rover."

Jules winced at the thought of the scary-named snake. Rick grimaced, as he too hated snakes. They drove for what seemed like forever and finally came to a small river.

"My camp is about a mile upriver past those Jackalberry trees. Don't get too close to the river. It's teeming with crocs. Just follow me and you'll be fine. Normally, I'd drive right to the camp, but there's a fallen tree on the two-track trail, and I haven't had a chance to have it removed. I always swipe a cane in front of me in the tall grass so we don't surprise any Boomslangs. If they know you're coming, they will slither away."

Rick checked his phone and only had one bar, but it was enough for a text to come through. He was super anxious to get the second DNA results back, knowing full well they would belong to Kirsten. He was just biding his time, trying to enjoy himself, but it was difficult. Jules could see something was bothering him and squeezed his arm to show support.

In the back of the Range Rover in a plastic case, Paul passed out the anti-bite leggings and put on a pair of boots. He placed the leather shoes he often wore back in the SUV. Paul took the lead down the trail. The brown grass was high on both sides of the track and even in the center. Paul swiped his cane back and forth on front of him as he walked. About a quarter mile down the trail, he raised his fist for everyone to stop.

"There's one," exclaimed Paul as he pointed at the snake.

They all saw its tail as it disappeared into the tall grass to their right. Rick tensed up. He could feel adrenaline starting to flow. Rick didn't fear snakes, but he certainly didn't like them. Especially highly venomous ones.

They continued to walk, and Paul pointed out a leopard highly camouflaged high up in a tree three hundred yards off of the trail. Rick looked at the beautiful cat through the scope on his rifle. It had its body draped over a large limb and was it licking paws the same way a domestic cat does.

Beautiful.

They continued their hike up the trail and stepped over the fallen Jackalberry tree that blocked the trail for the Range Rover. Paul pointed out the occasional wild game. He was so keen on spotting, after spending so many years in the bush. Once they passed the tall Jackalberry trees, the camp came into view. It was a rugged but expansive camp with bunk beds and had full electricity and water. The inside was quite plush, considering the rough-sawn logs that comprised the outer shell.

"Would you two mind helping me get that tree out of the trail so I can bring the Range Rover up? I can't get any tree company to show up, so I guess I'll have to do it myself."

"No worries," responded Gary.

"Jules, there are a couple of photo albums on the coffee table of some of the hunts and hikes we've done from here. Feel free to check them out. It won't take us much time at all with my big saw."

"Okie dokie, I'll chill while y'all take care of it," she responded.

"I'll join you!" said Kirsten happily.

Paul pulled out a huge Husqvarna chainsaw from a shed behind the camp.

"I used this puppy to cut most of the logs that built the camp. It took a painstaking two years, but it was a labor of love. The Jackalberry trees are dense and heavy and resistant to termites. I burned through a lot of chains building the camp."

"Cool, let's do this!" said Rick.

They walked back to where the tree covered the trail, and Paul began to saw. It only took about twenty minutes to make the two cuts necessary to clear the trail. The three of them rolled the middle log off of the trail with relative ease.

"Why don't y'all return to the camp? I'll run up and bring the Range Rover back. There's some Mad Giant beer in the fridge. I have it shipped in from Jozi, ahem…Johannesburg. It's my favorite microbrew in Africa. They have an amazing taproom in Blairgowrie, as small suburb just north of Jozi. Depending on how long you all stay, maybe we can make a run up there. We can take my Agusta 109 up there. It's my helicopter. The only way to travel!"

"Sounds like a plan, Paul," replied Rick.

Rick and Gary made their way back to the camp, making sure to avoid any snakes on the way. It wasn't even eight a.m. yet. Still plenty of time to explore the bush. Paul returned in the SUV and honked. They all hopped in, and he put it in four-wheel drive and left the main trail. He switched between the front and back cameras and the built-in GPS often as he drove.

"Wow, your nav system is about as high tech as a space shuttle," said Rick.

"It's pretty sweet. It records audio and video 24/7 even if the truck is not running. Theft in Cape Town and all of South Africa, I'm afraid, is high. I never go anywhere without a pistol. I got this ride and cameras after I was robbed at gunpoint in Jozi a few years back. I was in my old Jeep and I left the house without my sidearm. I swore I'd never do that again. There were no witnesses and they cleaned me out. That's when I sold the Jeep, did a ton of research, and ordered all of the Range Rovers with the high-tech security features."

"That's freaking cool," replied Gary.

Jules climbed up in the high chair again, and they crossed several streams going deep into the bush. Paul explained that most of the big animals were closer to the reserve where his property butted up to it. After an hour, he stopped the truck suddenly. He turned off the engine.

"Everyone, listen," said Paul.

They all held their breath and listened. Off in the distance, they heard a roar then what sounded like a cackle.

"You hear that? That's a male lion."

"And some hyenas!" chimed in Kirsten.

"Lions hate hyenas and kill them just for fun. I've seen it happen before," said Paul with a chuckle.

They all exited the Range Rover and began to walk forward slowly, following closely behind Paul. He crouched down in some tall grass and pulled out his binoculars. He passed them to Rick and pointed to the west. In the distance, under a small patch of trees, was a pride of lions. He counted ten females, two males, and the king. The males were juveniles and barely had manes. Paul told them that the king would one day either kill them or run them off to maintain his dominance over the pride. They were still too young to pose a threat to his reign.

Rick was enjoying the mini safari but kept checking his phone every few minutes for the text from Carson. Still nothing. *Dammit. Hurry up!*

Paul had everyone take a wide path around the lion pride. According to his map, they were inside the park and not on his property, so off limits to shoot. Rick didn't want to shoot a lion anyway. He only wanted to shoot something he could eat. He had no desire to bring home a trophy. He couldn't stop Paul, though, if he wanted to. It was his country and his rules.

Suddenly, Rick heard a sound he'd only heard on TV before. It was the trumpet of an African Elephant. In a watering hole just beyond a bluff was a herd of elephants blasting water in the air and rolling in the mud. A baby elephant was covered in mud and tugging at his mom's leg to join in the play. Paul handed Jules the binoculars, and a smile crept over her face.

"They're so cute. ¡Ay, Dios mio! Look at the baby," she said.

"We have to be super careful around them. They are extremely dangerous and unpredictable. They can run at speeds up to twenty-five miles an hour. If they charged us at close range, we could not outrun them. They are second only to hippos for the most human deaths in Africa. Take your rifles off safety and make sure one is chambered. We aren't gonna shoot one. It's just for our protection in case they charge. I've fired shots in the air to stop them before."

Rick wished Possum were with them to take in the experience and take photos with his Canon rig. The iPhone just wasn't cutting it. Paul pointed out the crocodiles on the opposite side of the watering hole sitting on the bank. Their gaze was fixed on the baby elephant, but they didn't dare enter the water with the giant male in between them and the playful baby. The scenery was inspiring and surreal. Rick hoped he'd come back under different circumstances. He knew having Kirsten arrested would be hard on Paul. Especially after just losing his daughter, but he also knew it was the right thing to do. She was a gold digger and a murderer.

"We need to head back. The last thing we wanna do is be here after dark. Plus, I'm hungry! I had my staff fully stock the fridge. We can have a feast tonight."

"Yay!" exclaimed Jules.

On the return to the Range Rover, Paul pointed out several Kudo, some gazelles, and a secretary bird. Rick was mesmerized by the long-legged bird. They were raptors that traveled mostly on foot. They could fly when they needed to but preferred to walk. Rick watched it stomp around and dig in the dusty ground with its long talons and pull up mole and devour it. He thought of Chief and missed him. Rick was always drawn to birds. All species, since he was a boy. Without even thinking about it, and almost automatically, he would often point out different birds to Jules everywhere they went. She thought it was so cute and loved learning about things Rick was passionate about.

They arrived back at the camp just before sunset, and as hot as it was during the day, the temps could drop drastically this time of year at night. Paul lit the fireplace and started preheating the oven. The main meal was already prepared by his staff and in a large aluminum-covered tray. To Paul it was roughing it, as he had to put it in the oven, but to Rick it was luxurious. Rick vowed to never take money or employees for granted. He had grown up poor and now that he had money, he intended to never forget his roots. In his opinion, Paul had. Gary was exactly like Rick and had far more greenbacks in the bank than Rick did. But he was just a regular guy who'd give anyone his shirt off of his back.

"Who wants wine or a beer?" asked Paul.

They all said yes. Jules shared a glass of Graham Beck Brut Rose with Paul and Kirsten, while Gary and Rick went for another local IPA. The meal wasn't wild game this time. Paul had his staff make one of Africa's favorite comfort meals: Denningvleis, which was prepared with a combination of lamb, garlic, onions, tamarind, allspice, cloves, bay leaves, and nutmeg. It smelled amazing when he set it on the center of the mahogany dining table on a warming plate. He explained it was better for it to cool down then warm back up. It brought out the flavors. It was also an excuse to drink more before dinner.

Rick woke up early the next morning and checked his phone. Still no update about the DNA. It was still dark outside as he peeked out of the window. He lay back down and tried to fall back asleep, but his mind was racing. He wanted the final proof he needed to confront Kirsten. Once he knew, he'd let Paul in on the plan. He didn't want any surprises. Telling Paul too early would be a mistake if he was wrong. It would cause undue trauma, and he had been through enough. Rick had almost let the cat out of the bag the night before after too many local IPAs and a couple of shots of white lightning, but he managed to hold his tongue.

He quietly snuck into the kitchen and pushed the button on the coffee maker. A sliver of light shone through a crack in the curtains. Either the smell of the coffee or Rick's cursing when he stumped his toe on the kitchen table woke everyone up. They all stumbled in like zombies—except for Kirsten. Somehow, she'd slept through the noise. Paul held his head, indicating he had a hangover. He looked for the aspirin and then his favorite glass. He cursed when he remembered.

"Ava smashed it. I just remembered. It was a glass she gave me for Christmas. It read Best Dad on it. But as usual Ava had a BPD split and smashed it to the ground to hurt me. If I had a dollar for everything she broke in a BDP rage, I'd have a lot more money. I miss her, but sometimes I'm actually glad she's gone. She caused us so much chaos over the years. I'm sorry, that's a terrible thing to say. I loved my daughter. She was just so unpredictable and violent. Well, her illness was. One in the same, I guess."

"I get it, Paul. Mental illness is hard on everyone. Maybe even more so on the caretakers," said Rick.

Paul heated up some biscuits and sausage. He wanted to take everyone out up past the river in the Rover for a short hike. Kirsten woke up just in time to join them, to Rick's relief.

"Get your gear on, everyone. Snakes don't sleep," said Paul with a laugh.

Rick got ready fast and walked out on the porch to take in the morning air. He placed his rifle in the Range Rover. Jules followed closely behind and climbed into the high chair she loved so much. She took out her revolver and polished it as she waited.

Gary and Paul came out, and Paul sat on the porch to put on his boots again. Gary walked to the back of the SUV and leaned his rifle against it, then came back and stood beside Rick. Before breakfast, he had gathered a few more pieces of wood for the fireplace and needed to take off his favorite shoes for boots. Rick leaned against the front of the Range Rover with his feet crossed, waiting for Paul to finish. Kirsten ran back inside to grab something she'd forgotten.

Rick's phone vibrated as Paul untied his leather laces.

> No match for DNA for Kirsten. But we got a hit. Paul Giovanni, plus his prints were on the shoes.

Rick's entire body stiffened.

> Prints where?

> On the outside was a full handprint.

> Thanks, Carson.

> No worries. Also, I'm sending an enhanced photo of the

impression in Ava's neck. There's a letter under the locking mechanism of the shoe. It is an M.

The text photo popped into his phone. The enhanced picture clearly showed an M under the locking part of the shoe heel. Rick was shocked. He'd been so certain Kirsten's DNA would be on the shoe. Paul was the one who'd packed the shoes and brought them to Rick in the first place. Of course, his fingerprints would be on it. *Right?*

He just sat there and leaned against the SUV and stared blankly into space, trying to make sense of it. Had he been going after the wrong person this whole time? He snapped out of it when Paul tossed his leather oxfords on the porch and started to slip on his boots. Rick looked over at them and saw a silver button at the heel.

"Why'd you do it, Paul?"

"Why'd I do what?"

"Why'd you kill Ava?"

Kirsten came back onto the porch just then, but froze in the doorway upon hearing Rick's words.

Paul tensed and stared at him. "Excuse me? Is that some kind of sick joke!?"

Gary and Jules perked up. Gary focused on Paul's rifle sitting next to him, pointed in their direction. His handgun was behind his back in his waist. Paul had the drop on them.

Rick pointed at the leather oxfords. The color ran from Paul's face.

"Why'd you do it?" repeated Rick.

Paul exhaled loudly as if a big relief was falling off his shoulders.

"Rick, you have no idea how hard it is to live with a person with Borderline Personality Disorder. I loved Ava, but she never got better. She's wrecked every good time we ever had. She caused the breakup of my first marriage because of her erratic behavior. She's destroyed family heirlooms, thrown pots and pans at me. She was insanely jealous of Kirsten, and it was causing major problems in our marriage Right, baby?"

Kirsten had a blank look on her face as Paul talked. She was in pure disbelief.

"But you killed your own daughter. How and why would you take it to that level?"

"I had just reached my limit. There's no other way to put it. After years of her black-and-white rage, I just finally broke."

"How? You were with me in the lobby waiting for the EMT..."

"I may as well tell you. I guess it doesn't matter anymore. That video footage you saw of a guy going back into the villa was me. I told you I was gonna use the restroom in the lobby, and I walked in that direction, but when you turned around, I ran back to the villa, took the diamonds, and went to Ava's bathroom. You don't honestly think this is the first time I stole my own diamonds, and double dipped from the insurance company, do you? Why do you think I sell them in crime ridden areas like Playa Del Carmen. Kirsten was upstairs. Ava was lying with her neck against the toilet, and years and years of her abuse hit me all at once. Everything turned red and I knew I had to finish the job."

"Finish?"

"Yeah, when we found her, I asked Kirsten to make Ava a glass of BC powder, and I ripped open a dozen of her Effexor capsules. Once Kirsten returned with the glass, I added the pile of it to her glass as Kirsten cried and covered her face with her hands. I didn't know Ava would throw it all up and survive. I just wanted her to be out of her misery. She was a living nightmare. For herself and all of us who had to deal with her. She was better off dead than alive. There was no healing her mental illness."

"But she was throwing up and still alive!" exclaimed Rick.

"I know. When I ran in, I slipped on her vomit and knocked my heel off. I was going so fast I didn't even know it. I shoved my right foot against her neck and choked her out. When I stepped back, I saw my heel and popped it back in and ran back to the lobby. I was out of breath when I got back to you. I was afraid you noticed, but you didn't. It was a sympathy killing. You understand, right?"

"It's still murder, Paul, and you need to face the consequences."

"I was afraid you'd say that, Rick. I'm sorry, but I can't let you ruin my life. I'm ready to live a life without Ava's chaos. I'm sorry, Rick."

Paul stood up and began to raise his rifle. Rick had no chance. Out of the corner of his eye, he noticed Kirsten rushing back inside to get away from all of them.

Boooooooom!

The sound of the gun's explosion bounced off of the hollow porch. The bullet ripped through the center of his chest, and Paul fell backward on the porch, dead before he hit the wooden floor. As if in slow motion, Rick turned around to see Jules holding the pistol and smoke coming out of the barrel. She had just killed Paul and saved Rick's life. Gary ran over to check Paul's pulse as he kicked the rifle away from him.

"He's dead," exclaimed Gary.

Jules climbed down from the Range Rover and threw her arms around Rick, weeping. Rick held her tight, still in shock.

"How are we gonna prove this, Rick? It's his word against ours. It's his country. We could be tried for murder."

Kirsten had witnessed everything too, of course, but they couldn't be sure she would speak up on their behalf.

Rick and Jules both looked back at the same time at the camera in the front of the mirror of the SUV. The front Range Rover camera had captured the entire thing.

"Get his keys," said Rick.

Gary pulled the keys out from Paul's pocket and tossed them to Rick. He started the SUV and hit the *VIEW* button on the big screen on the dash. He pushed *go back* thirty seconds several times and saw Paul sit on the porch. It began to play. He turned up the volume, and it was true confession caught in 4k and perfect audio. After they watched it, he popped the memory card out of it and put it in his wallet.

Without a word, Rick walked into the camp and came out with some plastic wrap and a large Ziploc baggy. He carefully picked up Paul's right shoe with a piece of the plastic wrap, pushed the button and removed the heel. On the bottom of the shoe was the exact same shape they'd found on the back of Ava's neck, plus the letter M. M for Men. They were the only shoes Passion Footwear made for men. Rick sat beside Paul's dead body holding the shoe, taking it all in. It was a family tragedy.

CHAPTER EIGHTEEN

It took about forty-five minutes, once Rick called 911, for the first of the authorities to arrive. Two cruisers from the South African Police Service, or SAPS, arrived just before the coroner. Rick met with a man who introduced himself as Constable Benji Kalil. He and his partner taped off the crime unit and called in forensics. Rick began to explain what had happened, and they collected evidence. They took the gun Jules used and separated her, put her in a car to question her. Rick started Paul's SUV and played the video that was taken of the incident. Before the first unit arrived, Rick had made a copy of the flash drive on his laptop for safety. South Africa had a reputation for corruption, and there was no way he was gonna let anything happen to Jules. She had saved his life.

Constable Benji watched the video as Rick sat beside him. Paul and Rick were clearly visible in the footage, and Gary stood on the far right of the screen. Jules and Kirsten were not in the video, but the fire from Jules's .45 flashed in the shot.

"If you run a DNA test on the underside of that oxford beneath the removable heel, you will find Ava Giovanni's DNA," said Rick.

After the video finished, it was a clear case of self-defense. Jules was questioned for over an hour, as were Rick and Gary, and Kirsten agreed to talk to the police as well. Their stories all matched perfectly. Once the coroner placed Paul's body in the van, several reporters arrived from the nearby city of Bloemfontein. Paul was an extremely wealthy, influential man. His death would make national news. Once the story got out about Paul being responsible for his own daughter's death, the story would blow up even more. Rick told the constable that they would stay in Bloemfontein for a couple of weeks if they were needed for more questions. Paul's Range Rover was towed in as evidence as well as all of the weapons.

Kirsten, still in shock, gave Rick and the gang a ride back to her and Paul's place. The air was thick with grief and they felt uncomfortable. She told them they were welcome to stay, but they decided to get a hotel near the airport. They got adjoining rooms at the Road Lodge, the same hotel Gary's pilot Clay was staying at, walking distance to the airport, where Gary's jet was waiting on the tarmac. It didn't take long for the press to find their location. They were hounded everywhere they went. Rick would speak to them but not about certain details of the incident. He and Jules's faces were all over media as the private investigators who'd brought down the corrupt Paul Giovanni. They met with the SAPS several times, and after a week and a half,

Paul's death was identified as death by lethal force and not murder. Jules was cleared, and they began to make plans to fly back to Florida.

Jules ordered some Chinese delivery as they tried to stay away from the press. There was a knock on the door, and Rick answered, thinking it was the delivery driver. He looked through the peephole and saw a young black man with bandages wrapped around both of his arms.

"Hello, are you Mr. Rick Waters?"

"I'm not answering any more questions. I've asked the front desk to keep the press away."

"I'm not with the press, Mr. Waters. My name is Junior Dlamini. My father's name is Bandile Dlamini, or I should say was. He was murdered. I saw you on the TV and I would like to hire you to find his killer or killers. You are the great Rick Waters, right?"

Rick didn't know how to respond to that and just said, "Yes, I'm Rick. Come on in."

Junior stepped into the room and bowed in respect to Jules. Rick pulled out a couple of chairs for them to sit. He opened the adjoining door and waved Gary over to join them.

"I'm very sorry to hear about your father. Has the SAPS conducted an investigation?" asked Rick.

"Yes, but they are corrupt. They ruled his death as an accident—a hunting accident. My father spent most of his life protecting animals from poachers. He made many enemies. He became aware of a large stash of illegal elephant ivory. The biggest collection in all of Africa. There is a seventeen-million-dollar Kwacha reward for finding the ivory and delivering it to the government to get it off of the black market. That's the equivalent to a million US dollars. My father found the stash and stole it. He hid it somewhere near the Zambezi River near the Kafue National Park. He told me if anything ever happened to him, that the proof of his death would be found with the ivory. He gave me a map to it, but it was destroyed when my dad's Toyota Land Cruiser was fire-bombed. He had just given it to me when his new Land Rover Defender arrived. I think the men who blew up my Toyota thought my dad was driving. I was lucky to get out alive. I have terrible burns on my arms. When the truck blew up, I had just opened the top and I was able to climb out before it burnt to the ground. The map was in the console. It was completely destroyed. Two days later, my father was shot in the back and died alone beside his new overland truck. There's no way it was an accident. No one would shoot that close to a vehicle accidentally."

"How can I help?" asked Rick.

"The SAPS has closed the case. I think they have some bad cops on the inside being paid off by the poachers. I can't pay you, but if you find the ivory, you can solve the case and get the reward. My father was a great man and he did not deserve to be killed like this. He loved the elephants and spent his life protecting them. Can you please help me?"

Rick sat there for a few seconds, looked over at Gary and Jules. "I guess we're going to Zambia."

THE END

ACKNOWLEDGMENTS

I'd like to thank my beta readers Bavette Battern, Mike Keevil, Carroll Scadden Shroyer, and Terry Gillard.

I'd like to thank my amazing editor, Stephanie Diaz Slagle.

I'd like to thank my proofreader, Carroll Scadden Shroyer.

Thanks to my graphic artist Les.

I'd like to thank my super awesome formatter, Colleen Sheehan.

Special thanks to Nick Sullivan, Wayne Stinnett, Cap Daniels for all their input and advise.

I like to especially thank all the readers of my novels. It's all about the readers. I appreciate your continued support on this journey.

ABOUT THE AUTHOR

Eric Chance Stone was born and raised on the gulf coast of Southeast Texas. An avid surfer, sailor, scuba diver, fisherman and treasure hunter, Eric met many bigger than life characters on his adventures across the globe. Wanting to travel after college, he got a job with Northwest Airlines and moved to Florida. Shortly thereafter transferred to Hawaii, then Nashville. After years of being a staff songwriter in Nashville, he released his first album, Songs For Sail in 1999, a tropically inspired collection of songs. He continued to write songs and tour and eventually landed a gig with Sail America and Show Management to perform at all international boat shows where his list of characters continued to grow.

He moved to the Virgin Islands in 2007 and became the official entertainer for Pusser's Marina Cay in the BVI. After several years in the Caribbean, his fate for telling stories was sealed.

Upon release of his 15th CD, All The Rest, he was inspired to become a novelist after a chance meeting with Wayne Stinnett. Wayne along with Cap Daniels, Chip Bell and a few others, became his mentors and they are all good friends now. Eric currently resides in Destin, Florida with his three exotic birds, Harley, Marley and Ozzy. Inspired by the likes of Clive Cussler's Dirk Pitt, Wayne Stinnett's Jesse McDermitt, Cap Daniels Chase Fulton, Chip Bell's Jake Sullivan and many more, Eric's tales are sprinkled with Voodoo, Hoodoo and kinds of weird stuff. From the bayous of Texas to the Voodoo dens of Haiti, his twist of reality will take you for a ride. His main character Rick Waters is a down to earth good ol' boy, adventurist turned private eye, who uses his treasure hunting skills and street smarts to solve mysteries.

FOLLOW ERIC CHANCE STONE

WEBSITE:

ERICCHANCESTONE.COM

FACEBOOK:

FACEBOOK.COM/RICKWATERSSERIES

Manufactured by Amazon.ca
Acheson, AB

11761376R00151